GRAVE PASSAGE

GRAVE PASSAGE

by
William Doonan

CARSON—
YOUR GRANDMOTHER THOUGHT
YOU MIGHT ENJOY A GOOD MYSTERY, SO I HOPE YOU LIKE
MY BOOK. LET ME KNOW WHAT YOU THINK — 916-706-0874,
THAT'S MY PHONE NUMBER. YOUR MOM AND I ARE OLD
FRIENDS. I MET YOU WHEN YOU WERE A BABY, AND
I HOPE WE CAN MEET AGAIN SOON.
—BILL

THE GLENCANNON PRESS

MARITIME BOOKS

Palo Alto
2009

This book is copyright © 2009.
Cover Art by Laurissa Doonan

Published by The Glencannon Press
P.O. Box 341, Palo Alto, CA 94302
Tel. 800-711-8985, Fax. 510-528-3194
www.glencannon.com

First Edition, first printing.

Library of Congress Cataloging-in-Publication Data

Doonan, William, 1965-
    Grave Passage / by William Doonan. -- 1st ed.
        p. cm.
    ISBN: 978-1-889901-49-7 (alk. paper)
1. Cruise ships--Fiction. I. Title.
    PS3604.064G73 2009
    813'.6--dc22

                                            2009028182

for Carmen

ACKNOWLEDGEMENTS

Many people have worked with me to help bring this project to life. I'd like to thank my agent Etta Wilson at Books & Such Literary Agency for having faith in me, Bill Harris at The Glencannon Press for taking on this project, and my family for working with me to bring it to fruition. My parents Bill Doonan and Marijanet Doonan provided invaluable support and read numerous drafts. My sister Laurissa Doonan helped me make sense of it all. The artist Dan Stuelpnagel has read and reread and worked with me for years to improve my work. My best friend Eric Love keeps me sane; he helped me figure out what I needed to say. Finally, my family; Carmen, Will and Huey, give me great joy, for which I cannot thank them enough.

CHAPTER ONE

Contessa *Voyager* is one of those new ultra-modern cruise ships that offer something for everyone, which for my money is a bad idea. Give people too many choices and they get confused. In the old days, and I'm sounding like an old man here, passengers played shuffleboard and sat by the pool. But times change; today's passengers can avail themselves of *Voyager*'s twin water slides, twin driving ranges, the mini-tennis court, or even the three-story rock-climbing wall where the body of legendary F.B.I. profiler Robert Samson was found hanging from a narrow ledge.

Voyager was midway through a ten-day Caribbean cruise and en route from Aruba to Martinique when I got the call. The

1

murder, which it presumably was, had taken place in international waters, and because jurisdiction at sea can be difficult to establish, I was called in to investigate.

Sakato-Kobe, the company that owns *Voyager*, flew me to Aruba and from there I took a helicopter out to the ship. I had the hip replacement surgery last year which made the ride a bit unpleasant but it was a short flight, a night flight. They insisted on a night flight so the passengers wouldn't be spooked when a helicopter landed. They were probably spooked enough already so I was hoping to be unobtrusive.

Voyager was scheduled to dock in Miami in five days, at which time U.S. federal agents would take jurisdiction. But if I wrapped things up before then, this ten-day Caribbean cruise could still offer something for everyone. Well, everyone except Robert Samson.

This was a last minute job for me. In my line of work, you have to be ready to pick up and move fast, and I can do that. I packed fast and drove fast. A briefing packet on Robert Samson had been delivered to me at the airport but I misplaced it somewhere, possibly at the little restaurant where I had the muffin. They faxed me another copy in Aruba and I planned to read it on the helicopter but ultimately I didn't. All I managed to get through was part of the background information.

Samson had been a celebrity of sorts, someone who had more than his fifteen minutes of fame. He was a senior profiler for the F.B.I. and worked on some big cases. Once retired, he cobbled together a comfortable living on the lecture circuit, which led him to *Contessa Voyager* for about six weeks each year. He worked on a couple of other ships too and he did some academic lecturing, speaking at law schools and such. He drove a Chevy Impala and lived in a rented condo.

That's as far as I got before we saw the lights of the ship below us. I'd sailed on *Voyager* before but I'd never seen her from that angle. She looked like a little toy, so lonely out by herself in the middle of the Caribbean. We came down fast. The helicopter set down only for a moment, barely long enough for me to gather my things and hobble out before it lifted off, leaving me on the deck with a sore neck and an aching bottom.

Six crewmembers wearing windbreakers were on hand. One stepped forward, and I knew from experience that the first ten minutes or so were going to be awkward. I was the outsider coming in to help someone who really wasn't at all interested in my help. I am a nice man, a lovely man really, and it always breaks my heart to have to go through the same dumb chest-thumping dance.

The guy didn't even shake my hand; he just ushered me inside a little vestibule and started talking to me. I couldn't hear a thing. Maybe the noise of the helicopter had blown out an eardrum or something. "Give me time," I told him as I checked my hearing aid. It was off. I must have turned it off during the ride, so I turned it back on. "That's better."

"Is it now? I'm Hugh Arlen," he said as he shook my hand. "I'm chief security officer for *Voyager*. Captain Erlander has asked that I bring you directly to his quarters."

I introduced myself. "I'll appreciate a stop at the *baño* on the way. The helicopter made me a little queasy."

"Of course." He led me down a breezeway toward the middle of the ship. I looked out at the pool and the waterslides, and then the rock wall came into view.

"That's where he was found?" I asked.

"Yes, just there by the top."

"Who found him?"

"Troop Two, Sea Scouts, six- to eight-years-old. We've been doing counseling sessions. I have to say I'm not really sure why you're here. We have the investigation under control."

"I'm sure you do," I told him. "I think I'm just a formality. It gives the company a reputation for responding quickly. I'll try not to get in your way."

"That would be appreciated." He pointed to the restroom.

I could see we were going to have some attitude to deal with. "I can meet you. You don't have to wait for me."

"Not a problem. You don't have a crew identification card, so I have to accompany you to restricted areas."

"Might be a couple of minutes here; maybe even ten."

"Take your time."

I flashed him one of my most winning smiles. "And I'm going to need one of those crew identification cards that gets me into restricted areas."

"That's up to the captain."

"That's up to Sakato-Kobe," I told him. "They are the captain's employer as well as yours. If you can have the card ready for me first thing in the morning, I'll put in a good word."

I can do attitude as well. I took my time in the bathroom. I like cloth towels; they're so much more refreshing than paper towels. The soap was nice and frothy, and they had bottles of cologne lined up under the mirror. I tried some. It smelled kind of minty.

Capt. Egil Erlander pointed me to a chair. He had a glass desk but the chairs were normal. His office was much bigger than I expected;

lots of windows. He had the place decorated with photographs of box-ers, famous boxers boxing with each other. Out of the corner of my eye I saw Floyd Patterson taking an upper cut from Ingemar Johans-son, but it was the glass desk that held my attention. I don't know why anyone would want a glass desk. I can't see the appeal.

Erlander was a big fellow, a big Nordic-looking fellow. He looked as though he'd have no trouble wrestling down one of those giant Alaskan sled dogs if a situation called for it. He might have even lasted a round or two with Johansson. I generally don't like to discuss people's physical dimensions and whatnot, largely because I wouldn't appreciate someone yammering on about my girth or gait, but the guy was a bruiser, really quite a big man.

"Glass," I said, pointing to the desk as I took my seat. "Very nice."

He was kind of staring at me. He turned to Hugh Arlen but got only a shrug by way of response. "I'm sorry," he said. "You are not what I was expecting."

"Story of my life," I told him. "My second marriage lasted all of two-and-a-half months before she figured out she didn't want to be married. Or at least married to me. That was Joanne. She was from Minneapolis, not used to the Pennsylvania summers."

They both stared at me.

Capt. Erlander opened a leather folder and read from a page. He had an accent that I think was Norwegian or Swedish. I can't tell the difference, and in my heart I believe that nobody else can either. "Please extend all honorable courtesy to Mr. Henry Grave. He is to have unrestricted access to all areas of the ship as well as full coop-eration from all personnel. It's signed Hiroshi Saito, Senior V.P. for

Public Affairs, Sakato-Kobe." He closed the folder. "Are you a police officer, Mr. Grave?"

"No. No," I said. "I'm an investigator for the Association of Cruising Vessel Operators in Washington, D.C."

"Retired police? Military? Law enforcement?"

"No. No. Nothing like that, though I was in the service as a young man."

"Are you armed?"

"I am not."

"That's good. I don't allow weapons on my ship."

"A sensible rule." I nodded sagely.

"We've been trying to find some information on you but we haven't had much success."

"I can certainly help you there," I told him. "I'm a Libra. Social by temperament, I seek out the company of others. I enjoy roller derby, the theater, and a good Scotch, a full-bodied Scotch."

"We Googled you," Hugh Arlen said, interrupting my train of thought. "That's a computer term. I don't know if you're familiar with the internet."

"I once had a number calculating machine."

"We learned some interesting things about you. You were a P.O.W."

"I was. It was the most intensive weight reduction program money can buy. I was quite thin by the end. Also, I lost four teeth, but that's a story for another day. I had them replaced. You can see just back here." I leaned forward and opened my mouth wide.

Both men stared at me. I was starting to think my tie was crooked.

"I'm sure your country owes you a great debt," Erlander said.

"You ran for Congress in 1972," Arlen continued.

"Yes, I lost. Badly. Looking back, I think my message could have been crisper. I'll be honest, I was kind of all over the place but I was a big advocate for ethanol. Ultimately, the good folks of Pennsylvania thought not to send me to Washington on their nickel."

"And you wrote a book," Erlander continued. He read from a sticky note on his desk blotter, *The Lost Mummies of Pachabamba*. You were an archaeologist."

"I was." I pulled out a copy of the book from my case. I never travel without one. I placed in on Erlander's desk. "Went to college on the G.I. Bill and I liked it. I stayed in college for quite a while and then I was a professor for a short time."

"Until you were fired."

"That's right. Shortly after the book was published."

"Fired for what?"

"I lost the mummies."

He frowned. He stared at my book. "But they were lost mummies to begin with."

"I lost them again. Look, it's quite a tale. I'll tell you about it one day. We'll get some Irish coffees and a scone and we'll shoot the shit all through the night, but I'm a little tired right now and my ass hurts from the helicopter."

Arlen leaned forward. "I'm not quite certain how we will introduce you to public life here. The atmosphere is already a little tense and someone showing up out of the blue might be noticed."

I reached into my case for a flyer that I had prepared. "The story is that I boarded in Miami with everyone else, but I've been ill in my cabin for the last few days. Now I'm ready to party." I placed my flyer on the desk.

"International dance champion," Erlander read. "Tango with Henry." I had written a few more details under a photo of me on the ballroom floor but he elected not to read them. "You are an international dance champion?"

I nodded. "Tango. I have awards."

"I think we'll just have you be one of the guests rather than an entertainer if that's alright with you. Are you really an international dancing champion?"

"Yes, I have awards from Bethlehem, Pennsylvania, and Hamilton, Ontario. Rolling Pines had an excursion up to Canada last year and we went out dancing. I got a ribbon."

"Rolling Pines? Is that a nursing home?"

I glared at him. "It's a community of active seniors."

Erlander smiled. "How old are you, sir?"

"I'm eighty-four years old."

Arlen shook his head. "Are you really sure you're up to this?"

I smiled at him. "I am. Now please get my crew identification card taken care of. I will need to be able to move freely about the ship, the public areas as well as below decks. I'll need a passenger manifest right away and a list of the crew and their stations. Bring me whatever bio you have on Samson as well as the incident report. I also need some juice and a muffin or two. I'm a little diabetic so you might want to get on that first off. And no raisins, they give me the trots. Which one of you can help me find my cabin?"

CHAPTER TWO

I took a little nap but I generally don't sleep for more than about two hours at a time. I'm not sure why but I've been like that for more years than I can remember. It was getting to be light outside and I had about half an hour before the early risers' breakfast. They have omelets.

I puttered about, checking out my cabin. *Voyager* is a large ship. She can accommodate up to 1,684 passengers in 770 cabins, the vast majority of which were billed as deluxe suites, sporting little balconies with lounge chairs. Twenty-four of those cabins were called Ambassador Suites and had large balconies in addition to separate living and sleeping quarters.

Two of those cabins were majestically titled Parliamentary Suites. Each of these relatively palatial apartments consisted of a large bedroom, elegant living and dining rooms, separate bar area, and a balcony big enough to sport its own hot tub.

Fourteen cabins were known as Junior Suites, one of which had been assigned to me. My Junior Suite had no balcony but it did have a window looking out onto a lifeboat, which hung just in front of it, ready to be lowered, presumably, in case of emergency.

It wasn't a bad little cabin. I had a full bathroom and a couch and a TV and a refrigerator, all nicely appointed in tasteful green and gold, the signature colors of Contessa Cruise Lines. I made myself a pot of coffee and sat down on my little couch to look over the material that had been slipped under the door.

You have to give it to the marketing folks at Contessa; they cram a lot of people onto their ships. The cruise was almost full, and some of the passengers were staying on board for the next cruise and even the one after that. I got out the passenger manifest. Exactly 1,532 people had booked passage. Twenty-two nationalities were represented, though eighty percent of the passengers were American.

Six hundred and forty crewmembers called *Voyager* home. More than half were Filipino, making up the custodial technicians and the housekeepers and the busboys and the other service jobs. The dining room and bar personnel appeared to be largely eastern European, and the officers, with the exception of Hugh Arlen who was American, were all Scandinavian. Quite the ethnic profile, I told myself, but it was more or less standard for most large cruising vessels.

All of this force was put in service for a wealthy, largely conservative population of passengers who were willing to pay a great deal of money to a Japanese company to pamper them as they stood on their balconies and admired the Caribbean Sea as it passed by six or seven stories below.

Sooner or later I was going to have to read through the crew and passenger manifests. In all probability, I'd find someone I knew from a previous cruise and that might be useful. But first I picked up Robert Samson's folder. Samson was a snappy fellow. I had met him some years earlier after he retired and began lecturing for the cruise industry.

I read the fifty-word bio that Contessa requires from its lecturers.

> Robert Samson is a world-renowned crime fighter. A former lead profiler for the FBI, Mr. Samson is best known for his apprehension and arrest of Harlan Odette, better known as the Crossing Guard Killer. Mr. Samson has received numerous awards and citations from state, federal, and international law enforcement agencies.

The folder was filled with additional promotional material. Samson was scheduled to deliver a series of three lectures. He'd delivered two already; one on the Crossing Guard Killer, and one about his ongoing work with an unsolved murder on Cape Cod. In the third lecture, he was going to reveal the identity of the Cape Cod murderer. That I found interesting.

The first time I met Samson was a good number of years back on a *Carnival Odyssey* trans-Atlantic cruise. He was talking about the Crossing Guard Killer and how he tracked him down and then wrestled him down. I thought he was a blowhard but he had the audience all wrapped up. A couple of years later I chanced upon him having lunch at a House of Pancakes in Albuquerque. I said hello but he looked down right away at the crossword puzzle he was working on. I think he was drunk.

I read for another half an hour, until I came to the photos of Samson hanging from the little ledge up on the rock wall. His lips were pulled back in a grimace and his eyes were open, bloodshot. He'd been strangled with a towel and then hoisted up the wall with a belaying rope. Now that's a terrible way to die, and an even worse way to kill someone. It's flashy, risky. That was an open deck. Someone could have seen something, even if it did happen in the middle of the night.

I was familiar with standard security features of ocean-going vessels, familiar enough to know that open decks are monitored by surveillance cameras. I'll tell you a secret; I've been there on the bridge with the guys monitoring these cameras, panning about, zooming in here and there to look at this woman and that woman. If someone is drowning or going over the railing of a cruise ship, they had best do it early in the morning or late at night when there are no bathing beauties about, or they will go undiscovered.

But Samson was killed in the middle of the night, so no bikinis. The incident should have been caught on camera. I dug through my case to find the protocol manual for *Voyager*, and sure enough, I found the page with the drawing of each deck and the little cone of gray that indicated which areas were monitored. And just as I thought, the rock wall would have been in full view of the security officer on the bridge at the time of Samson's death, which was listed as 3:30 A.M. I was going to need to get a look at that security tape, and I was going to need to ask Hugh Arlen why he had not brought it to my attention.

But first I was going to need some breakfast. I freshened up in the bathroom of my Junior Suite. The soap was called Blood Orange and smelled something like a lime. The towels were among the fluffiest I had ever encountered.

Feeling rested, ready, and hungry, I made my way out into the hallway. I had the passenger and crew manifests with me so I could do some work, but I forgot about my new crew identification card so I stepped back inside to retrieve it from the folder. It featured a file photo of me that Sakato-Kobe must have sent, and listed me as a consultant. I had all-access clearance, which was going to come in handy.

I needed to find the Lido Deck. There are seventy-three large cruising vessels out there sailing passengers around this sea or that, and I suspect that every last one of them has a Lido Deck. *Voyager's* Lido was three flights up. With my knees, I wasn't about to climb three flights of stairs, so I took the elevator.

The main theater was on the Lido Deck, as was the shopping area, the disco, and the Bistro, where they did the early risers' breakfast. I passed a few people strolling around here and there, but when I reached the Bistro, it was packed. I hadn't seen so many senior citizens in one place since the time Rolling Pines invited Sunrise Assisted Living over for movie night. We had pizza and watched, *A Bridge Too Far*.

I couldn't find a single free table. I considered getting a plate to go when I heard a voice calling out to me.

"Why don't you join me, young man?"

I couldn't help but smile. She was a pretty thing. Her eyes sparkled.

"Young man? I'm a good deal older than you," I told her. "My name is Henry. Henry Grave."

"Helen Ettinger," she said, as she held out a delicate hand. "I'm seventy years old. I like to get that out of the way right up front. I look every day of it too, so don't bullshit me. Have a seat."

We made some small talk. I was enchanted. Let me tell you something about myself; I like meeting women. I always have. I'm smooth, too. "Enjoying the cruise?"

"Oh my goodness, yes." She waved a hand to which a waiter quickly responded, bringing me a pot of coffee and a menu card. "Have the waffles with peaches and whipped cream. They do the whipped cream really nice. I like the potatoes as well but I have to watch my salt."

"Me too." I ordered the waffles as she suggested, along with a small egg-white omelet and whole-wheat toast with low-fat margarine along with some juice. "Diabetes," I said.

"Type II?"

"But of course. Just a touch, however. I have to watch what I eat is all. It's the blood pressure I'm more concerned about."

She laid her hand on top of mine. "Me too."

I smiled.

"So how come I haven't seen you around?"

"You know, I've mostly been keeping to myself. Then I was under the weather so I've spent a lot of time in my Junior Suite. Today is my debut, you could say."

"Where are you from, Henry?"

"New York, originally. I've moved about quite a bit. Right now I live in Bethlehem, Pennsylvania, but I'm thinking one day I'd like a little condo in Paris. I might have to check out San Juan when we get there. I had a friend move there and he likes it quite a lot. Where are you from?"

She buttered her toast slowly. "Montreal but I live here now, and we're not going to San Juan. I've lived aboard for just over a year now."

I had heard about such women but I'd never actually met one. "How interesting."

She frowned. "You mean expensive. And yes it is. And no I'm not rich, not really, but this is actually cheaper than a retirement home. And the service is first rate."

"And the scenery changes every day," I added.

"That it does."

"Tell me, do you go to the shows?"

She took a sip of coffee and daintily patted her mouth with a cloth napkin. "Not the cabarets. I'm usually in bed by nine but I do go to the recitals in the afternoons. They have tea and cakes and cucumber sandwiches. It's very nice."

"And the lectures?"

She threw her head back. "Yes, of course, the lectures. The day you stop learning is the day you stop living. My mother used to say that. I'm not sure why, since she never left the house."

"Did you go to Robert Samson's lectures?"

"I did," she said. "Poor soul. You know, I hate to speak poorly of the dead but he was more show than substance. He really didn't have much to say. Just tooting his own horn as to that Life Guard Killer. That must have been twenty years ago, but he kept talking about how he tracked him down to his ranch, and how he had to fight him in the end. That terrible man killed six children."

"Crossing guard killer." I nodded. "Four children." I remembered the case because I was living in California at the time. Harlan Odette had some super-low I.Q. but somehow managed to pull off a respectable living breaking and entering. I remember at the time thinking that they had the wrong guy. The evidence was pretty slim. No bodies, only the school bags that he collected from his victims.

"Is he still alive? I think Samson mentioned something about him dying but to be honest I think I nodded off toward the end of the lecture."

I smiled. I understood all too well how sleep calls to a mature individual at the peak of the morning. "He died of lung cancer in Folsom Prison about five years ago. He claimed he was innocent until the day he died. I believed him."

"But then they found the bodies."

"Then they found the bodies," I agreed, "all four of them when the county took the Odette Ranch for back taxes and started digging foundations for condos. Odette's DNA was on the clothes."

Helen shook her head. "Crazy world," she said, biting into a cream puff. "And now it would seem we have a murderer among us."

"It would seem."

"It could be you," she said, wagging a finger at me.

"I have an alibi; I was in my Junior Suite. You, on the other hand, are a prime suspect."

"I was asleep at the time."

"Can anybody confirm that?"

"Aren't you a flirt," she said blushing. "I'm not prepared to answer that question. If you're going to interrogate me, you might have to get rough."

I chuckled. I've had decades of flirting practice but apparently so had she. We chatted a bit as we finished our breakfast, and I arranged to meet her for a drink later at the Copacabana Lounge. Then I went off to do a little reconnaissance.

Let me tell you something about mature individuals like myself; we like to walk. If and when we can, we take walks regularly. You miss out on so much when you're young because you rush. I've learned this from paying attention to my life. I haven't learned much else.

I had work to do, an investigation to pursue, and I like to start my investigations by walking around, getting the lay of the land, or the ship as it were. It was my intent to walk the halls and decks of *Contessa Voyager* from top to bottom but that proved to be a larger task than my bladder or muscles could accommodate. I took the elevator to the top, to the Vista Deck and stepped out into the warm Caribbean air.

It was beautiful. I looked down at the bow of our ship, some four decks below. I never get over that feeling; every time I'm on a cruise I feel like I'm standing on the top of a skyscraper. And to be honest, I really don't understand for one minute how big ships float. Why they don't just sink to the bottom and drown us all is beyond me but I'm sure glad they don't.

Cruising is a wonderful experience. It's not for everyone. It's not for most. But it is very much for the mature traveler – folks like me who are not ready to throw in the towel, folks who want to ride a gondola around Venice and take a nice bus through a Puerto Rican rain forest but who no longer have the knees or the energy to make their own intricate arrangements. A cruise is a very comfortable way to travel gently in a community that blooms anew each time the ship leaves port; new friends and new prospects. We're old but we're not dead.

We're not all old either, not anymore. Although most cruises feature an abundance of senior citizens, plenty of other demographics can be found on board. You have your families and your kids, and the teenagers who try to get drunk and the newlyweds who succeed, but overall, our community is a mature one.

The Vista Deck wasn't really much of a deck. Lounge chairs had been artfully arranged but it was still too early in the day for lounge chairs. Mini-tennis was already being played on the mini-tennis court. Beyond that, the deck was little more than a narrow jogging track overlooking the pool complex two full stories below.

The rock-climbing wall towered over everything. I'm tempted to suggest that it looked ominous, all grey and steep and kind of pointy, but I suspect it probably always looked that way. Out-of-Service signs sprouted from many of its contoured surfaces. Behind it were the tops of the waterslides that snaked all the way down to the pool.

I kept walking; the air was nice. I felt like the circulation was returning to my legs and back. As I approached the stern, I discovered that the helicopter landing pad was actually the driving range, two driving ranges in fact, which had evidently been reconfigured as such some time early in the morning.

Both were occupied by gentlemen dressed for the sport. Seniors approach golf the way zoo pandas approach the obviously fake bamboo groves that dot their enclosures – nonchalantly at first, but soon enough they think of little else in life.

Golf has never been my thing. The idea of flailing after a little ball all the damn day long on a golf course does not appeal, and the idea of doing so on a ship appeals even less. But you have to have something for everyone, that's Contessa's motto. It has never been mine.

I took the stern stairway down one flight to the Sky Deck and entered the gym. Already, the treadmills were milling as passengers did their best to shake off last night's Baked Alaska. You have to keep moving in this life. And as you age you have to keep moving more and more just to keep from getting older too fast.

I counted sixteen identical treadmills lined up along the starboard side of the gym. Each sported its own flat-screen TV. Across from them, rows of recumbent bicycles and elliptical trainers beckoned. Nobody was working the weight machines yet, but it wouldn't be long.

"Can I help you set up a training regimen?"

I turned around to find a young Filipino fellow smiling at me. He consulted a clipboard. "I don't have any appointments set up until nine so I could fit you in."

I have a little treadmill back at Rolling Pines. I swore I'd use it every day but I never use it. I make plans to but it never happens. I like a good walk and a good swim, but other than that, I don't very much like the idea of programmed exercise. "That'd be great," I told him. "Do you have anything open at about nine?"

His nametag said, 'Fred, Manila.' Crewmembers wear their home-towns pinned close to their hearts. He looked at me for a moment then glanced down at his clipboard. "Ouch," he said, "I'm afraid I'm all booked up until about three."

I shook my head sadly. "It's just my luck. Perhaps another day." I walked past a couple of women working with tubular abdominal frames. I tried not to stare but how can you not?

Next to the exercise area and through a low doorway was the reception area for the Ambrosia Spa. I stepped inside and admired the plush couches that lined the waiting room. I decided I was going to be hanging out there a lot because those had to be among the nicest couches I'd ever seen. I tried one. I sat back and kicked off my shoes and put my feet up on the little ottoman. The air smelled like lilacs or something Asian, and there was nature music playing, the kind with little crickets and a waterfall. I'm pretty certain there was an owl in there somewhere. That must be quite a job trying to record that sort of thing, since you can never count on an owl showing up when you need one. Maybe you can. I don't know anything about owls.

I thought about my first cruise; Niagara Falls back in 1943 with Emily on our honeymoon. That was just a few months before I set sail for England on my second cruise, this time aboard a naval ship with a couple thousand other scared American teenagers. Let me tell you something: the first cruise was so much better.

I must have dozed off because all of a sudden there was a young woman leaning over me patting my arm. And unless she just willed herself into existence right at that very moment, I had to have been doing a little sleeping.

"Sir, are you all right?" The accent was Slavic. I was pretty certain she was from Belgrade and that her name was Mina. I put a lot of faith in nametags.

"I'm well, thank you, Mina. I think I just had a little nap."

"I think so."

She was so cute. Her eyes were dark and kind of big. I fall in love at least once per cruise, and Mina was lined right up there to be my number one crush.

"Can I interest you in a massage or a Balkan steam bath?"

I had no idea what a Balkan steam bath was. My mind was not quick to conjure up an image. I gave it a moment and soon enough I had a vision of myself lying on a bearskin rug drinking spiced Vodka from an earthen tumbler as Mina's naked sweating body pressed against mine.

Weren't expecting that from me, were you? I'm full of surprises. I'm not dead, I'm a man even still.

"Most tempting," I told her. "Have you had a lot of takers so far on this cruise?"

"Oh yes. Every day at sea, we're booked full. It's a little slower when we're in port." She looked down. "And ever since, well … it's been a little slow."

I felt sad for her. I wondered if she worked for commission or just tips. Somewhere in my paperwork, I probably had her contract specs written down, so I could check that out, but I felt sad even so. You don't come all the way from Belgrade to the Caribbean just to talk about Balkan steam baths. You come to give them. "Sure then," I said. "Why not the steam bath? Sign me up. How about this afternoon?"

She lit up as if it were Christmas. I wondered if she smoked. She probably did, I decided as she consulted her schedule. Then she frowned. "Nothing. How about tomorrow after, say eight-thirty, right about this time?"

"Perfect. Should I limber up first, jog, drink lots of juice or something?"

"No. Just bring yourself. You'll enjoy."

I promised to bring myself. Then I headed out into the fresh air. There wasn't much else for passengers to do on the Sky Deck. Other than the gym and the spa, there was just a little bit of space for deck chairs but the rest was open to the Tropicana Deck below where the pool and main recreation areas were located. I take that back. There was a little something else if you ignored the 'No Admittance' sign and walked down a narrow path of decking on the port side. If you did that, as I did, you'd come to the bridge. A crewmember perched up on the tower waved me back and called something out but I kept going.

CHAPTER THREE

I suspect that the door to the bridge was probably always locked so I had to knock. Actually I had to knock a couple of times before an officer opened it and started off with a paternal shake of the head, but I wasn't in the mood. I held up my ID card which he strained to look at.

"I'm sorry," he said, "but not on the bridge. Officers only on the bridge. You might have a crew card but it doesn't get you onto the bridge."

I didn't really need to get onto the bridge but I was curious to have a look. Bridges generally have great views. Also, I was interested in testing the limits of my unrestricted access. There was another reason I wanted to go there but it eluded me at the moment. "Yes, it does get me on the bridge," I called out to the officer as he closed the door. "It says all access. That means I can go anywhere, including the bridge." I suggested that a call to Hugh Arlen or to the captain might clear up his error.

Then I had to wait a bit. I heard voices but I wasn't sure if the conversation was transpiring in Swedish or Norwegian or perhaps some hybrid Swahili of the Sea. I was certain however, that the subject matter included both myself and some measure of irritation. A second officer opened the door, a more accommodating man who gestured grandly for me to step onto the bridge.

"Please watch your step," he said, and he grabbed my arm to help me up the step. "I'm Soren Nilsen, staff captain of *Voyager*. I'm told to offer you any assistance you require."

"Well that's a grand thing." I smiled. He seemed a nice enough man, comfortable with himself. That's something I pay some attention to, having moved through life as long as I have, sometimes gracefully and sometimes not. I've spent years being uncomfortable with myself, years interspersed with other years of great comfort. Lately I've been just fine, and I think the staff captain was, too. He was kind of a little guy but in really good shape. On any cruise ship, the staff captain is the person who carries out the captain's orders and oversees the day-to-day operations of the vessel. It's a big job, an important job.

"Can I sit in the chair?" I asked, pointing to one of the three expensive looking Scandinavian chairs lined up in front of an immense control panel. I think I was expecting to see a lot of knobs and levers and dials, but instead it was mostly monitors with images of knobs and levers and dials. Everything was computers these days; even the toaster I got at Target last year had a thing where you can program in your desired degree of toasting.

I sat down in the chair. I've never been a big fan of Scandinavian design, especially when it comes to chairs. I'm a cushion man at heart. Give me lots of padding and just a few options for back support and recline. The chair was all pipes and webbing, but man, once I sat down, I stopped being a cushion man. It was comfortable. I made a mental note to get one when I got back to Rolling Pines. "How do you not fall asleep just sitting here?"

"We do our best," Nilsen said. "Very nice though, isn't it?"

There were three other crewmembers on the bridge: the guy who told me I couldn't come in, another officer sitting next to me who appeared to be doing the actual sailing of the ship, and a security officer who sat behind me in front of a smaller panel.

"What does that one do?" I pointed to a gauge on one of the monitors that was oscillating between 19.6 and 19.7.

"Our current speed in nautical miles."

I liked him. He was the first member of the crew who wasn't obviously irritated at me. "So do you ever sail the ship or does he get all the fun?" I asked, pointing to the officer next to me. "Do you have to keep an eye on him, make sure he doesn't fall asleep?"

Nilsen shrugged. "It depends. Mostly we use the autopilot. A ship like this sails itself. We spend more time at the bar than up here."

"You're joking." I caught myself a moment too late. Of course he was joking.

He grinned. "Currently Mr. Larsen has the helm. We have busy waters today. You can see seven vessels if you count them." He pointed to a large flat panel display above the forward windows. "There we have some information on each of them. Four are private watercraft, yachts or such. The larger vessel starboard is *Makanto*, a freighter out of the Port of Hong Kong headed for the Panama Canal. Beside her, *Amoco Hudson*, a tanker out of Galveston, Texas bound for Barbados."

"What about that one?" I pointed to a large icon on the starboard side of the screen.

"That's *Crystal Serenity* bound for Martinique. Another big cruise ship; we'll be berthed alongside her tonight."

"We're going to Martinique?"

"Of course."

"I thought we were headed to Puerto Rico in three days."

"No. We're not going to Puerto Rico. We have Martinique to-morrow, then a day at sea, then St. Thomas. After that, we'll have another day at sea en route to Miami."

"How about that. I've never been to Martinique. I was in St. Thomas years ago. I had a beverage I quite liked called a piña colada. Have you ever had one?"

"I have. They make them at the bar."

"Is that right? Do you ever sail the ship yourself?"

"I do."

"From this chair or the other one?"

"I usually stand." He picked up something that looked like a huge cell phone. "I use this. Remote control. I can sail the ship from any-where on board."

"Well I'll be god-damned." I remembered the other reason I want-ed to see the bridge. "Tell me something, can you screen security tapes on the big screen up there or do you use one of the ones here on the panel?"

"Not on the big screen. That's always used for tracking nearby shipping. We'd monitor any security files on one of the monitors just in front of you."

"Let me have a look at what he's looking at," I said, pointing to the security officer who sat behind me staring at a bank of monitors.

Leaning over, Nilsen touched a couple of icons on the screen and brought up the security camera data. I watched as what looked like a Tic-Tac-Toe board appeared, splitting the screen into nine tiny monitors, each of which looked out onto a different part of the ship.

The top three were different views of the pool and the area around it. The other screens shifted from one camera to another. I saw the casino in one, though it was closed at that time of day. Also featured were the Bistro, the main ballroom, the library, the daycare, and lots of deck.

"Why do some of them have flashing borders?" I asked.

"Motion. Those are areas that have current activity. Pick one you like and touch the screen."

I pressed the panel that included the waterslide and the rock-climbing wall and watched it expand to fill the screen. I saw a few people strolling about. On any cruise ship you'll find people walking around the deck at almost any hour of the day. The waterslides weren't yet open and the rock-climbing wall, of course, wouldn't be opening at all. It didn't look so big from where I was standing. A young couple with arms around each other's shoulders stopped to point at it, likely talking about where the body was found.

"Who do you think killed him?" I asked.

Nilsen grinned. "Isn't that what you're here to find out?"

"Sure, sure. But you have to have some suspects." I pressed the screen again and the panel shrank back to its smaller size.

"No suspects. Not yet."

"It might have been a member of your crew."

"It might have been."

"I'd like to see the surveillance footage from the night Samson was killed. You should have his murder recorded, right?"

"There is no surveillance footage, of course. If we had a tape of the murder we wouldn't need much of an investigation."

"So why don't you have it?"

"The camera was disabled."

"By who?"

"Who do you think?"

I smiled at him. "You have somebody monitoring the cameras twenty-four hours a day. How does someone disable a camera and not get caught instantly?"

"Very cleverly, I suppose. He would have cut the feed cable to the camera, staying out of the frame, of course. The duty officer filed a work order and switched to another camera. By the time maintenance got to the camera in the morning, Samson was already dead."

"You don't have security patrols on the decks?"

"We do. They noticed nothing out of the ordinary. Look," he said, sitting in the chair next to mine. "We have an acknowledged security failure here, but we did follow company protocols. They will be revised, of course, but we acted appropriately."

"How come I've never seen a security camera? I've been on dozens of ships and I've never seen one."

"They're hidden or disguised. Many of the indoor cameras are set into light fixtures. The exterior ones are often incorporated into the trim."

"How many total?"

"Sixty-two."

"Do they ever malfunction?"

"Rarely."

"When was the last time one malfunctioned?"

"Probably months ago?"

"Can you find out?"

Nilsen fired off a burst of Norwegian to the security officer, who soon produced a log book. Nilsen spent a few moments looking for the appropriate page, then he frowned. "That's interesting."

I peeked and read the entry. A camera on a small patio on the Executive Deck malfunctioned a couple of days before Samson was killed. "What was the nature of the malfunction?" I asked. "I don't have my glasses with me. You keep all records in English?"

"Yes. It says here a string of lights shorted out. This camera was disguised as a light bulb."

"Reason for the short?"

Nilsen shook his head as he read. "Nothing is indicated. It was repaired within the hour. The following day, a camera in the library failed. One of the wires was severed, possibly due to contact with the sharp edge of the ceiling panel."

"Or possibly due to contact with the clippers someone used to cut it," I said. "So within a few days, three cameras were disabled: on the patio, in the library, and by the rock wall."

"We can't know that for sure. The first two could have been genuine malfunctions."

"No they weren't. Look, whoever killed Samson was trying to figure out how he was going to do this without getting caught. He did a couple of test runs and he learned enough about maintenance rotation to know that the camera on the rock wall wouldn't be repaired until morning."

"No. No." Nilsen shook his head, trying to piece it together.

"Yes. Yes. You said the deck camera was repaired within the hour. But I'll bet the library camera was disabled at night, not too late. The library would still have been open, but it was late, maybe nine or ten. He was checking to see if someone would be sent just then or not until morning. The answer is not until morning."

Nilsen said nothing. He just stared at the logbook. "In fact, I'm not the person to be working on this. Hugh Arlen is in charge of security. He's probably already working on the details we just discussed."

"I'm sure he is," I said. I found my glasses in my pocket and I scanned the page in the maintenance log. "The wire that was cut in the library was only an inch from the camera itself. That doesn't sound like it would be easy to do. He'd have to get right up close, so maybe the camera got a look at him before he disabled it."

"It's possible."

"Can I have a copy of it? Of the surveillance file from that camera?"

He thought about that for a moment. "They're large files. We could burn it to a CD."

"That would be swell. Send that over to my Junior Suite. I know what I'll be watching in the evening before I nod off!"

"Maybe you'll get lucky."

"Now is not the time to be thinking about romance," I said. I stood up and stretched. "I guess I'll be leaving. Hey, this has to be a nice job, spending your days up here on the bridge. Do you ever worry about icebergs?"

"No. Not in the Caribbean."

"No. I suppose not."

CHAPTER FOUR

I knew instantly that the Tropicana was going to be my favorite deck. These cruise lines go all out decking out their big ships, and they have to. Ten major cruise lines are out there lined up at the dock waiting to sail away with your money. There are probably a few dozen smaller lines too but each of these ten major lines has between two and eleven ships in the water. Not since the days of ancient Greece, when sleek triremes rowed by chained slaves rammed into each other, has maritime competition been so intense.

I don't care how old you are, how wrinkled, fat, shy or just plain ugly you are, you are going to sit in a lounge chair by the pool. The pool is the soul of any cruise ship and souls are perfect, dainty things. Or maybe they're loud boastful things, I don't know, but they're central to it all.

That's what I was thinking as I came down from the bridge onto the Tropicana Deck. I found myself in an elevator lobby right in front of the daycare, the children's activity room. Next to it was what looked like daycare for older kids, young teens maybe, several of whom were already lined up at the controls of some video games. I don't play those myself. I don't really know how anyone can since they have more buttons and knobs than I have fingers.

The warm breeze hit me as I swung the door open. I looked around quickly, but really I was just ready to be outside. Later I would get out my swim trunks and my cap and have a dip, but not just yet.

There must have been five or six hundred lounge chairs right out on the deck. Alternating rows of green and gold cushions gave way here and there to bathers who were already out in some force. About fifty or sixty people were taking advantage of the morning sun.

I passed the base of the rock-climbing wall and almost ran straight into one of the waterslides. I gave a little bit of thought to trying out the slide. It really did look fun, but honestly, it probably wouldn't be the best idea for a mature man. I wondered if you'd get turned around in there.

The pool itself was glorious. A younger couple splashed around, playing at drowning each other. I walked along the edge of the pool and then across a little bridge that passed over it. Beyond the bridge, the pool expanded greatly, surrounding a little island where more lounge chairs were laid out like the petals of a flower. A big hot tub formed the center of it all.

What kind of a person do you think is going to lay out on an island in the middle of everything? Oh, a pretty one, I guarantee you that. Several lovely petals had already unfolded from their slumber to begin their daily tanning photosynthesis. The hot tub was empty but I made a note to check back later.

If you were in the pool, and you swam past the island, you could swim right up to an underwater barstool and order one of those piña coladas which would probably be a nice thing to do in a pool.

I found myself staring out at the sea, the beautiful Caribbean. It was calm, even serene. I saw the large freighter they pointed out to me on the bridge, and another cruising ship. I wondered how many people were on board. Some of the larger ships can accommodate more than three thousand people. I must have daydreamed a little because I nearly bumped right into the Tai Chi in the Morning group.

"Well hello again!" It was Fred from Manila from the gym. "Would you like to join us for some Tai Chi?"

A dozen people were lined up there, holding a pose. Their arms were outstretched, hands pointing down, as they balanced on one leg. It wasn't for me. "Not today," I told Fred. "I'm more of a kick-boxer."

"We have kick-boxing at four."

"Oh, bullshit."

"No, we do. Really." Fred assured me he wasn't kidding. "Have you studied the martial arts?"

"Not since I was in the service, and I wasn't a big fan then either."

"Maybe we could find something that you would like."

"Do you know what time they have Bingo?"

Fred shook his head. "Let me know if you change your mind."

I took the outdoor stairs down to the Penthouse Deck and walked down the hall, one long hallway from stern to bow. Well, really there were two long hallways, one on each side of the ship but the Penthouse Deck was all penthouse suites, much larger than my Junior Suite. The middle of the deck, between the hallways, was storage areas, compact galleys, maintenance rooms, and a couple of small crew lounges where the penthouse butlers hung out.

Most of the passengers were already out and about, either finishing breakfast or figuring out what to do for the day. The stewardesses were hard at work, their carts partially obstructing the hallways, piled high with towels and fruit bowls. I peeked into the suites as I passed by. They were nice, I'll tell you. Nice big balconies. The beds were bigger too, King-sized probably, and they had much bigger TVs.

Near the midpoint of the ship were the parliamentary suites, one on the starboard side and one on the port, and the door to one of them was open. I saw the cart with the towels and cleaning supplies in the hall but I didn't see the stewardess, so I peeked.

I took just a half a step inside, and man, it was really something. It was at least as big as my condo at Rolling Pines. It had a separate living room with a big wrap-around couch. A flat-screen TV took up nearly a whole wall, and out on the balcony, I saw a private hot tub. I wanted to see what the bar looked like so I took a couple more steps inside. God, you could have a party in there. The bar was a thing of wonder, bigger even than some pubs I've been to. It was all wood and chrome and had four wood and chrome stools. Behind it I spied a

Sub-Zero refrigerator and one of those counter-top wine chillers with the glass door.

"Is there something particular you're looking for?" The voice came from behind me.

I spun around, kind of unsure what to say. "Sorry," is all that came to mind. He was a short man with a bit of girth to him. He was a younger man, too, maybe early seventies with a Spanish accent. He could have used a shave and some pants. "I didn't know anyone was home."

"So you thought you'd just intrude."

He had me there. "Again, I'm sorry. I was just curious. I have a Junior Suite down below that looks out onto a lifeboat. I was curious to see what a Parliamentary Suite looked like, and I have to say I am impressed. It is truly presidential, regal even. Senatorial in the Roman sense."

"I'd offer you a drink but it's a bit early."

"Had I intruded later, would things have been different?"

He stared at me. "Perhaps."

"I could come back."

"Perhaps another day."

"Well hold on." I got out my little day planner book. "What about tomorrow? I'm free tomorrow. Tomorrow we'll be in Mozambique"

He continued to stare. "Martinique."

"That's what I said. Is that a staircase?" Just next to the bedroom I saw it. I've never seen a two-story suite on a cruise ship.

"Yes it is."

"Where does it go?"

"It goes downstairs."

"As I expected. What's down there?"

He shuffled a bit and reached down to pull up a sock. "A den more or less, with office space."

"Is there another bar?"

"Yes."

"So are we on for tomorrow? You could show me the downstairs."

"I'll have to check my agenda," he said.

I gave him my number and belatedly introduced myself. He shook my hand but said nothing. I asked him his name.

"Duarte."

"Just Duarte?"

"Duarte, yes."

I didn't have my glasses on so I squinted a little to get a good look at him. "You look kind of familiar. Were you in some films or something?"

I couldn't be sure if he grinned or if it was something involuntary. "No," he said. "I was not in some films. I would like to dress myself now, if you'll excuse me."

I stepped back into the hall and the door closed behind me. I could have walked a bit more but I was getting hungry. It was about lunchtime and I'll tell you something; one thing these cruise ships do well is food. I've been on quite a few cruises and I don't know any that don't do food exceptionally well. I took the elevator down to the Avenue Deck and headed for the dining room.

Including myself, 1,533 passengers were currently aboard, and I'd have been willing to bet that close to a thousand of them were gathered right there, waiting for the dining room to open, waiting to be fed. I got there just as they opened the doors and the herding began.

One thing I like to do on cruises is to estimate the average passenger age. I spotted some families, even some babies amongst the older ladies and dashing gents, so I'd say the average age was about forty-eight. A couple years back I worked a drowning case on one of the Cunard ships, and I put the average age at a hundred and three.

Lunch was open seating, meaning a fellow such as myself could sit just about anywhere. One of the waiters came to escort me. He was Andres from Dubrovnik and he had a quizzical look on his face; he didn't remember seeing me before so he couldn't greet me by name as his supervisors would like. "A small table by the window or can I seat you with a group?" he asked.

"A group, please." He scanned his assigned section of the room before deciding on a table. It was an eight-seater, and already two couples were at work on the basket of rolls. I could already tell that we were going to need more butter.

By the way one of the men took charge of the introductions, I knew they were friends. It's not uncommon for couples to cruise together. "Elliot Powell," he announced, holding out a hand. "This is my wife Donna and those two midgets over there are Doug and Opal Baxter."

I told them who I was. I decided to profile the little group here. It's what I do, where my talent lies. "Let me just have a look at this menu," I said. I love looking at menus, always have. I like eating my food thinking about the fact that there was something else I could have been eating instead. It makes me feel happy.

Opal Baxter was a tiny woman, though not a midget in any real sense. She was in her mid-sixties, and was about half the size of Donna Powell, who appeared to have spent a great deal more time on wardrobe and makeup than her friend. I concluded that Elliot and Doug were the operative friends, and the women had possibly become vague friends over the years as they spent more and more time together.

"Can I recommend something?" Donna leaned over and tapped a meaty finger on my menu. "Shrimp cocktail. Sometimes I don't even eat the entrée. I just have them bring more shrimp cocktail. We don't eat a lot of shrimp back in Marysville. That's up by Sioux Falls."

I knew right then that she was a woman of substance, a woman who paid attention to culinary temptations. Two appetizers was an inspired idea. "I think I will have the shrimp cocktail. I like also the sound of the featured entrée: Scandinavian Venison," I read from the menu. "Slow-roasted with rosemary. Served with garlic mashed potatoes and fresh New England miniature beets. I had no idea they grew miniature beets in New England."

Donna chuckled. "I guess I didn't either."

Continuing with my profile, I decided that Elliot and Doug owned neighboring farms. They kept cows and chickens and hearty Scandinavian deer. Often at dawn, the two men would meet at the barbwire fence that divided their properties. They'd be riding mustangs and drinking coffee from earthenware mugs, and they'd discuss the day's chores. Elliot was a big man, big-boned, but also a fat man. He threw his weight around some, using it to bully Doug when they had a disagreement. Back home, Opal worried about mildew. And in the other home, Donna snacked.

Andres from Dubrovnik came to take our orders.

"Doug and I generally have a beer or two at lunch," Elliot said. "How about you join us, Henry?"

"Oh, I don't know. I don't really like to drink alone."

A look of confusion passed over his face. "I can't see as how you'd be drinking alone since you'd be joining us."

He had a point.

"What sort of work do you do, Henry?"

"Retired," I told them. "I did a little of this and a little of that. I was a teacher a long time ago."

I heard Doug's voice for the first time. It was about as soft as I imagined it would be. "I almost went into teaching myself," he said.

"A retired teacher," Elliot concluded.

"No, that was a long time ago. It was only for a short time. I did home inspections for a number of years and then I worked private security. I ran for Congress in 1972. I was in *Time* Magazine."

"Were you now?" Elliot asked.

"I did. I was the endorsed Democrat. I carried much of the district too if twenty-eight percent can be called much."

Elliot made a circling motion with his finger. "We're all Republicans."

"I won't hold it against you. How about you, what do you do for a living?"

"We're veterinarians. Doug and I started our practice twenty-three years ago, large animals mostly."

I wasn't far off.

It took no more than a minute for Andres to bring our beverages. The women drank iced tea.

"You play poker, Henry?" Elliot asked, leaning back in his seat.

I shook my head. "Not in years."

"That's a shame. Doug and I found a late night game. We've been playing most nights."

"Is that right? Let me ask you something, you ever have anyone bring in something really strange, like an octopus?"

"To the poker game?"

I frowned. "No. To be fixed. I thought you were vegetarians."

"Veterinarians," he said.

"That's what I said. How about a circus animal, like a dancing bear or one of those talking seals?"

"Well, no, nothing like that, but about a year-and-a-half ago, a man brought in a porcupine that had advanced periodontal disease."

I shook my head. "So sad."

"No, no. We fixed him up."

"You fixed him up? What did you do?"

"Well, we cleaned his teeth."

"Just like that? He didn't shoot poison at you through his spines?"

Doug nudged in at that point. "A porcupine in actuality is not a poisonous animal."

"No. I remember a television program where the porcupine shot out a little dart and hit a bear and the bear ran away."

Elliot and Doug exchanged frowns.

"No? In any case, this porcupine just sat there and let you brush his teeth?"

"Well, no. We had to knock him out for that, just as you would a cat or a dog. Most animals don't really like it when you poke around in their mouths."

"I imagine not," I said. "Let me ask you something, are any of you at all nervous or kind of scared knowing that there's a killer on board?"

Glances were exchanged.

Opal decided to end her silence. "I'm terrified," she said. "I want to go home. This has been a terrible cruise, just terrible."

Doug put his hand on hers. "We've talked about this, honey. It wasn't a random killing. And they definitely have more guards now patrolling. People get killed. It's the world we live in. This is about drugs, I'll bet you five dollars."

"I don't pay it much mind," Donna said. "People get killed in Marysville too, like that Mexican fellow that held up the Purple Rose."

Opal was clearly becoming frustrated. "He was shot by the police, Donna, when he wouldn't drop his gun. That's a little bit different."

"All I'm saying is that people get killed all over the place."

Opal wasn't giving up. "Well since I'm not going to be holding up a Bar and Grill, I'm not too worried about the police shooting me. What I am worried about is some insane lunatic strangling me with a towel."

Elliot held up his empty beer glass, indicating to Andres that we'd like a refill. I had barely started mine. "My position is this," he said. "Whoever killed the F.B.I. investigator knew him and hated him. There's lots of easier ways to kill someone than that. Just push him overboard."

"Someone would have seen that," Opal insisted. It was clearly part of a conversation they had had before.

"Probably not," I said. "If someone goes overboard at night, they would very likely go unnoticed. And once in the water, they wouldn't be able to yell loud enough for anyone to hear."

"That's my point," Elliot said. "It's personal, so it doesn't have anything to do with us. We signed up for ten days here, and at better than $9,000 a couple, I'm disinclined to let it spoil my fun."

Opal shook her head grimly as Doug tried to comfort her.

"Opal writes the obituaries for the *Gazette*," Donna whispered to me. "That's part of why she maybe is a little sensitive."

"Did any of you go to Samson's talks?" I asked.

Elliot shook his head. "Doug and I golf, but Donna checked out a few of the programs."

"I did," she confirmed. "I went to the first one where he talked about that killer he tracked down, the one who killed those kids. I meant to go to the second one but my beauty appointment went over so I only made the last ten minutes or so. He was talking about the homosexual fellow in Cape Cod who ran the Bed and Breakfast."

"Harvey Cotton," I said. I had read about him earlier, back in the Junior Suite.

"Right. He was stabbed to death on his patio one night coming home with the groceries."

"They dumped his body in the ocean," Opal added. "I was at the lecture too. The police figured it as part of a series of hate crimes targeting homosexuals but Samson said it wasn't that at all."

We paused as Andres brought our meals, delicately placing Donna's twin shrimp cocktails in front of her. She clapped her hands in delight.

"He also said it wasn't part of a robbery either," Opal continued, "that the robbery was just a cover-up."

The conversation was getting interesting but so was my Scandinavian venison. I waited as long as I could, cursing as Andres fiddled with Opal's snow crab. I took a bite. I'll tell you something; I have never tasted anything quite so oddly delicious coming from a land mammal. I really love food. Not just food, but the eating of it. I have a little belly that I've had for quite some time and it's always been a source of pride. The New England miniature beets tasted quite a bit like regular beets, though they were somewhat smaller. "Who did Samson think it was?" I asked, between mouthfuls. I reached for another roll.

Donna's eyes were closed and she appeared to be praying and chewing at the same time. "Divine," she said finally. She took another minute to digest. "Well, he said it was someone who knew Cotton for a long time. He was going to tell us who it was in his next talk."

"Did you go to that one?"

She stared at me for a moment. "No, I didn't. He died."

"True. Very true."

Opal hadn't touched her snow crab. "He said he was prepared to turn over his notes to the police in Massachusetts if we found his argument convincing. I had every intention of going to the next talk."

"So you think maybe the person who killed Cotton came on the cruise and killed Samson too?" I asked.

Both Donna and Opal nodded.

"Samson must have left some notes behind. He must have written it all down somewhere."

"His cabin had been cleaned out. The killer took his keycard."

"Is that right?"

"They told us in the interview. The cruise director and the chief security guy here interviewed us all, all of us who saw the talk."

"Is that right?" I had a lot to think about here but at the moment, I needed to concentrate on my food. Concentrating on one's food is important.

Good food has a life of its own quite apart from the life it had before it was killed to become food. It is demanding and consuming, requiring attention and praise. The better the quality, the greater the gravitational pull. Once in Munich, after the war, I ate a schnitzel that tasted like a breaded angel. It was like a culinary black hole – pulling in all attention, all thoughts, all words. I complemented the cook but I don't think he could hear me.

We talked a bit about obituaries, Opal and I, but I couldn't concentrate too well. I had been up half the night and I was tired. Since no other theories were immediately at hand, I was willing to believe that Harvey Cotton's killer came on board and killed Samson because he was closing in on him. And since nobody had disembarked since, the killer was still on board.

CHAPTER FIVE

I napped. I'm an old man and we do that. I napped longer than I planned to, and if the light coming in through my window, after passing through the window of the lifeboat hanging just outside was any indication, the afternoon was already more than half over. Very likely there was a clock around somewhere.

I flipped through the TV channels without finding anything of interest. The CD I was waiting for had been delivered while I was at lunch. I meant to watch it as soon as I got back to the Junior Suite, but as I said, I napped. It came in a little CD envelope that said, "18 hrs, 11 min."

I put it in the player and turned it on. It was the surveillance footage from the hidden camera in the library. The camera itself

45

was positioned across from the desk. It captured the one part of the library that couldn't be seen by the librarian at the desk. At the far end of the frame was a big comfortable chair with a table next to it underneath a window. It was a nice cozy reading corner. Other than that, the image was just bookcases. I wondered if the camera was really necessary. How many people pay ten grand for a cruise just to steal a large print copy of *The Da Vinci Code?*

The thought of spending all day watching the tape was starting to bring me down. I was on a cruise, after all, and I had no intention of spending it in my Junior Suite watching heads bobble in and out of a library. I switched tasks and began looking at the crew assignments to see if I had any friends on board. I glanced at the pages of biography abstracts on the 640 members of *Voyager's* crew.

Most crewmembers on any ship work contracts, generally about six to eight months long after which they go home at company expense, for a few months. Almost everyone completes multiple contracts, and most work several cruise lines over the course of their careers. The lowest paid scrubbies on *Voyager* made about $800 a month, and even that far exceeds what an unskilled laborer could earn in Manila. I'd probably sailed with some of these guys before but I wouldn't recognize their names or even their faces.

The cruise director I did know; Ron Gibson, a British fellow. I last ran into him a couple of years back on one of the Carnival ships, but I've been in the business for a few years now and so has Ron so our paths have crossed here and there, kind of like cars in the night.

I knew Inga Hess from Entertainment. Inga was a one-woman cabaret act. I'd seen her show a number of times. Entertainers can make really good money at sea; far more than they can make on land.

Who goes to cabaret shows anymore? You know who – people like me, mature people. And people like me aren't about to get behind the wheel of the Oldsmobile and drive to a show they might sleep part way through anyway. But they do go on cruises, and most of them have nothing better to do before dinner than go to a before-dinner cabaret show. Inga would remember me. I'm charming.

My Junior Suite was starting to feel a little cramped so I headed out and took the elevator up to the Lido Deck. I like to watch people but I get self-conscious because I worry that I might be staring.

The Lido was crowded. There's a lot you can do on a cruise ship, and the Lido was the deck to do a lot of it on. I wandered through the casino, which was surprisingly busy. There were maybe a hundred slot machines chiming away, and the Blackjack tables were full. Let me tell you something: if you want to gamble at a casino, you'd do better to stick to the ones that are on land. Go to Atlantic City, they've got ten or so, and those ten casinos compete with each other. On a ship there's no such market force at play. A slot machine here will drop a quarter maybe once every six months but you wouldn't know that from all the ringing and banging. I'm not a big gambler myself.

I headed for the atrium, the expansive two-story heart of the ship. A miniature rainforest dominated the atrium. I took the little winding path through it, passing two waterfalls, trees with giant fanning leaves, and a toucan that I suspect wasn't real.

Beyond the rainforest was the reception desk. The atrium was ringed by shops with jungle themes: Amazon Apparel, Tropical Treasures, and disappointingly, the Piranha Cabana. I kept walking. I passed the Bistro where I had my breakfast, and finally I came to the library. It was closed. It would likely reopen in half an hour if the sign printed on the door was any indication.

I kept walking until I came to a nice looking little bar. The Steamboat Saloon was all dark wood and shutters, like something vaguely British colonial that had been put out to sea. I found a comfortable table and chair and got my papers organized.

Lana from St. Petersburg took my order. I kind of felt like having a cigarette, though I hadn't had one in about forty years. Let me tell you something: most murder cases are not complex. Most are solvable. I know what you're thinking: the cops don't have the time to investigate. That might be true. But I do, and I can find a killer. I pay attention to details.

Unbidden, Lana brought me a plate of little sandwiches with my Merlot. It's that kind of detail that brings a passenger back time and time again.

So I made some notes and I made a list of the things I was going to need. I needed to know if Robert Samson had submitted copies of his speeches, or if they were recorded. I would need Hugh Arlen to cross-check the passenger manifest against other cruises that Samson worked on. It's possible, I was thinking, that the killer might have tracked him before. If so, I might be able to get a name, even if it was a fake one. I would also need to know why Samson was alone since an entertainment contract always allows for a spouse or guest.

I waved to Lana and she came back promptly, eagerly even. Maybe she liked me. "Can I get a couple more of these sandwiches?" I asked. "And can you call Hugh Arlen and ask him if he will meet me here."

She looked a little unsure right then. Passengers don't usually summon the officers. "We can page him but he's probably on duty."

I showed her my crew identification card which seemed to surprise her a bit. "Tell him it's important, please. He'll understand. The Merlot is first rate, by the way."

He made me wait close to fifteen minutes, which is the outer marker of what I was going to let him get away with. "I'm a busy man," he told me, straight away. "And I'm not available at your beck and call. If you need to contact me, you can leave a message at reception."

I assured him I would. Lana crept up behind him but he shook his head. I handed him the list I just made.

He shook his head again as he read it. "Passenger information is confidential. And in any case, I don't have the staff to do this research. Much of what you're requesting is already part of my ongoing investigation."

"And it will become part of mine," I assured him. "I'll also need you to be watching tomorrow to see who gets off in Martinique and doesn't re-board. You'll need to coordinate with the police and airport control."

He was getting a little hot. "Let's understand each other, Henry."

"Let's, Hugh."

"We have a very delicate situation here that we are pursuing with the utmost diligence. You are here so that our parent company can put on a helpful, caring face so that people such as yourself will still book the Autumn and Winter cruises and not be scared off by the idea that we have a murderer on the loose."

"You do have a murderer on the loose," I reminded him.

"I know that. And we are following some leads, so if you leave me alone, I can perhaps do my job."

"Let me tell you something," I told him. "When I was in the service, I was a corporal. There was this private who behaved much as you do, misunderstanding the nature of things, and it fell to me to correct his behavior which I did in short time."

I paused there to sip my Merlot. "Nutty," I said, "but it has a nice finish. Look, I'm here to solve a crime and you're going to assist me in any way you can. If you have a problem with that, I'll call Kenji Sakato himself in Kobe, Japan. He's the guy who owns this ship and therefore owns you, and I will request that you be replaced. I've worked for him before. He'll agree because if he doesn't, my next call will be to C.N.N. Have you met Mr. Sakato?"

Arlen glared at me. "I haven't had the pleasure."

"Well, we're old buddies," I lied. I'd never met the man nor had any direct communication with him. "We talk frequently. I'll probably be giving him a call this evening as a matter of fact." I stood up to go. Arlen wasn't looking at me; he was too angry. "Do you know if it's O.K. if I take my drink out of here and carry it around?"

He looked up at me. "You don't have to be such a hard ass."

"I know," I said. "It pains me."

The library was just opening when I got there, and Jewell from Manila asked if she could help me find a book. "We have DVDs too."

"Do you have DVDs of the lectures that were given on this cruise?"

"I'm sorry we don't." She made a sad face. "But we do have some educational titles if you look on aisle three."

I looked on aisles three and two and one. It was a nice little library. Not a huge number of books, of course, but there were some nice fat chairs for reading and a couple of tables with magazines fanned out across them. I took a seat in a big comfortable chair by a window. I couldn't spot the camera at first but it didn't take me long. It was a tiny thing right up there looking like part of the sprinkler system. I wondered how long it would take me to find it if I didn't know more or less where it was.

I made my way back to Jewell. "Very busy these days?"

"Not so much. We get a lot of traffic in the morning."

"Mostly the same old people day after day," I offered.

She smiled. "Sure, we do have our regulars which is nice because then I can get to know people by name."

"That's a lovely thing," I told her. Leaving the library, I passed the Bistro again and I walked the misty path through the rainforest. I tried to find the toucan but I couldn't. I walked back through the casino and played one quarter in a slot machine. It rang and rang; I'd won a quarter. I was in a fine mood when I got to the Copacabana Lounge. I was after all, a winner.

Inga was at the piano singing something from the standard song-book that all entertainers seem to have memorized. I've always wondered what goes through a singer's mind when she's working her way through the theme song from *Cats* or *Grease* or whatever for the millionth time. I made a note to ask Inga when she finished with her Beatles medley.

If I had another drink at that point, I would probably just float off the ship, so I just sat and relaxed. Inga spotted me and smiled. It was a little dark so I couldn't read the nametag of the fellow who came by to attend. I declined the drink, the nuts, even the sandwich. It was too close to dinner and I wanted to try the swordfish with porcini mushrooms.

So I sat and listened to Inga sing. I had always liked her. She came right over when she finished. She gave me a big hug. "Henry, I've missed you."

"We'll always have Princess Cruises 'Spring Mexican Riviera Four Night Escape,'" I told her.

"Here's looking at you, kiddo! What are you doing here, Henry? I didn't know you were on board."

"What do you think I'm doing here?" She knew what work I did.

"Of course. Yeah." She sat across from me. "Yeah, that was something. And the killer is still onboard, obviously."

I nodded. "And he'll get off tomorrow in Martinique. He'll get off and then a few hours later, he'll walk right back onto the ship. Not doing so would attract suspicion. Why take a cruise and not visit the ports of call? So tomorrow I'm going to rule out the people who stay on board."

"You haven't figured out who it is yet?"

"I haven't."

She called to the waiter. "Jewell, will you bring me a Vodka Tonic, and a Kahlua and Sprite for my friend."

"No, no." I waved my finger at Jewell. "I don't drink that anymore. That was just for a few months but it gave me gas. I'll have a Merlot please."

I hadn't figured out who did it yet, but I was getting close. "I have it narrowed down to about four hundred and fifty people."

"How is that?"

"The killer is a man, I'm sure of that, so I excluded the women and children. If I took out the aged and infirm I'd be down to about eleven suspects so I'm not prepared to do that just yet."

"Henry, I heard you were on the Belgravia ship when the guy went overboard near Mykonos."

"Don't try to blame that on me," I said. "He was already dead by the time I got there."

"Don't make fun of me." She sat back, almost floating into the chair, and lit a cigarette. Her hair fanned out behind her. She was probably in her early forties and she'd been living at sea so long she seemed to belong. "He was drunk or something, right? He took a nosedive off his balcony, right? Did they find the body?"

I nodded. "Yes, a sponge diver pulled him up a couple days later. The guy's wife sued Belgravia for not working with local authorities. She filed the suit before he was even found."

"Did she get the money?"

"No she dropped the suit the next day after I had a talk with her."

"What did you say? Did you think she killed him?"

"Yes I did. He had his girlfriend in another cabin. He had brought her along for the cruise. The wife found out about it and pushed him over the side."

"She told you that? She confessed?"

"Yes she did, after I sat her down and told her that her husband hadn't jumped after all but was alive and well, starting a new life on Mykonos with his gay lover."

"And you made that up."

"I did."

"She didn't believe you, though?"

"Of course she didn't. She killed him, or she thought she did, but it got her thinking that he might have survived. I told her we'd arranged to fly in her kids to see him and his new lover, Thor."

"Thor?"

"Yeah, then she started to come apart. 'If there's one thing that asshole is not, it's a homo,' she kept saying."

"So how did you get her to confess?"

I didn't even notice that my Merlot had arrived but there it was on the table beside me. I don't see very well without my glasses and I thought I had them but I didn't, and it was kind of dark. "I just kept with that story for awhile and then I shifted. I just asked her point blank why she pushed him. I told her he was willing to testify that she pushed him. Then she confessed."

"And then you told her he was dead."

"That's right."

Inga made quick work of her Vodka tonic. "You're bad, Henry."

"I'm a bad man."

She smiled. "It's not that far-fetched a story though, guy realizes he's gay and leaves to start a new life on an island somewhere."

I thought about that for a moment. "No, it's not bad." I thought about it for a moment more. Cape Cod is kind of like an island. What if something from Harvey Cotton's old life came back to haunt him? "Let me ask you something, Inga. Did you talk with Robert Samson at all?"

She lit another cigarette. "Not much, just to say hello. He drank in here a lot, and once he bought me a drink. He was already drunk and talking about his wife leaving him. New wife; they were only two years into it."

"Did he say why she left?"

She shook her head. "No, he was just drunk and complaining. He kept asking if he could buy me a drink and I kept pointing out that he already had."

"Did you ever see him with anyone?"

"No. Now and again passengers would come up to him to say they liked his talk or something, but he wasn't very social. Ron gave him a bit of a hard time about that. Our contracts do require us to be social. Have you talked with Ron yet?"

I hadn't. Cruise directors tend to know more than most people so I was due to call on him. "Are you still dating the fellow who takes the snapshots?"

"The photographer, Henry. Photographers take photographs not snapshots, and no. I'm not. My heart belongs to Manuel from Hotel Services."

"A keeper, is he?"

"We'll see. We'll see. And you? Did you make an honest woman of Bernice from Biloxi?"

"Candace from Colorado Springs," I reminded her, "and no, I'm too young to settle down."

CHAPTER SIX

Dinner on a luxury cruise ship is something quite extraordinary. It's tuxedos and gowns, real ones, the kind of tuxedoes and gowns that haven't been seen at dry land affairs for decades. I'm talking about sequins, mink stoles, diamond collars, ivory buttons, that sort of thing. If you took all the cufflinks from a single cruise and lined them up, you would have a fourteen karat chain long enough to reach the moon and back fourteen times. You don't see those kinds of garments and finery on dry land anymore, not for decades. There's a genteel elegance at sea that has been lost elsewhere, and that's why people come back again and again.

The line to get into the dining room was long but the herding moved at an acceptable pace. Each tuxedoed waiter took a lady by the arm, holding her drink as he escorted her to her table. And I promise you she has a drink. Every last one of them does.

That waiter will remember her name and will take good care of her. In return, he has a more or less guaranteed gratuity of $5 per dinner. And at the end of the cruise, that lady will almost certainly slip him an extra $20 or $50, so he'll do well to remember her beverage of choice. Every couple of months an angel will come along. She'll be an older woman, wiry, and at the end of her cruise she'll give him an envelope with $1,000 in it.

This is an interaction between haves and needs, between the wanting and the willing. It's the magic show of economic inequality – there's simply no way to make that kind of money in Manila or Bucharest, or Riga or Lodz. And there's simply no way to get that kind of service in Omaha or Trenton, or Oakland or Sioux Falls.

Andres from Dubrovnik offered to hold my wine but I didn't let him. I can hold my own wine. I needed to circulate. I told him I was interested in sitting with someone other than my lunch companions, and he had a quick chat with the maitre d' that turned into a longer chat. The dining room was crowded. Would I care for the late seating at 8:45?

I was alarmed. "Do I look like I'll be awake at 8:45?"

Andres took my response back to the maitre d' and they made me wait. I've financed cars with less back and forth. Finally he came back with a smile. He made another failed grab for my drink and then led me to a window table, a four-seater, where a very pretty young woman sat across from a man who was clearly a bit older. I was willing to bet they'd had the table to themselves so far, and they wouldn't be happy about me showing up.

I made an instant profile of their relationship. It was an office thing. He was the boss in an advertising company, or something like that, and she was the secretary. Not the secretary. I forgot that they don't have those anymore, nor typists, nor even receptionists. At the bank I go to they got rid of the girl who sat out front and put in a computer that you type your name into. They named the computer Holly. Call me old-fashioned but I'm not going to call a computer by name, and if I did, it would be Titus or Rex or something with numbers in it. In any case, I decided that he was the boss and she was the administrative associate. Maybe they were both working on the pudding account and fell in love.

"Hello, Hello," I called out as I took my seat. "I'm Henry. I won't be a bother, I promise. They put me on the late dinner list but I've got a little diabetes so I have to eat earlier."

The woman gave me a great big smile. "Shelley Tobin," she said, shaking my hand. "This is my husband Jack."

She was pretty. I thought I forgot my glasses but I found them in my pocket so I put them on. "Hey. You're beautiful. I mean gorgeous. You could be a model. If you were a model, I'd buy stuff from you, like socks or powder."

She smiled but she didn't blush. Jack had a strange look on his face.

"You look familiar. Maybe you are a model. Have I seen you in the *Reader's Digest?*"

"No," she said, "but you're close. I play Jasmine on *Quickly Deadly.*"

"Say what?"

"I'm an actor. *Quickly Deadly.* Thursday nights at nine."

"You're an actor? You mean an actress."

"An actor," she corrected me.

"Well I'll be god-damned." I leaned in closer.

"No, that's not what I mean," she said, a little alarmed now.

Jack jumped to her rescue. "Actor is the preferred term now for both men and women. She is in fact a woman."

"Ah ha. I see." My heart was racing a bit. "That makes more sense. An actor. I didn't know this. Well how about that. So what do you act at on *Thursday Bloody?*"

"*Quickly Deadly*. I'm a demolitions expert."

"Well I'll be god-damned."

Andres arrived just in time. I couldn't take the confusion. I had barely glanced at the menu but I already knew what I wanted. Shelley and Jack both ordered the rack of lamb, but not me. "I'll have the porpoise with the sordini mushrooms," I told Andres.

Andres frowned.

"I don't think they're serving porpoise," Jack noted.

Andres stared at me. "You mean the swordfish with porcini mushrooms?"

"That's what I said, and the onion soup." I looked around at the room. It was quite full, quite festive. My new friend Duarte was sitting alone at a window a couple of tables down. I waved to him but he wasn't looking. He was probably thinking about getting back to his Parliamentary Suite.

I snapped my fingers. "The *TV Guide*. You were on the cover of the *TV Guide* maybe?"

She nodded, sipping her wine. "Yes, it was a couple of months ago."

I decided to pretend Jack wasn't here and she and I were on a date. I moved my chair in closer. "Is your character a good girl or a bad girl?"

"Well," she began, gesturing at her husband, "at this point it's not entirely clear. You'd have to ask Jack. He's the lead writer."

"Lead writer; that sounds impressive. So that's how you two got together? He chased down his leading lady?"

Jack laughed and almost coughed up a roll.

"Quite the opposite," Shelley said. "I won him over, slowly but surely."

"Is that true?"

Jack nodded, though not terribly enthusiastically.

"He didn't like me at first," Shelley said. "He doesn't much like me now either, but for awhile he did, very much."

"Can we not do this, Shelley?"

"He was afraid of being just another one of my playthings, that's what he told me."

"Are you kidding me?" I asked Jack. "Why the hell didn't you want to be one of her playthings. I'd stand in line to be one of her playthings."

Shelley reached over and gave my hand a squeeze. "It's complicated," she said. "We were both in relationships."

"I see. So is she going to wind up being a good girl or a bad girl?"

"We'll have to see how the vacation goes," Jack said.

"I meant the show."

"I know."

"Fair enough. So you solve crimes on the show?"

Shelley nodded as our soup came. "Every episode, more or less."

"So how would you write an ending to this one?" I gestured at Jack with my soup spoon. "Retired F.B.I. profiler comes back for one last case. He goes on cruise to give lectures, in exchange for a free cruise, and promises to reveal the identity of a killer but he gets killed before he gets the chance? You think you could write your way out of that one?"

"I think I could," he said.

Andres was back so I ordered a bottle of Merlot for the table. "So who did it?"

"I didn't mean I could do it right now."

Shelley rubbed his arm. "Come on, let's give it a try."

He shook his head. "You always do this."

"I always do not. Come on, we could use this in the show."

We had about a minute-and-a-half of terrible, terrible silence before Andres arrived with the Merlot. I had him fill Jack's glass first. Before long, I refilled it and that seemed to get him to another place.

"First we'd need a back story, some history," he said.

"Like what?"

"This F.B.I. profiler; we can probably assume he's not really welcome around the Bureau anymore. They're tired of his ranting. He was a hero a long time ago and he wants that again."

"Go on." I leaned in. I decided to pretend Shelley wasn't there and he and I were working a case together.

"His marriage is failing or his wife died, or something like that. He's getting old, and his pension is adequate but unremarkable. Plus he gambles or he likes whores. He misses the spotlight so he does these lectures. He gets a little attention that way, but it's not exactly prime time."

I nodded, unsure where he was going.

"So he's getting lonely, getting depressed. He wants that one last shot at fame but he's also a big drinker which makes him prone to mistakes."

"How did you know he was a big drinker?" I asked.

Jack stared at me. "I don't. I don't know anything about him. I'm just trying to write a plausible scenario."

"So you just made up the part about the whores, too?"

"I did, yes."

"Well, you had me convinced. So who's the killer?"

"I don't know. And I don't think Robert Samson knew either."

Shelley frowned. "Well that's not much of a story, honey."

"I agree with Shelley. If I was watching your show on TV, I'd change the channel. I had the cable TV installed, which has a great many channels. I watched a show about a woman who was so fat that they had to cut off her skin after they sucked out the fat because she had too much skin. Hey, did you ever write for *Murder She Wrote?*"

He shook his head. "I didn't have the pleasure."

"That's a shame. Have you met Angela Lansbury?"

"No, and I'm not saying I can't figure out who did it. I'm just saying that Samson didn't know the killer."

"Why do you think that?"

"He would have told someone."

"But he must have had an idea." I drink a lot of wine when I get excited, often, too, when not excited.

"I'm sure he had some idea, but his plan would have been to draw the killer out. He's been on the case for years, so the killer is very likely watching his moves, paying attention. Samson would have counted on that."

I spent a few moments eating my soup, thinking about that as Shelley refilled our glasses. "So Samson figured he could draw him out. He made it clear that he's going to reveal the killer's identity on the cruise, hoping he would be curious enough or crazy enough to show up?"

"Exactly. He'd be in disguise and under a fake name, but Samson figures he's still enough of a cop to flush him out."

Andres came for my soup bowl. "Too complex," I said. "For the killer to sign up for the cruise would be an extraordinary risk. Once on board, Samson could profile him from the passenger manifest. He'd be a sitting duck."

"No," Jack said firmly. "This is actually a pretty controlled environment. You have to pass through metal detectors every time you re-board. There's no way to get a gun on board."

"What about a towel?"

He stared at me. "You can never control for everything."

"I could kill with my bare hands," I said as my swordfish arrived. "Or at least I could at one point in my life. They taught us to do that in the service."

"And they probably taught Robert Samson how to do it in the F.B.I. academy," Jack noted.

"Look at this," Shelley said, admiring her rack of lamb. "This is too pretty to eat."

I have to tell you something; my swordfish was delicious. I'm not a huge mushroom fan. I can take them or leave them, but swordfish, when done well, is exquisite. And it was done well, tasting like the two sticks of butter it was probably cooked in. "I'm not convinced," I told Jack. "Angela Lansbury would never take that kind of risk."

"Angela Lansbury never worked alone, nor was she nearly broke, paying two alimonies, and drinking heavily."

"No, nor the gambling or the whores." I nodded. "I'm going to have to think about this."

I did just that as I ate my swordfish. I take a pill for cholesterol every day and I think at that point, I was going to be needing two. Shelley was busy with the desert menu when I left. I would love to have stayed but I had a date.

CHAPTER SEVEN

When I got to the Copacabana Lounge, I found it to be quite a bit darker than it was during the afternoon, probably due to the sun no longer being out. Inga was back at the piano playing something jazzy that I didn't recognize. I think she nodded at me but I don't see well in low light.

On a cruise ship, there's no quieter place than a lounge during the second dinner seating. Demographics reveal the reason for this; older passengers have their dinner at the first seating, and then they go to the show, or they go to bed. And because the younger passengers have their dinner during the second seating, they're not in the lounge either.

I found Helen sitting at a table by the window. I'd kept a lady waiting and that was never good.

"I didn't see you at dinner," I said, kissing her cheek. "I looked for you. I had the swordfish."

"I had it too, it was delicious. I had dinner with the captain tonight in the officers' dining room. It was very nice."

"You must be special." I sat next to her and examined the bottle of champagne chilling by the table. "This looks expensive."

"I am special and it is expensive."

She wore a sparkly gown. She was a beautiful woman. She must have been quite the looker back in the day, and by back in the day I mean yesterday and the day before. I know some men chase young women, but for my money, give me the texture of a life richly lived. I had plans for Helen, plans and intentions, I'll get that off my chest right now. My plans were quite vague but my intentions were not. She would be substantial, fragile maybe. But God willing, she would be yielding.

"Do you dance, Henry?"

"I do, yes. Would you like to dance?"

"Not now," she said as a hostess came to pour me a flute of champagne. "Perhaps tomorrow evening. There's a cocktail party. It's for repeat offenders – passengers who have been on more than one cruise. You can be my date."

"I'd love to be your date." We clinked our glasses.

"Tell me you're not married."

"No, no. I'm a single man, a bachelor. I have an apartment with etchings on the walls, and I have a stereo phonograph for my Dean Martin albums. A nice artificial fire in the hearth, some Campari; it can get quite cozy."

She laughed. "I think you're all talk. You were married though?"

"Yes. Twice."

"Widowed or divorced?"

"One of each. Both a long time ago." I was starting to feel tired now, not to mention a little drunk.

"How did your wife die?"

I'll tell you something; that is not really a topic I enjoy talking about. "I don't really know," I told Helen, "even now. We had a baby, my son Teddy. She had the baby and then she just never got better. She died about six months after he was born. The doctors didn't know what she died of. It was a long time ago, probably some kind of cancer."

Helen put her hand on mine. "That must have been terrible."

I am a fortunate man, a blessed man, and when I pass from this earth many years from now, I will walk boldly into whatever realm awaits me. And although I suspect no realm awaits me, and that I will simply expire like a candle flame does in time, I hope against all reason that I am wrong and I will walk into Emily's embrace even if just for a single moment. Just to apologize.

"It was terrible," I told Helen. "I wasn't even there. I was in the service when she died. I was overseas."

"Oh how awful. They don't send you home for something like that?"

I nodded. "They do when they can but I was a guest of the German government at the time and they were not accommodating. I didn't find out until afterwards, until we were liberated and shipped home. I met my son for the first time; he'd been living with my parents. He was just sixteen months old."

I must not have said anything for some time. I remember looking over at Inga at the piano and trying to remember the name of the song she was playing. I think I was a little drunk, but perhaps not. As a rule I get coarser when I drink and I was feeling softer instead. I started thinking about Teddy, how we had a rough time coming to know one another.

"I think I put a damper on our evening," Helen said. "Shall I leave you for now?"

I held her hand. "I won't hear of it. Tell me about yourself. If you're married, tell me now so we can get you a quickie divorce tomorrow in Martinique."

She laughed. "I was married for twenty-four years to a wonderful man who went and died on me just when disco was getting big. I've had two long term boyfriends since, but not for some time."

"So you're about ready for number three?"

"You couldn't handle me."

"I know how to tie seven kinds of knots."

She blushed. We talked about her children and her life in New York. Then I walked her to her cabin, a Deluxe Suite on the Executive Deck.

I kissed Helen Ettinger gently on the cheek and she hugged me. We had shared something. Maybe another night I'd be invited into 390 square feet of elegant opulence, and I'd recline on one of two comfortable sofas or perhaps even on a lounge chair on her private balcony, or perhaps I'll stop for now. It was ten at night. I was exhausted and I still had another stop to make.

I'll tell you something about cruise ships in general. I don't care if your ship is named after a Princess or a Countess or a Duke or a

Goofy, at heart it's a floating cask of ale, a membrane between a sea of salt water and a sea of alcohol. Every cruise ship is at its core a booze cruise. In fact, the entire industry owes its existence to alcohol. Recreational cruising became popular in the 1920s with prohibition. You couldn't drink on land, but you sure could tie one on afloat.

I found Ron Gibson at the Pirate's Cove, the open air tiki-themed bar up on the Tropicana Deck. If you want quiet on a cruise ship late in the evening, don't bother going to the pool because it's not going to be quiet. Some people were still swimming, even that late at night, but from the looks of them, being fully dressed and all, it probably wasn't something they had planned on. There must have been a hundred people hanging around the pool and the bar drinking rum out of plastic coconuts through straws a foot and a half long. There was going to be some sex that night, I can tell you that much.

The rock wall loomed heavily above us. Just a few nights before, someone was killed right there, but that wasn't going to stop the partying. I counted four security officers with their regulation windbreakers, little Indian guys not exactly blending in.

Ron was leaning against a round chest-high table that sprouted a fake palm tree. His uniform jacket was hanging kind of sloppy, probably because he was a little drunk. He was chatting up a young lady who I'm certain was not old enough to drink at any tiki-themed bar that wasn't floating in international waters.

Ron waved at me and said something I couldn't hear. The band was loud and I didn't have my hearing aid with me.

"Look what the catfish dragged in," he said as I approach his palm tree. He turned to the young woman. "Claire, I want you to meet my dear friend Henry. He was an archaeologist. Ask him about his mummies."

Claire liked Ron. I could tell by the way she was looking at him, barely looking at me. And she should like him; Ron is a good guy. And he's good at his job. The cruise director is as important to the cruise ship biosphere as the captain is, arguably more so. The captain sails the ship, but it's the job of the cruise director to keep spirits afloat. Keep the music playing and the jugglers juggling, Ron told me once, but it's more than that. A cruise is like a good brandy. It will refresh you and make you tingle. But some people aren't refreshed by brandy and they don't tingle well. A cruise is a terrible place to be sad, an awful place to be lonely, and an unforgiving place to be belligerent. It's the job of the cruise director to keep his eyes open and remember all that.

Claire smiled and kissed me on the cheek like a French girl would. "Tell me about your mummies," she said in the sweetest little English accent. I would have sworn she was American.

"I will. I promise," I told her. "But not right now. We'll get together you and me. We'll have some soup and some hot cocoa, and I'll tell you about the mummies, but right now I need to borrow Ron for about fifteen minutes. Will you lend him to me?"

She frowned playfully but she left us. Ron frowned too. He called to a server wearing a flower print blouse. "Another Heineken please. And for my friend, you're not going to believe this, a Tequila and tomato juice. Isn't that right, Henry? I remembered."

"No." I shook my head. "I don't drink that anymore. It was starting to give me a goiter. Also, I'm really quite drunk. I'll just have a club soda."

He ordered me a beer anyway. "I can't believe you made her go away."

"She'll be back. Tell me things. How the hell have you been?"

"Good. Good, all things considered. Nice cruise. Love the weather. We have an all-star cast on board; a TV actress, the usual gaggle of rich old ladies, a Venezuelan general fighting extradition, and a cosmonaut. Oh yeah, and a murdered F.B.I. profiler."

I stared at the rock-climbing wall. It was very prominent. "Everyone seems to be holding up quite well given there was a murder just a couple feet from here just a couple days ago."

"They do, we've put a lot of work into it. We have counseling sessions. For those who aren't interested in counseling, we have free upgrades on future cruises. For those who have vowed never to come back, we have some deposits to their shipboard accounts. They'll buy more wine and forget about their troubles."

"Amazing. You'd never know anything happened here."

"You would," he said, "if you looked carefully." He pointed to the band, which had set up on the little island in the pool. A good-sized crowd was dancing on one side of the pool but the other side was pretty desolate. "Usually you'd see people all over the place. But look how people are avoiding the climbing wall. Everyone is huddled together, staying in the light."

He was right. "How many security people are out here?"

Our beers came and we toasted. "Seven or eight. Everyone is working long hours."

"How well did you know him?" I asked.

"Samson? I guess I knew him about as well as I know you. He'd been working the cruise circuit for years, so I'd run into him here and there on different lines."

"Did he seem any different this time?"

Ron shifted to keep Claire in sight. A guy in a Hawaiian shirt had already pounced on her. "He did seem different, yes. For one thing, he was traveling alone. He usually brought his wife. I think there were two or three wives through the years but he was alone this time. He mentioned going through a divorce."

"Did he get close to any of the passengers?"

"He did make some friends. A couple of older ladies were quite upset, quite in tears, but I don't think there was much to that. You know, he spent a lot of time with Vasily. I think they were drinking buddies."

"Which one is Vasily again? He sounds familiar."

"Vasily Orlov, the cosmonaut. He lived on Mir for almost two years."

"Is that right? I didn't see him on the list of entertainers."

Ron took a long drink from his bottle, and I guess I did too because when I looked at mine, I found it to be empty. "He's not on this list. He got in a fight with the captain so the captain moved him to crew quarters and cancelled his lectures."

"What was the fight about?"

"It was dumb. Vasily is a really popular lecturer when he stays on topic but he gets sidelined easily. A couple of weeks ago he had a packed house but he just yammered on about Sputnik for half and hour and nobody cares about Sputnik."

"Sputnik was the one that had the monkey for a pilot?" I asked.

Ron frowned. He made eye contact with a bartender and held up two fingers. "No, it was just a little satellite. No monkey. Anyway, the captain at one point suggested that he talk more about life as a cosmonaut and less about the minutia of the Soviet space program. So Vasily blows a gasket, tells him that he commanded the most advanced vehicle ever known to humanity and was not going to take suggestions from a tugboat captain."

"And the captain didn't respond well?" Our beers took about a second longer to arrive. I felt about ready to pass out.

"That's right. So maybe you could talk to Vasily if you get the chance."

"Can you set that up for me? Tell him who I am and that I'll be calling on him some time tomorrow."

Ron nodded. "Hey, you know who's got a thing for you?"

"Claire?" I said, my eyes lighting up. "You can tell already? I've never been with a British girl." I thought about that for a moment. "No, I have."

"No, no," Ron said, waving his hand. "That's not what I mean. I mean kind of an attitude when it comes to you. Hugh Arlen."

"I've met him," I said. "He's the fellow who teaches karate."

"No. Hugh is the head of security."

"That's right. He is."

"He's a little ticked off. He has some of his people now doing work for you, watching who comes and goes tomorrow. You really think someone is going to jump ship in Martinique?"

"I don't, but you never know. The guy could just get off, make like he missed the boat and just disappear, then take the next flight to New York or Memphis. People get left behind all the time by cruise ships, don't they?"

"No. Almost never."

I shrugged. "Then he'll probably walk right back on board, having bought a few souvenirs. Arlen doesn't need to get in a huff. It's not like he wasn't going to be tracking who gets on and who gets off. Don't you do that all the time anyway?"

"All the time, yes. We scan your keycard when you disembark and scan it again when you come back."

"Then you'll be scanning the killer's keycard tomorrow. It's strange to think he could be right here at this bar."

Ron looked around. He had lost sight of Claire and was becoming agitated. "I don't think he's here, Henry. I think he's back in his cabin sleeping like a baby or watching TV."

I shook my head. "No, he's right here, somewhere in this crowd, maybe at the bar, maybe even dancing. He's feeling good about himself, feeling pleased."

"Why do you think that? Why would he come back to the scene of his crime?"

I looked over a couple of guys dancing. At the bar, men stood tall and looked at women. "Because it's nice here. Because he did a really good job."

By the time I got back to my Junior Suite it was late. I'm not sure how late. I turned on my TV and watched a little of the library surveillance tape and then I flipped through the channels and found C.N.N. I watched for awhile but I couldn't concentrate. I had work to do but I was too tired, and I think a little tipsy. I made a mental note not to drink for the next couple of days. I had only four days to catch a killer.

I was thinking, as I got into my pajamas, that the killer would almost certainly be traveling alone. Not because killers are dangerous loners or anything like that; they rarely are, but because he had a clear and well-executed plan that would have required time and attention to detail. Having the wife along for the cruise might make things difficult.

I got a bottle of water from my mini-fridge. I opened it and took a drink and realized that it was a bottle of beer instead. Nuts.

I made some notes of things I needed for the morning. I'd need a list of all male passengers traveling alone. I wondered if there was maybe a satellite overhead when the murder happened. Wouldn't that be something! Imagine getting caught because you did your killing in full view of a camera hovering thirty miles over your head, or fifty miles, or whatever. I wondered if they had satellites that did that. Maybe Vasily Orlov would know. He flew in space with a monkey. I would have to ask him. But first I needed to sleep. I tucked myself in and took a final drink of my water but it was still not water. Nuts.

CHAPTER EIGHT

I'd never been to Martinique before. I learned from my complimentary shipboard newsletter that we docked at about five in the morning. Looking out my window, past the edge of the lifeboat hanging there, I made out a sliver of coastline. I'd seen a lot of islands in my day, but this one was something else. It looked like a mountain had been uprooted from somewhere and then set down on a beach.

It was nearly six by the time I got myself together. I had planned to be up earlier but things didn't work out that way. I didn't have time for a full breakfast, so I made a dash for the Bistro. It wasn't crowded at all. I got my coffee right away, stuffed a couple of croissants in my pockets, and took the round staircase down past the rainforest to the gangway.

Quite a crowd had gathered there, all anxious to set foot on Martinique, and I got jostled a bit standing there in line. Soon enough, a security officer scanned my keycard, and as he did that, I felt a sharp pain in my right side. I figured I must have bumped into a railing or something but with people all around me, I couldn't really see anything so I walked down the steep gangway with everyone else. Maybe it was appendicitis or some other horrific malady which I didn't want to be thinking about right then. But it sure did hurt all of a sudden.

"Sir!" A crewmember walked up to me as my feet touched Martinique. He had a concerned look on his face. "Have you hurt yourself?"

"What are we talking about?" I asked Lyndon from Manila.

"Have you cut yourself?" He pointed to my side.

I looked down and saw a little red stain on my jacket. "I think it's just the jelly from my croissants," I said. I felt confused all of a sudden. I handed him the croissants which looked remarkably intact and opened my jacket to find a larger red stain on my shirt, about the size of silver dollar. "Well I'll be god-damned." I'd been stabbed.

"Sir, just sit here a moment," Lyndon from Manila said as he reached for his radio. "We'll get you back on board in a moment and the doctor can take a look at you."

"No, no. No, no." I told him. I sat on a plastic folding chair next to a table on which rows of identical bottles of spring water perspired. I very discreetly took off my jacket and folded it over to hide my wound. Considerably more effort was spent on hiding my sense of alarm, which was growing exponentially. I had started shaking, breathing too fast. You can't do that at my age; you can get yourself in trouble very quickly.

I really didn't know what to do. I felt kind of confused, as if maybe I was dreaming and this didn't really happen. And I started leaning toward that direction, trying to make it a dream so that I would be O.K., but I couldn't. As the confusion started to wear off, it became clear that this had really happened, and then I got scared.

I could tell you that I felt angry at that moment, angry and determined to find whoever did this to me, but all I felt was fear. I knew that if I went back up that gangway and looked around, I'd never find him, but I was absolutely terrified that I would.

So I sat there and I bled. I pressed tightly through my jacket, keeping pressure on it like they taught us in the service. My heart was racing too fast. I needed to calm down. I'd been stabbed once before, many years ago in a produce warehouse in south Philadelphia, and that time I nearly didn't make it. Using that incident as my barometer, I judged my current condition to be not life-threatening. The wound didn't feel that deep, but then I wasn't a doctor and I hadn't even yet looked at it. I would have to get back on board for that.

I breathed deeply. A colored fellow walked up to me and asked if I wanted to see the volcano, which I did not. I've never had the least bit of interest in volcanoes. I sat there for a few moments and then stood. I folded my jacket over my arm so that it would cover up the blood and I headed up the gangway, which was a chore because it was crowded with passengers climbing down. Back on board, my keycard was scanned again and my picture appeared on the monitor. I walked through an airport style metal detector and set it off. "Titanium hip," I told the officer. "I had it done last year. It's made a world of difference."

He waved me in.

Back in the Junior Suite, I took off my shirt and had a look. There was a little hole there, right above my right hip. As luck would have it, an ample layer of fat seemed to have shielded my inner workings from damage. I washed off some of the blood so that I could take a look. It was still bleeding a little so this was no easy task, especially since my hands were still shaking. The little hole appeared to be a knife wound but a very small one, maybe an eighth of an inch long and not too deep. I washed it with soap and then with a little alcohol pad from my first aid kit. And when I finished and applied a nice dressing, I got very angry.

I sat on the edge of the bath tub and tried to take some measure of what had just happened. Why would someone stab me? And why a tiny knife? Presuming this person had something to do with the murder of Robert Samson, which I did presume, why would he take that kind of risk? What kind of a man stabs someone in the middle of a crowd, I asked myself but I already knew the answer; the same kind of man who strangles a federal agent with a towel and hangs him on a rock wall; a man who knows no fear. A man who knew I was hunting him and wanted to send me a message, maybe scare me. Message received. I knew right then that I was going to kill him.

I told nobody what happened. This was between him and me.

I took three aspirins and headed back out. I walked back to the reception area and passed through a small recessed doorway marked crew only. A security officer stood up to intercept me but I showed him my crew ID. He was a young guy, Hispanic. He didn't look more than sixteen years old. He smiled and let me into *Voyager*'s security office. It was a small room, maybe six by ten feet; it was Hugh Arlen's office. I sat at his desk. I knew it was his desk right away. It was orderly, nothing out of place, fastidiously clean, and featured a nameplate with his name on it.

"What can I do for you, sir?" the young security officer asked.

"You know who I am?"

"Yes, sir. You just showed me your ID."

"That's quick work."

"Excuse me?"

"Nothing."

"Sir, Mr. Arlen has authorized me to give you any help you request."

"That's wonderful. Let me ask you a question. You're a member of the security staff, right?"

"I am, yes."

"How the hell old are you?"

"I'm twenty-three, sir."

"You look like you're about eleven years old."

"I have heard that I do look young for my age, but I assure you, I can do my job well."

"Well that's grand to hear." Far be it for me to discriminate on the basis of age.

I had a look around. It was a crowded little room and clearly not meant for passengers. The walls were plain white. I couldn't spot even a single decorative touch except for a few photographs here and there on the bulletin boards, lost among lists and bulletins. There were no windows but a door at the back led to a smaller more secure room, which functioned as a holding area should anyone get out of hand. I've been on dozens of cruise ships and most of them have such a room.

"Do you ever have to use the torture room?" I asked pointing to the door.

"Rarely."

"That's not the brig is it? You do have a brig somewhere in the bowels of the ship, don't you?" I watched the monitor on the desk flashing images of disembarking passengers.

"We do have a brig in the bowels, by the engine room. I only remember it being used once about a year ago."

"What happened?"

"You'd have to ask Mr. Arlen."

"All the help I requested, isn't that what you've been authorized to give me?"

"Yes, sir. A married couple got into a fight and the wife started beating on the husband. It was at one of the shows. One of the bartenders tried to hold her back and the husband hit him, hit the bartender."

"Well I'll be god-damned. What happened to the woman?"

"We left her off at the next port. Him too. I think it was in Panama City."

I leaned back in Hugh Arlen's chair. "Can I get room service here?"

He stared at me. "I don't see why not. Just call reception and they'll patch you through to catering."

I did that. I ordered myself an English muffin with some bacon, and an orange juice and a coffee and a Bloody Mary. "I didn't have any breakfast," I said. "I'm a little diabetic so I have to be sure to eat something at about this time."

"I see. So what is it I can help you with?"

"I'm glad you asked. Do you have a pen?"

He took a pen from the desk and held it out for me. I shook my head. "No, it's for you. Take notes. I'm going to make a series of assumptions here. First I want a list of all male passengers traveling solo. Our killer, and I'm going to call him Hector so I don't have to say 'killer' every three minutes, is probably traveling alone."

He frowned at me.

"What's the problem?"

"Hector is my name."

"Nuts. Well then, I'll just refer to him as the killer."

"I'd prefer that."

"Fine. Crewmembers too. I want a list of all male crewmembers traveling solo."

He shook his head. "No, you'll need to use a different search parameter. Only about five or six of the male crewmembers are traveling with wives who also work on the ship. The rest would turn up as traveling alone."

"OK, remind me of that again in five minutes. Another thing, see if you can find someone at the main office back in L.A. who can look into the possibility that there was a satellite or something like that looking down the night of the murder. Maybe we can get lucky."

"You mean like a spy satellite?"

"Yeah, do they have those now or is that science fiction?"

"They probably have them but not in the middle of the ocean."

"Can you check?"

Hector shrugged. "I would have no idea how. Hey, are you a cop or what?"

He was warming up to me. "No, no. I'm just an investigator."

"Do you have a badge or some kind of official ID?"

"I have a laminated ID. I'd show it to you but I forgot it at home. I wanted a badge, something metal, but I was told it would be inappropriate."

"So you don't really have any ID?"

I showed him my crew ID again.

He stared at me. "That's cool."

"How about that list of male passengers traveling solo?"

He started typing away. "I can bring that up right now."

"While you're doing that, can I look at passenger profiles? Can you set this computer up so that I can just scroll through them?"

"Oh yeah," Hector said. "Very easy. Watch."

There was little to watch, but soon enough, Hugh Arlen's computer screen was alive with information. Pictures and more pictures.

"This will take you awhile," Hector said. "We have about 1,600 passengers on board."

"We have 1,533 on board," I reminded him as I pulled up the first passenger, Wilton Abelard of Cape May, New Jersey. "I got you, you fucker," I told Wilton's bald head. "Thought you could get away with it, didn't you?"

"I think Wilton did it," I told Hector.

He looked up only for a moment. "I don't think I've met him, but he's not alone. Look at the link on the side."

Next to the photo of Wilton's head was a blue plus sign. "It's a blue plus sign," I said.

"Yes. It's a link for accompanied passengers. It tells you who the passenger is sharing a cabin with. Click it and you'll see who Wilton sleeps next to."

I did just that and the screen brought up an image of Bernice Abelard, listed as his wife. "I got you, you fucker," I told her. "You might have fooled Wilton but you can't fool me."

"I thought you said it was a man."

Hector had a point. I left Bernice for now and scrolled through a few more passenger profiles. "Check out this guy, Mason Cornish of Avalon, California. I wonder if his friends call him Corny." Mason Cornish had a blue plus sign next to his photo as well so I let him be. "This is going to take all the damned day. What's the name of that town out there, do you know?"

"That's Fort of France, the capital of Martinique."

"Lots of taxi cabs are lined up out there. I read in the newsletter that there's a volcano and a couple of other nice little towns and some city that got blown up a hundred years ago. Get one of your guys out there by the taxi stand. Hand out some $10 bills or whatever. We want to know if anyone asks to be taken to the airport. Your guys should also be looking for anyone walking off the ship with a suitcase. Maybe get two guys, or three. Anyone with a suitcase or heading for the airport needs to be followed."

"I'll need to get authorization from Mr. Arlen."

"Yes, you will," I told him, "and you'll need to do it right away. Where is he anyway?"

Hector pulled a clipboard from the wall and flipped a page over. "He's meeting with the harbor master right now. I can get him on the phone."

"Good. You work on that." My breakfast arrived so I worked on that as I typed the name 'Orlov' on the keyboard. Nice picture; nice smile. Vasily Orlov of Miami Beach, Florida. Russian national, fifty-two years of age. I played around with the buttons. I learned that

Orlov had a $690 tab, almost all of which was the result of purchases of Johnny Walker Black at various onboard establishments.

Orlov was listed as a special interest lecturer which meant he got his cruises for free, probably his airfare too, maybe $1,000 a month on the side, and half off his bar tab. All of this meant that Vasily Orlov has been drinking quite a lot. Someone needed to talk to him about that.

I heard only one side of Hector's conversation but that was enough to know that Hugh Arlen was not happy with the latest turn of events. He didn't really have a choice though; I needed to do my work and he needed to help me.

"It's getting set up now," Hector said, putting the handset back in the cradle. "Four guys on the ground with some cash. I told him you wanted to be notified if they turn anyone up."

"That's great."

"Hey, have you ever caught anyone? Any killers?"

"I have. I'll tell you about it later. We'll order a pizza, stay up late." I pointed to the designation E022B on the screen. "Where is this?"

Hector chuckled. "I forgot about that. Orlov got downgraded. His cabin is all the way down on the Engine Deck. It's an inside cabin near the stern."

"Sounds nice. OK, I'm going to go talk to him. Don't touch my bacon."

CHAPTER NINE

The elevator didn't go down to the Engine Deck. I took it as far down as it went, down to the Sea Mist Deck and then I walked through a pair of heavy doors marked 'Crew Only.' Just inside, a heavy plastic curtain hung from the ceiling. The first time I walked through one of those curtains I had no idea what it was for. But it took only half a second to learn. The most salient difference between the world of the passengers and the world of the crew is smoke. I don't know if it's fair to say that every member of every crew smokes cigarettes, but I'll say it anyway. Without that curtain, the heavy smoke would surely waft up into the public decks, killing everyone in its path.

Passing through the curtain was like passing into a different world. It was self-contained, sealed, and in every way crappier than the world that existed above it. I walked down a narrow hallway and down an even narrower staircase to the Crew Deck, which was smokier still. The walls were industrial blue and looked like they had been painted a hundred times, and the linoleum floor was so badly scuffed that some kind of artistic pattern was spontaneously forming.

I found myself in a long hallway cluttered with boxes and carts and laundry bags. There were people everywhere; crewmembers hurrying and staring at me while they hurried. It was loud down there. Before I walked twenty feet, I heard twenty different kinds of music blasting from inside the little crew cabins. I passed the crew mess hall which was mobbed. It was smaller than I would have expected. Little tables were crammed in close to each other, and each table was filled with Asian men and eastern European women smoking and eating rice and probably other foods too, but I sure saw a lot of rice. And judging by the amount of smoking going on, there was probably a lot of ash mixed in with it.

It was loud – just trying to have a conversation over the noise of the generators and the music and the shouting seemed like an impossible feat, but they managed. I heard high-pitched voices speaking Tagalog, and I heard some Russian as well. I picked that up from some fellows in the service and I still understand a few words but I didn't have time to listen.

"Excuse me, sir." The voice came from right behind me. Then quickly there was a gentle but firm hand on my arm. "This area is for crew only. I'm sorry."

He was an Indian fellow. He didn't have a name tag but he was wearing the insignia of ship security. You'll find Indian or Nepalese security officers working throughout the cruise industry. They're short and sweet-looking so they don't intimidate the passengers, but they're all ex-military, they know six different kinds of karate, and they're very effective under pressure.

I showed him my ID. "I'm sorry, too. I'm going to be all over the place for the next couple of days. Check with the captain if you have any questions."

He nodded. "Yes, yes. I was told about you. Can I offer you some assistance?"

"I'm looking for cabin E022B. Do you know where that is?"

"Of course," he said, leading me down the hallway. "We have to go down one flight of stairs."

I held onto the railing as he skipped ahead of me down the steepest flight of stairs I think I had ever seen. "Let me ask you something," I said when I caught up with him. "Do you guys get the same food down here as the passengers get upstairs?"

He grinned. "No, sir, we don't."

"Filled croissants, maybe? I mean it's not just gruel, right? Not like today is oatmeal day and tomorrow is turnips and pumpernickel is it?"

"No, sir. We eat very well. Very well. They prepare a few main choices for each meal. A lot of Filipino dishes as you might imagine."

"What did you have for dinner last night?"

"I had chicken with mushrooms."

"Were they porcini mushrooms?"

"I don't know, sir," he said. "We're almost there."

The hallway was narrower down on the Engine Deck. It had to be in order to accommodate the engines as well as the massive water tanks that a cruise ship carries. The Engine Deck was the loudest part of the ship and a dismal place to live. Only the lowest-ranking crew members lived there. Usually.

He stopped in front of a door marked E022B. "Here we are, sir."

"Thanks," I said, knocking on the door. I waved goodbye.

There was no answer from within so I knocked again. I heard something but I couldn't make it out. "I don't have my hearing aid with me," I called out. "I don't know what you are saying."

The door opened a moment later and a disheveled Vasily Orlov appeared. "Who are you?"

I told him.

"Yes, yes."

Both Vasily and Ron Goodman are night owls, so evidently Ron was able to tell him about me last night. "Can I come in?"

He backed up to let me in. "Mercy," I said, taking in the view. Orlov was clearly not the kind of person who enjoyed tidying up. There was no maid service down in the crew quarters, but what really struck me was the cabin itself. It was awful. Tiny like a jail cell, it had a chair and a desk and a sink and an actual bunk bed. And there was no window or porthole, of course, since it was underwater. I couldn't see into the bathroom but I suspected it was equally grim. "This is just terrible," I told him.

"I know," he said in a thick Russian accent. "I had more room on Mir."

Once inside, I moved a pile of clothes out of the way and sat down on the chair. I was having trouble with the scene before me. "At least you don't have a roommate."

He sat at the edge of the bed. "I did. His name is Wolfie. He had face like a ham. He is working somewhere in accounting. He did not enjoy being roommate."

"Ron tells me you got to be friends with Robert Samson," I said. "Can you tell me about him?"

He looked up. "You are investigating, yes? You think I kill him?"

"I don't, but did you?"

"No, but maybe I would if he kept talking at me constantly and not stopping. I wish not to speak poorly of a dead man but he possibly needed to be killed."

I noticed two bottles of scotch on the desk next to a half-eaten cup of pudding. "That's quite a statement," I said. "Why would someone possibly need to be killed?"

"I've seen it many times. Many of my colleagues, Gorodish, Tupelova, Ruchov, others too, maybe me, I don't know, we are famous. The whole of Soviet Union loves us because we have flown above world. We come home safe, and for more than one year I never buy my own drink. Always someone to buy my drink.

"I have nice apartment in Moscow, have color television with VCR, and Toyota car with sunroof. Women stand in line, not for soap or mutton, but to spend time with cosmonaut in nice apartment watching *Rocky* movie on VCR. Maybe tomorrow we take ride in Toyota car."

I shook my head in admiration. "That is the life I have always wanted."

"And then nothing. World changes, government changes. Have to pay for apartment now with what money? VCR one day eats movie of Steven Segal, and Toyota needs clutch which closest is in Helsinki. Women not so fast to line up.

"Gorodish and Ruchov drink more and smoke more and so kill themselves because good days are gone. Me, I think better to go. Move to Miami Beach and become visiting professor, talk about Mir. American students line up to sleep with cosmonaut. Very nice. This time Hyundai car, but OK. Then no more money for visiting professor, work on cruising ships and get cabin small enough to die in. Maybe I too need to be killed."

I was getting a little depressed. "So Samson was past his glory days, you think, just drinking himself to death like your colleagues and yourself?"

He looked up at me. "Not me. Not yet. Maybe one day, but for Samson, yes. Too much problems with women, no more money, nobody pays attention anymore."

"It's possible that his murder is related to his lectures," I told him. "Did he ever talk with you about what he was working on?"

Orlov nodded. "When he is drunk, and he is always drunk, he says that he will be famous again, that world will notice. Killer finally will not get away. And yes, I ask who is killer. He say he will not tell me. I ask him even if he worries that killer will throw him over edge of ship to kill him. He laughs only, says he has mafia on board to protect him. I do not know what this means. You know what I think?"

"I do," I said.

"You do?"

"No, I mean I want to know what you think."

"I will tell you. I think he does not know who killer is. He has only some ideas and he will tell audience. But killer does not know this, so kills him."

I nodded. "That makes a lot of sense to me. Let me ask you a question, do you have any snacks in here?"

"Snacks?"

"Yeah, like food."

Orlov looked around, his eyes resting momentarily on the half-eaten pudding. "I think I have no food. You can go to crew dining room and eat bullshit just upstairs one flight."

"I'll do that," I said, pulling myself up from the chair. "Hey, what was it like up there, in space, in Skylab?"

He stared at me. "Mir. It was Mir. Skylab crashed in Indian Ocean in 1979. Australian government gave fine to United States for litter. United States have to pay $400."

"That's expensive. Well Mir then, what was that like?"

Orlov's face lit up. "It was something. Very quiet. Take bottle of Vodka and look out window at earth. It's nice. Get horny though."

"Let me ask you one more thing," I said, stepping out into the hallway. "What exactly did the monkey do? Did he get to drive the ship?"

He frowned. "Space station, not ship. And not monkey. What monkey are you saying?"

"I heard you had a monkey up there to run some tests, walk in space in a space suit for a monkey."

"No monkey," he said forcefully. "Not ever on Mir. And not ever do space walk on any mission."

"Is that right," I said but he had already closed the door. I knocked again. "One more question, OK?"

I heard a grunt from inside.

"Are there any satellites that can take pictures from space? I'm thinking maybe if there were, one took a picture of Samson's murder."

He opened the door. "US government have fifty-one Keyhole satellite, which have resolution of five inches. So yes, can take picture from space, but not of middle of ocean. No spying on middle of ocean. And NASA not give you picture anyway."

Nuts. "Do they...."

"No," he yelled, closing the door. "Keyhole satellite not have monkey either."

When I got back to the security office, Hector was gone. Hugh Arlen let me in.

"Your hunch paid off," he told me.

I looked around the room. "What happened to my breakfast?"

"What are you talking about?"

"I had my breakfast waiting right there. I only ate part of it."

"You know, I've been in and out, several people are working on this, so I don't know what happened to your food. Now do you want to hear what I'm telling you?"

"I do," I assured him, "but I need to get some food."

"We'll get something on the way out. One of our passengers showed up at the airport."

"Where is he now?"

"He's being detained at the airport. I'm going. I'm thinking you'll want to come."

I nodded. I was very hungry.

CHAPTER TEN

"Who is he?" I asked. We drove in a taxi on the coastal road toward the airport and I was finishing an English muffin ham sandwich. Martinique was really quite pretty. A little corner of France in the Caribbean, yet it had an essence all its own, a peaceful West Indian warmth. I knew that because I read it in my newsletter.

Arlen handed me a folder. "His name is Norman Gellerman. He's a retired postal inspector from Chicago, and he's sailed with us several times before. In fact, he's been to Martinique with us three times already."

"How about that. Has he ever skipped out before?"

Arlen shook his head. "There would be a notation if he didn't complete a cruise."

"Is he on my list?" I asked. "I asked Hector to make me a list of male passengers traveling alone."

He nodded and brought out the list from his case. "No, Gellerman isn't on it. He has a roommate."

"Then he isn't the person I'm looking for."

He scanned Gellerman's profile. "Not so fast. See this notation in the corner?"

"The one that looks like a toe?"

"It's a thumbs up, the Contessa Community icon. It's a roommate matching program. This means that Gellerman asked to be matched with a roommate with similar interests. You tell the computer if you're a night owl and other things and then it matches you with someone else so that you don't have to pay the single supplement."

I frowned. My side was starting to hurt again and I was getting irritated. "I'm still fairly certain he's not the person I'm looking for. Samson's killer traveled alone. He'd have to be one bold and frugal son-of-a-bitch to want a roommate."

Arlen nodded. "As for now, however, we have to be very careful how we deal with Mr. Gellerman. He is a paying passenger and we have no legal right to detain him."

"That's why I'm going to talk with him by myself."

Arlen took a deep breath. "No. No you're not. I'm going in with you to make sure this is processed appropriately. I don't want him walking because of an improper arrest."

"Arrest?" I said. "I'm not going to arrest him. I just want information. If you come in, the cruise line becomes involved. But if I walk in alone and he doesn't know who I am, he has nobody to complain to."

"So you think you can just walk in as a private citizen and he'll just open up and start talking to you?"

"Who are you calling a private citizen?" I pulled out my fat wallet and took out an embossed card which I handed to Arlen.

"Drug Enforcement Agency," he read. "This looks real. Is this real?"

"No it's not. I have a friend from the service I've kept in contact with. He forged ID papers for the British during the war, and now he sort of keeps it up as a hobby. He has a condo in Connecticut and poodles that he shows in poodle contests. I can get you one if you want?"

"A poodle or an ID?"

"An ID. He shows the poodles. He doesn't sell them."

"So you plan to walk in and tell him you're from the Drug En-forcement Agency?"

"That's right."

"I don't want to offend you, but you look a little old to be a D.E.A. agent."

"Then I'll say I'm the boss of it. Or how about this?" I pulled out another card.

Arlen read it. "Associate Justice, United States Supreme Court. I'm not sure that would be appropriate."

"Oh, bullshit. I could pull that off. Imagine what trouble he'd think he was in."

He grinned. He was warming to me. "What else do you have?"

I handed him a third. "Chief Inspector, United Nations High Commissioner for Smuggling," he read. "I'll bet that doesn't come in that handy."

"This is my favorite," I said, handing him the yellowed card covered in Arabic writing that framed a photograph of yours truly wearing a black turban.

"What does it say?"

"Republican Guard. Iraqi. It is much less useful than I had hoped. Take your pick, Arlen, but I'm going in alone."

The airport was a lot smaller than most I've seen. I was surprised when we passed the main terminal and parked in front of general aviation. If Gellerman was interested in flying away, why would he be at a terminal reserved for private planes and charters? Did he have his own plane waiting?

Arlen spoke with a couple of colored police officers. They didn't look too happy so I figured I'd interrupt. "Bon jour," I said, walking up, flashing my Drug Enforcement Agency ID. "I just need to have a few words with the subject and then I'm pretty sure you can just let him go. If there's any problem, I'll call my embassy and we'll do an official transfer of custody."

I don't know exactly how or why that worked but it did. Let me tell you something: people say you can't do as much when you get old, but that's just not true. You'd be surprised at what you can get away with, and I'm not talking just about getting extra liquor on airplanes, which is child's play. I'm talking about walking in to sold-out Broadway plays without paying. I spent the better part of a year doing that. All you do is ask to see the manager. You say you want to file a complaint because the bartender in the lounge was rude to you. Once you're in, you start acting a little confused, and ask if they use real cats in the show. Invariably you get a free cocktail and sometimes an ice cream sandwich.

In any case, I was in. They led me down a small hall and into a bare interview room. Norman Gellerman was a smaller man than I had expected. He looked to be about five-eight, maybe a hundred and sixty pounds, but whippy, probably fast with a hard punch. He was good looking too, striking. He stood against the wall, behind the small metal table, his arms crossed. He had a grey backpack on his back.

"Who the hell are you?" he asked.

I held out my ID. "I think this is a big mistake," I told him. "I don't think you're the guy I'm looking for."

"That's a relief."

"We have thirty agents here at the airport. You probably passed six or seven already without ever knowing. You ever hear of Carlos 'The Robot' Zapato?"

He shook his head. "No. Who is he? What does this have to do with me?"

I sat at the table and motioned for him to do the same. Interrogation is all about getting someone off balance, and I was just about ready to tip him over. "Zapato runs the largest drug cartel on Martinique. Heroin, cocaine, opium, goof balls. He has a shipment due in today but so far the plane hasn't arrived."

He stared at me. I can read a man pretty well, sometimes. I didn't know if he killed Robert Samson or not, but he was guilty of something. He had that look to him, like the British fellows at the prison camp who worked in the kitchen. You knew they were stealing a little food and they knew it too. They had that look. And you wanted to forgive them because they were starving and it was just a potato. And you wanted to kill them with your hands because you were starving too and it was a potato.

"Why do they call him The Robot?" he asked.

"Who?"

"Carlos 'The Robot' Zapato?"

"Him, yes." I coughed a few times. I wasn't expecting that. "He walks like one. He's very stiff. Can't use his knees. A rival cartel on the other side of the island broke them with a cricket bat. His elbows too."

"Jesus."

"Sit down, Mr. Gellerman. I think we can have you out of here in no time."

"Why am I even here?" he asked, but he did sit. "What does this have to do with me?"

"Probably nothing. We'll just get through a few questions and then you can be on your way."

"I don't know anything about a drug cartel. I just took a cab out here because I heard you could hire a plane to fly you over the island. I picked up a brochure; they take you right over the volcano."

"Why would you want to fly over a volcano?"

He shrugged. "To see it. It sounded interesting. Can you tell me why I'm sitting here right now?"

"Like I said, we have a sting here in place at the airport today. One of our agents got a little jumpy and had you picked up, that's all."

"For what?"

"Well," I began. The interview was going a little rougher than I had expected. "He thought you fit Zapato's profile."

"He thought I looked like him?"

I nodded. "I'm afraid so. Now if you just show me some ID, we can have you on your way."

He stood up; getting a little irritated. "You're telling me that a federal agent mistook me for a guy who can't move his arms or legs?"

"I'll tell you something; he's just about the worst agent we have." I shook my head. "Any other day, he'd be back in the office guarding the safe with the drugs in it, but we needed him out here today."

"I don't believe this."

"Listen, I have to be straight with you; I really need to pee and sometimes it can take me the better part of an hour, so do you want to do this quickly or you want me to come back?"

"Fine," he said. "What do you want?"

"ID."

He pulled out a wallet and showed me an Illinois driver's license.

"What's the card in front?" I asked.

He pulled out his Voyager keycard. "It's my cabin key. I'm taking a cruise."

"A cruise," I said. "How nice. One of those big fancy ships?"

"Yeah. We're just here on Martinique for the day."

I sighed. "Ah, shit. We'll then you're definitely not part of this. I'm sorry for all the trouble, Mr. Gellerman."

"Me too. I think I'll pass on the sightseeing plane."

"I think that's for the best. Hey, was your cruise the one where that guy got strangled? We just heard about that on the wire yesterday."

"Yeah. He was an F.B.I. agent."

"Tragic." I stood up. "Come on, I'll walk you out. That must have been pretty scary having a killer on board. I heard they didn't catch the guy yet."

"It's a little creepy."

"Does it make you scared, walking around alone at night?"

"Nah. I'm a big guy."

I was fairly certain he didn't do it. He was too easy around my line of questioning. I put my hand on the door and hesitated.

"What now?"

"I forgot, I'm supposed to look in your backpack, make sure there's no goofballs in there."

"What the hell is a goofball?"

I leaned back into his space. "Drugs. They're very popular with the kids today. Just let me have a look inside, OK?"

"I don't have any drugs. I did some shopping, that's all, to get some things to bring back for my girlfriend."

"Can I see them?"

"No, I don't think so." He pulled on the straps to tighten them. "I don't think you have probable cause, so I don't have to show you anything."

"Yes. Yes you do. You're at an airport. We can search anything we want, even X-ray you. Sometimes the cartels pay people to smuggle the drugs by swallowing them in little balloons or even condoms. I think that would make me throw up. Have you ever done anything like that?"

He stared at me.

"Just a quick peek and we can be on our way. Look, I have to go pee, so you want to do this now or later? If that backpack doesn't have drugs in it, then I don't care if its filled with endangered tree frogs, I just want to get back out to my sting, see if we can nail Zapato before I pass into the next life."

He stared at me for a few seconds longer and then made a face like he was angry. "I'm filing a complaint with the State Department when I get home."

"You do that. Now open the backpack."

He did. There was jewelry in it.

I found Arlen outside the general aviation terminal talking with a couple of policemen. "He didn't do it," I told him. "He's a thief, but he didn't kill Samson. He's carrying a substantial amount of women's jewelry and it's not new. He's got it taped up in little plastic bags. I'll bet you dinner you've had a passenger report a recent theft of jewelry."

Arlen shook his head. "Nothing recently."

"Nothing at all? Nothing fishy? There's a parcel mailing service in the terminal. I think his plan was to ship the jewelry back home and then get back on the ship. I'll bet he's done this before."

Arlen's face fell.

"What?"

"I think there's something you should see," he said.

We headed back.

Deep in the ship, on the Sea Mist Deck, was *Voyager*'s infirmary, and tucked away behind it, in an area completely off limits to passengers, was a three-bed morgue. Let's face facts; cruising is a mature person's game, and mature people die. I rather like the idea that folks who are 99 percent into the grave are out and about eating Lobster Thermidor and touring sugar plantations. Better to die there than in some nursing home.

All of the larger cruising vessels have morgues, and they do come in handy, especially when people die, which happens about once every few weeks. *Voyager* seemed to be having a spell of bad luck.

The ship's doctor was waiting for us. "Jens Knutsen," he said, shaking my hand. He opened one of the doors, rolled out the bed and lifted a sheet. Robert Samson was lying there. His face was purple.

"Sorry," Knutsen said. "Wrong one. I don't think we've ever had two at one time before." He put Samson back and rolled out a second bed. When he lifted the sheet I saw the body of an older woman. She had a smile on her face. She looked like she might have been sleeping.

Arlen stood beside me. "Dorothy Kent," he said. "She died four days ago in her cabin. Housekeeping found her."

"Cause of death?"

"Heart failure." Knutsen pulled the sheet back over her face. "I did only a provisional post-mortem. We're not really equipped to do autopsies. We'll hold her until Miami and then transfer her to the coroner. Her family has been notified but I had no cause for suspicion. She was elderly and had a history of heart problems."

"She was rich, wasn't she?"

"She was," Arlen said. "Very. She'd been onboard for seven months. Her plan was to die at sea, though I think she was hoping it would be a long-range plan."

"When you cleared out her cabin you would have done an inventory of her possessions, right?"

Arlen nodded.

"I'll bet you found some jewelry but not a lot. Gellerman would have left some behind so it wouldn't look suspicious."

Kutsen rolled her back and shut the door. "He could have drugged her or smothered her."

"This is all just speculative," Arlen said. "We don't yet have any reason to believe that Gellerman killed her, or even knew her."

"No, no," I said. "I don't believe much in coincidence. He killed her for her jewelry."

"You can't know that."

"I have a nose for this sort of thing," I told him. "Try this: make a list of all the old ladies who died onboard over the last few years. Then see if Gellerman was onboard."

"We could check that easily enough. The last death I remember was Doris Alexander in Lisbon." He still had Gellerman's folder with him so he opened it and read off the list of his recent cruises.

As the color drained from his face, I knew I was right. He looked up but he didn't say anything.

Knutsen tapped at his temple. "What was the name of the lady who smuggled in the dog? Remember, we had to send the dog back."

Arlen shook his head. "I don't remember that."

"Marie Deveraux. Remember, in Ireland? Room service showed up and found her unconscious. She died right after."

"When were we in Ireland?" Arlen asked.

"No, sorry. That was our sister ship, *Contessa Explorer*. I did a tour with her last year. It was a transatlantic to New England. My wife wanted to see the leaves changing."

Arlen checked the folder. He looked up and nodded.

"I think I found your killer," I said. "Just not the one you were looking for."

We spent the next half hour or so back at the security office. The captain was ashore and we were trying to find him. Arlen contacted the airport police and the American Embassy to arrange extradition for Gellerman. Things were about to get difficult for *Voyager*. Passengers get skittish when one of them is killed. Kill two of them and the mood can deteriorate quickly.

"You know what's kind of funny?" I said. "Whoever shared a cabin with Gellerman got hooked up with him through your roommate matching service."

"Why is that funny?"

"Well because it matches people with similar interests. So unless the roommate is a killer too, I'd say your system made a pretty poor match."

"Yes, that is very funny," Arlen said. "We probably should have a conversation with the roommate first. I'm not sure what exactly we tell him, or the rest of the passengers for that matter. Ultimately that's going to be up to the captain."

"We don't want to say too much," I said. "Not just yet. Have a little talk with the roommate. Tell him that Gellerman was detained by police on suspicion of robbery and you'll get him more details as they become available."

He nodded.

"And this can't become public knowledge at this point; nothing in the newsletter. I don't want to spook people."

"When it comes out, people are going to start calling this the Death Cruise," he said, shaking his head. "I can see it now."

That made some degree of sense. "We have a day at sea tomorrow," I told him, "and we need to set up a panel of interviews."

"Interrogations, you mean."

"Call them what you want, but we're having a private little chat with every male passenger traveling alone."

CHAPTER ELEVEN

I normally like to take my lunch early but it was noon by the time I got to the dining room. I felt like I'd already worked a full day. I spotted Doug and Opal Baxter and went over to sit with them. "Where are your comrades?" I asked.

Doug shook his head. "Elliot and Donna went on the excursion, the one to go see the volcano."

"Yes. Everybody loves a volcano. You all didn't want to go?"

Opal looked up timidly and shook her head. "We did actually. We did want to go but we felt, kind of ..."

"We needed a little time on our own," Doug said, jumping in. "Elliot just doesn't shut up."

"And Donna is a drunk," Opal added as I ordered a Bloody Mary.

"Is that right?"

"You should have seen her last night."

"They dragged us out to the disco," Doug said. "We're not disco people, you see. But Donna was hammered."

"Elliot tried to slow dance with me," Opal said.

"I'm an expert tango dancer," I told her, "an international champion."

"They didn't have tango dancing at the disco. Just disco music or whatever, and it wasn't slow and he just grabbed me."

"Swingers is what they are," Doug said loudly. "Donna was rubbing herself against me, telling me how much she valued my friendship."

"Yeah and you've already gone down that route, haven't you!" Opal said.

"That was a long time ago, honey. We've been through this." He turned to me. "So I grabbed Opal and we left."

Opal shuddered. "I went with Elliot in high school, you see. He wasn't so fat back then, and it was before I met Doug. I don't think Donna has ever really trusted me even after she evened the score."

Doug fumed. "I hate that son-of-a-bitch."

I closed my eyes for just a moment in hopes that they would both disappear. When I opened them, Andres from Dubrovnik hovered over me. I hadn't even looked at the menu yet. "This is going to be worse than the stabbing," I told him.

"What's that, sir?"

"Nothing. Give me a second here. I have to look at the menu." Veal with white sauce could be nice. And I was going to need the cream of tomato soup. Fettucine with grilled chicken just called out to me. I ordered that and sat back as my table mates ordered.

"Aren't you fellows in business together?" I asked. "You and Elliot? Gondoliers or something like that?"

"Veterinarians," Doug said. "We've been in business for years. And it's a good business but we stopped being friends a long time back only they haven't figured it out yet."

"Why the hell would you go on the cruise with them if you don't like them?"

"See, they gave us the cruise as an anniversary present, so what could we do? I could kill him."

"There's room for one more in the morgue," I said.

"What?"

"Nothing. Let me ask you something, Opal. You write obituaries, right?"

She nodded. "Yes, for the *Marysville Gazette*."

"How do you know what to say about someone?"

"Oh, you just do a little research on what they were like as a person."

"I see. Do you have to confirm that the person is really dead? I mean, you don't want to write an obituary for someone who turns out to still be alive, right?"

"That's right," she said. She seemed more comfortable now. Maybe talking about her work was calming her down a bit, even though we were talking about dead people. "The *Gazette* has a subscription to a database that tracks records from hospitals and funeral homes and coroners. That way we can make sure that someone is actually dead, and we can find out a little information about the person's life. About two-and-a-half million people die each year in the U.S, so this way there's a central file."

"Kind of like the internet," I suggested.

"Yes, it is on the internet but it's a restricted service because you can get a lot more information. And it's expensive. You need a password to get in."

"A password?"

"Yes, a password. Why do you ask?"

Our soup came so I had to take a bit of a breather. Good soup can give you hope, can save your life. Even if all you have is a couple of carrots and a turnip and the mushrooms you found, you can make a little soup. "I'm working on a project," I told her. I took out my wallet and fished around for the card I was looking for. "This is actually a working vacation for me. I'm a reporter and I'm doing a story on crimes aboard cruise ships. Could you maybe help me out?" I handed her the card.

"What's this?" she asked. Doug leaned over to read it.

"It's my press ID. If I gave you a couple of names, could you look them up in that database you were talking about?"

"*Penthouse?*" Doug said. "You work for *Penthouse?*"

I frowned. I looked at the card. I think it wasn't the one I was looking for. "Just freelance. An article here and there."

"It says here you're the senior editor." Opal pointed to the title under my name. I found my glasses and had a closer look. So it did.

"It's a thankless job," I told them. Opal backed off a little. "I had grand ideas when I took the job. We were going to move into whole new areas; more focus on the environment, alternative energies, orphans and koala bears, that sort of thing. I felt the magazine had gotten off track with all the nudity."

"But it's a pornography magazine," Doug insisted. "Nudity is its track."

I nodded. "Which is why they fired me as senior editor, but I still get to write hard-hitting articles. Last month I wrote about teenage runaways in Egypt. They leave their families and then go to the pyramids to try to make it there but they can't find work so they just sniff glue at the pyramids. It's very sad. You have no idea how young these kids are."

"Well, they're teenagers," Doug said.

"Very true." I shook my head sadly and waved for Andres. It was clearly time for a new Bloody Mary.

We ate a glorious lunch, the three of us. My fettucine was first rate. I had the flan for desert, and before I left, I slipped Opal a page of notepaper on which I had written two names: Robert Samson and Harvey Cotton.

I decided that I needed to spend a little time on Martinique, so I was headed out when Capt. Erlander waved me over. He was talking with a woman behind the reception desk but he came out and motioned me over to a sitting area by a large window facing the ocean.

"I want to thank you," he said. "I don't know if Mr. Gellerman killed the woman or just stole from her after she died, but this is nonetheless a tragic event for our ship."

"I'd have to agree," I said. "And not just for your ship, for the whole industry. You'll lose millions. Not just Contessa, but all the lines. Just think of the implications for Disney Cruises; Goofy could be a cold-blooded killer."

He stared at me for a moment. "Do you think it's possible that Gellerman killed Samson too?"

"No."

"But it's a possibility, right?"

I shook my head. "You just asked me that. Look, it's also a possibility that you killed him. In fact, of all your passengers and crew, I'm the only one who isn't a suspect. What are you getting at?"

"I am under pressure to show progress in this investigation. And so far things have not improved. In fact, they have gotten somewhat more dire. Are you not under the same sort of pressure?"

I leaned back in my chair. "You know, I haven't checked my e-mail yet. Besides, I still have three days left. I'm going to need more assistance though. I need to conduct a series of interviews."

Erlander nodded. "Interviews of passengers?"

"And of crew."

"How many?"

I took out the list that Hector prepared. "There are nintey-three male passengers traveling alone. This includes, mind you, twenty-two who used your matching service to find them cabin mates to avoid paying the single supplement. We wouldn't have even thought to check these people had not this issue with Mr. Gellerman come up. Of those ninety-three, eleven are beyond my suspicion due to age or infirmity so that leaves us with eighty-two people who need to be interviewed."

"You're going to personally interview eighty-two passengers before we get to Miami?"

"Oh no, I'm not going to personally interview any of them. I'm going to just watch the interviews. That way I'll know who to concentrate on. And it's not before we get to Miami. It has to be done tomorrow."

"Tomorrow!"

"Yes. We'll be in St. Thomas the following day. If the killer gets spooked, he'll get off there, and we'll lose him. U.S. territory; it's an easy flight back home to wherever."

"Why can't we just leave this to the F.B.I. when we get to Miami? I'm sure they have more experience interviewing suspects."

"No doubt, but jurisdiction over crimes at sea is a little tricky. That's a Bahamian flag flying off your stern. Any F.B.I. investigation will be far from comprehensive. We'll lose him."

He stared out the window and shook his head. "I don't know how we're going to set up interviews for that many people. We don't have the manpower for that, or the training. We're over-extended as it is with all the extra security."

"There's more. There are also thirty-four crewmen I want interviewed. These are guys who are on their first or second tour and who were not recommended by other crewmembers."

"That's simply too many. As I said, I can't pull any of my security personnel, not now."

"Give me four guys. If you can't spare the security people, then give me petty officers. Give me one of the head waiters or the dance instructors or a couple of the gigolos."

He glared at me. "They're hosts, not gigolos. They dance with women."

"So do I. Look, I don't need people with special training. I just need four live bodies. And I'll need Arlen to watch with me. They'll be simple interviews, maybe ten minutes a pop. We'll knock it out in twelve hours."

"You'll upset all the passengers. I'd be surprised if half don't refuse. This is a vacation, remember. They paid for this."

"I don't care. Give everyone who participates $100 in their account or something, an extra fruit bowl, a free photograph. Tell them that you've been asked by the authorities to expedite the issue. Tell them you're sorry for the inconvenience but you're trying to keep them alive."

"And if they still decline to participate?"

"Then thank them for their time, and let them know that we'll be informing the authorities that they declined to assist a homicide investigation. And tell them to be sure to change their airline reservations because they'll be detained at least eight to ten hours in Miami to talk to the F.B.I."

"This is going to bankrupt the cruise line. We'll be belly up by the end of the year."

"Maybe. But that's not what I'm focusing on right now."

He seemed to calm down a bit.

"OK, the interviews will be very simple, just five questions. Do you have a pen?"

He fished out a gold fountain pen and held it out.

"It's for you," I told him. "Here are my five questions."

He reached for one of the embossed Contessa notepads that were strategically placed on almost every flat surface of the ship.

"Question one: We've all experienced a terrible event; is there anything we can do to make the remaining days of your cruise more comfortable or enjoyable?"

I waited for him to finish writing. "Question two: What security features could we put in place to reassure you that future cruises will be safe?"

I really only had one question that I cared about, but I wanted to make sure it didn't just pop put of nowhere. "Question three: How do you feel about the idea of armed security personnel on board?"

He shook his head. "Nobody brings a gun on my ship."

"You already have guns on your ship," I told him. "I read the security specifications. In a locked safe in the security office you have six 9mm automatic pistols, one twelve-gauge shotgun, and assorted pepper spray canisters. This is in addition to the water cannon under the tarp on the bow that was put in place last year after the *Seaborn Spirit* was almost boarded by pirates off Somalia."

"We have them in case of an emergency."

"A murder is an emergency. Question four: Do you have any knowledge of who might have killed Robert Samson?" I waited. "And question five: We don't have the personnel on board to pick out all of the faces from our surveillance tapes, so to make it easier to find you, can you tell us where to look for you at the time of the murder?"

"We don't have that many tapes or that many cameras," he said.

"The killer knows that, but most people don't. Most of the people will tell us they were asleep, so we'll check keycard activity to see if their door was opened within an hour or so of the murder. This is the most important question. If anyone fusses, I'll follow up."

CHAPTER TWELVE

I left Capt. Erlander on the couch and headed for dry land. I passed through security and walked the plank back down to Martinique.

A colored fellow walked right up to me. "Welcome to Martinique," he said. "Is this your first visit?"

I shook my head. "No, I was here about an hour ago." I waved him away. I really just wanted to sit down and watch the action. I spotted a little café just across from the dock. I know that doesn't sound especially nice but it was. It was lovely with little round tables and an ocean breeze. Not much of a view, I couldn't see much more than our ship and the smaller *Crystal Serenity* docked just behind it.

I spotted a few crewmembers lounging around a bank of pay-phones. Anytime you see payphones in the vicinity of a cruise ship, I promise you, they will be crawling with crew members eager to talk with people back home in Manila or Belgrade or wherever. Making a phone call from a cruise ship is an expensive proposition. It will run you about $10 a minute because, I'm told, satellites are involved. Just thinking about that makes me realize how old I am. I was already a young man when Sputnik was launched. We didn't even have viable commercial air travel back then. Hell, back then everyone traveled by ship. What a change. Nowadays you can dial a number right from your Junior Suite, and somewhere two hundred miles above the earth, there's a monkey sitting at a keyboard routing your call.

I found a good table from where I could watch the gangway and maybe have a little something to eat. I ordered a coffee from a pretty girl and stared out at my ship. Even early in the afternoon, people were climbing back aboard. Martinique is a land of culinary delight, an exotic fusion of Caribbean, African, and East Asian cuisine, if my menu wasn't lying. But half the passengers were still going to scamper back to catch the tail end of the lunch buffet because it was free, rather than shell out a couple of bucks to sample the local fare.

I had a little pair of binoculars that I stole from one of the Broad-way theaters. Looking through them, I had a pretty clear view of people moving up and down the gangway. I saw the security men too, more than you would ordinarily expect, which is how I wanted it. The cabbies were all lined up at the curb and the vendors were every-where, selling postcards, key chains, and the standard souvenirs that you can pick up on any Caribbean island, like a section of coconut palm painted to look like a can of Red Stripe Beer.

Other than the cabbies and the vendors, a nice little crowd of younger guys had assembled. They appeared quite agitated. Several held signs up but I could only read one of them. It read, "*Ferocité.*" I didn't know what that was but it sounded scary. I wondered if we'd docked in the midst of some local election, or a coup. Maybe rival drug lords were vying for dominance.

Turning back to the ship, I saw my new friend Duarte moving down the gangway. He stopped the moment his feet hit the ground. He turned and looked in my direction. I waved but he didn't see me. Waving at someone while you're looking through binoculars is kind of a strange thing to do. You have to remember that the person you're looking at is far away. Duarte didn't even move off the curb. He took a few steps and headed right back up the gangway.

He was a character, for sure, but I didn't think he was the killer. I was pretty sure it wasn't Duarte who stabbed me. I was looking for another kind of oddness, like a guy walking down the gangway trying hard to look normal. A normal guy doesn't have to try. He's going to be looking around at the scenery and at bosoms. A guy trying to look normal would never peek at bosoms because he's too conscious of drawing attention to himself. But I didn't see any guys like that.

The girl brought my coffee. She was carrying some alluring baked pastries on her tray, destined for another customer, but I couldn't take my eyes off it. "What are those?" I asked.

"Puff pastries stuffed with curried shrimp," she told me. And because that's something I'd never had, I really had no choice but to order some. When I looked back through my binoculars, I saw a huge head coming my way. And as my eyes focused, I saw that it belonged to Ron Gibson.

I've always found British people to be quite cheery. "Henry," he called to me. "Don't tell me you're just going to sit here on your ass all day."

"I'm working," I told him. "I'm solving crimes."

"So I hear. Just not the one you came to solve. You're going to have us all out of a job. What do you have in store for us next, kidnappers on board, a plot to blow up the Lido Deck?" He sat down at my table.

"Do you know what *Ferocité* is?" I asked him.

He shook his head. "I bring a message from Arlen. Norman Gellerman was just transferred to U.S. custody. He's claiming that your interrogation and search was illegal."

"Never met the man," I said. "Did he remember anything about his alleged interrogator? Did he get a name, perhaps?"

Ron smiled. "Strangest thing, but he didn't remember a name. He said something about Drug Enforcement Agency, but the embassy confirmed they have no D.E.A. personnel on the island. He also said it was a really old guy with bladder trouble."

"Fucker. I'm mature, not old."

"The embassy also confirmed that they have no really old guys on duty because foreign service personnel enjoy more or less standard early retirement ages."

I frowned. "That's such bullshit. It's age discrimination, pure and simple. People figure that once you hit your eighties you should just roll over and play golf. Or stand in front of a Wal-Mart waving like some living advertisement for senility. I'm out here keeping people safe. I'll retire when I'm god-damned ready, when I get old."

Ron stared at me. "Sorry, mate."

I shook my head. "Yeah. I get a little sensitive sometimes." I waved the girl back over and ordered Ron and me a couple of Red Stripes. "What are your plans for the day?"

"I was planning to just have a bit of a walk around but I've been put back on the duty roster. Most of us have, anyway. Your fault, I might add."

"Is that right?"

"Your interview program. Arlen was kind of hemming and hawing about it but the captain pushed him to rush up on it. So we are to have a training this afternoon."

Our beers arrived, as did my plate of puff pastries with curried shrimp, which I generously shared with Ron.

"It's not funny, Henry," he said, all serious now. "We've had to rotate people around to free up guys for your interviews. And tomorrow is a sea day. You know what that means? It means all the passengers are on board looking for something to do. We usually have at least two or three events going on at any given time but I've got blocks of afternoon time tomorrow with nothing because of you. They pulled Eddie & Lane to work with you."

"Who are they?"

"They're the dance instructors. They had a full schedule tomorrow too. I'm having a tough time filling in. We're going to have some down times."

"When?"

"When what?"

"When are your down times tomorrow?"

He pulled a folded up sheet of paper from his pocket. "We've got movies all day long. The casino is open. High tea. We have martial arts in the morning and in the afternoon. We have 'A Tribute to Cole Porter' at 7:30 and again at 10:00. I've got nothing at all at 1:00. And nothing from 3:00 to 4:30."

"What about open bar? Captain's cocktail hour?"

Ron shook his head. "That's your solution to everything, isn't it? Free liquor."

I nodded. "It is, Ron. It is. Free liquor. I even like the ring to it. I like saying it, the way it rolls off your tongue. Free liquor is what our country was founded on. Did you know that? The main reason the American Revolution was fought in the first place was to get your greedy grubby British mitts off our rum. Hey, I've got a joke for you: What's the quickest way to a kraut soldier's heart? With a bayonet! Ha ha!" I frowned. "No that wasn't the one I was thinking of. I can't remember the other one. Listen, Ron, I have an idea."

"What's that?"

"Let me worry about 1:00 and 3:00 to 4:30."

"What do you mean; you worry?"

"I mean since I have you kind of doing my job, let me do a bit of your job."

"What did you have in mind?"

I opened my case and pulled out a folder of the flyers I made up at the copy place. I handed him one. "Tango with Henry," he read. "International dance champion." He looked up at me. "Are you serious?"

I nodded. "I have awards."

"You're going to dance all afternoon?"

"No. I'm going to dance for an hour. But I think I know someone else who would be willing to give an exciting and relevant lecture."

"Who's that?"

"Someone who is anxious to be extradited from his cage near the Engine Room and repatriated to his former suite."

"Orlov." Ron shrugged. "I'd say no but maybe you'll have more luck convincing the captain."

"I'll take care of it. Hey, do you want to share another plate of these puffy shrimp things?"

"Can't," he said. "I have interview training to attend."

"Sorry." I watched him head back to the ship. By that point, the flow of traffic on the gangway had slowed. Anyone who was coming back for lunch was already back, and anyone still on shore was probably going to stay on shore until evening. I looked back over at the crowd and saw even more young men. Some of them were shouting now. I had left my hearing aid back on board so I couldn't hear them. I waved over the girl and asked.

"*Ferocité*," she said. "It is a television show. It's an American show. It's very popular here."

"I've never heard of it."

"A woman has been accused of killing the vice-president and so now she is on the run. She has a small group of friends also on the run. They drive from town to town on small roads in a camper and they rob banks sometimes but mostly they help people in small towns get rid of criminals and things like that."

"Oh brother!"

"Have you seen it?"

I shook my head. "Doesn't ring a bell."

"The woman, Jasmine, is an expert at blowing up buildings which is why they think she killed the vice-president, because he was blown up. But the thing is, even though she is a good person, she might have actually blown up the vice-president, who is probably not a good person."

"Still not ringing a bell," I said. "But why are those boys yelling about it?"

"The actress who plays Jasmine is on one of the ships. She was in here this morning. Her husband wanted coffee and I got her autograph. Those boys are hoping they can get her autograph too."

Something was ringing a bell but it was a distant bell, and as I said, I didn't have my hearing aid with me. I spent another hour or so watching the gangway but I didn't see anyone who looked to me like a killer.

I was getting a strange feeling about a little Mexican boy standing by the foot of the gangway but then I realized it was Hector. From time to time, one of the cabdrivers would approach him but each time he shook his head. Probably someone trying to get a few bucks for a tip that wasn't quite what we were looking for.

I felt I wasn't accomplishing much here other than a small buzz from my Red Stripes, so I headed back to the ship. I made the metal detector sing as I always did when I came on board. By that time, however, some of the crew knew who I was, so when I told them about my titanium hip, I wasn't telling them anything they didn't know.

CHAPTER THIRTEEN

I needed a few things. Most of all I needed a nap, but I also needed to have a look at the surveillance footage from the library. If I napped right away, I knew I'd be down all afternoon, and if I watched the surveillance footage, I'd probably wind up napping. So I decided it was time to hang out a bit. I headed to the reception desk and asked if anybody knew where Inga was. They didn't, and they were disinclined to page her unless it was urgent, which it wasn't. Since Ron was already a little pissed at me, I felt as if I were just about out of friends. Almost.

I stopped off at the Steamboat Saloon and found it completely empty except for Lana from St. Petersburg who seemed quite happy to see me.

"I'm going to need a bottle of something," I told her as I showed her my crew identification card to remind her that I wasn't a passenger. "There's a fellow on board called Duarte," I said. "Do you know him?"

"Of course," she said. "He's been in here almost every day for at least a year."

"A year? He's been on board for a year?"

She frowned. "I think so, yes. He has one of the large suites. He lives there."

"He lives there, you say. What's he like?"

She filled a bowl with cashew nuts and set it in front of me. "He's a very nice man. Very big tips. He's handsome and has lots of girl-friends, new ones each cruise."

"He brings them with him or he finds them on board?"

"I think that he meets them on board. There are many single la-dies on board."

"What does he drink?"

She didn't even have to check. "Canadian Club. Always. He's a general or something like that. They're trying to arrest him in Ven-ezuela but he won't go back. He never leaves the ship either. He's afraid he'll get sent back."

I ate a nut. "Is that right?" My friend Duarte just got interesting. "Let me have a bottle of Jack Daniels," I told her. "And we never had this conversation, right?"

She nodded and swiped my keycard, then handed me the bottle. It was time to visit my new friend Duarte.

He looked good when he opened the door of his Parliamentary Suite, a good deal more put together than he was yesterday. He wore a charcoal grey blazer that looked expensive. I heard music in the background, so I wondered if he had company.

"Hey there," I said. "Remember me? We met yesterday just there inside your suite. You mentioned we might have drinks sometime so I brought you a little present. I don't know if you're a whiskey man but I sure am."

He nodded and opened the door wide to let me in.

"God this is glorious. This is bigger than my condo back in Rolling Pines. Can I look downstairs?"

"Why not," he said. He took the bottle and led me to the spiral staircase. The lower level wasn't as big but it had its own balcony. I suspect that the room might normally be decked out with couches, sectionals and such, but Duarte had turned it into an office.

"I spend a great deal of my time down here," he said, making his way to a small wet bar next to the staircase.

He had three big screen television sets on the wall, and three computers on a desk that ran the length of the room. File boxes lined the walls and stacks of paper covered just about every flat surface.

"Most people take a cruise to get away from it all," I told him. "It looks like you took it all with you. What is it you do, if you don't mind me asking?"

He handed me a drink and we sat, he behind the big desk and I in front. He held his glass up and stared at it in the light coming in through the sliding door. "I don't understand why you would bring me Jack Daniels. Can you tell me how you arrived at your choice?"

That was an unexpected question. It threw me off. If I were interrogating Duarte, that's exactly the sort of question I would ask.

"It's my favorite," I told him. "I keep a couple of bottles in the condo at all times."

"Was that your helicopter that landed two nights ago?"

I was burned. There was no getting around that fact. "Yes," I said. "I'm a private investigator. I'm looking into Robert Samson's murder."

"And you suspect me?"

"Actually, no. To be honest, I didn't until just now."

He stared at me quietly. I've known guys like that, guys who think they can learn about people just by looking at them. I'm not one of them. "You have access to the ship's passenger manifest, correct?"

"Correct." I nodded.

"So you've read about me."

I leaned forward and held up my glass, hoping he'd do the same so we could toast, and he did. Men must be civil, even in dense times. "I haven't read about you. As a male passenger traveling alone, you do fit my base parameter for suspicion, but my interest in you thus far extends no farther than my curiosity."

"But you surely will read about me when you leave here."

We drank. I smiled as he refilled our glasses. "I surely will."

Duarte opened a folder on his desk and read from a sheet of paper. "Dr. Henry Grave. You were born in 1925. You served in the armed forces during World War II, and spent five months in a prisoner of war camp. You hold a Ph.D. in archaeology. You have one son who is a cardiologist in Boston. You've made a career in private security. You live in a retirement home in Bethlehem, Pennsylvania, and you work for the company that owns this shipping line."

I felt my heart beating faster. "It's not a retirement home," I told him. "It's a community of active seniors."

He made a notation on the page before he continued. "In 1959 you suffered what was then referred to as a nervous breakdown for which you were briefly hospitalized."

He paused to give me a chance to respond, but I didn't say anything.

"I think the subtext here is not hospitalized, per se, but institutionalized. At which time, you were fired from your position as assistant professor at the University of Pennsylvania, and for the next thirty years, you did nothing of interest except for a failed foray into politics. I don't know if there is anything more. I've only been working on this since yesterday, you are aware."

I was not at all happy with how things were coming along. Now and again people stumble inadvertently into someone else's drama. I had just stumbled into Duarte's and he apparently had a great deal more juice than I did.

The information that he just shared with me should not have been possible to develop in such a short time. Secrets are meant to be hard to reach. They're hidden, protected; that's the point. Some secrets are protected by computers and by codes of ethics taken by medical professionals who work in beige offices in north Philadelphia, but clearly mine were not among them.

Looking at him just then, a memory jogged. I had seen his face before, in the paper maybe, years ago. "Indulge me, please," I said. "If you didn't kill Robert Samson, then I have no interest in you other than a gentleman's curiosity. But you do look a little familiar."

He smiled, kind of proudly. "You want me to believe you just walked into my home by chance."

I held up my right hand.

He took a cigar from a box on his desk and lit it carefully. "Can I offer you one?"

"Cuban?" I asked, leaning in to take one.

"No. I don't know where they're from. I am General Porfirio Duarte. I was chief of staff of the Venezuelan army, and the leader of a military party that governed my country from 1975-1979."

"Well I'll be god-damned. I thought you were in prison in Miami."

He stared at me for a moment. "That's Noriega. I'd been living in Australia for decades but the Venezuelan government secured permission for my extradition. I left instantly. My plan was to find a motel and hide and figure out a plan. As I was driving, I passed Sydney harbor and saw a ship. This ship. So I found the nearest travel agent and booked a passage. That was a year ago last Thursday. Nobody yet quite knows how to extradite someone at sea."

"Well I'll be god-damned. Why do they want you back so badly?"

"They say I murdered hundreds of people and stole a few hundred million dollars."

"Did you?"

Duarte puffed on his cigar. "The exact numbers elude me."

"I see."

Then he turned right into me, lined up on me, his eyes wide open. "Were you hired to get to me? Did Sucre send you, or Nestor Cuevas?"

You know, that kind of sudden thing can give a fellow a heart attack, or cause a nervous breakdown. I had enough to worry about already. But that's how nervous breakdowns work – the stress just keeps up until a couple of your main gaskets blow.

One day you're directing an excavation on the coast of Peru, and the next day you're curled up in a ball with your mind shorting out, wrapped up around the Russian kid you killed fourteen years earlier because he took your food. *Dosvedanya*. And all the mummies you dug up over the past three years get stolen because you forgot to lock them up, and it feels like the whole world is catching on fire.

"No, man," I told him. "I never knew you existed until yesterday."

He rocked back in his chair and stared at me. "I don't believe you. The helicopter made me nervous."

I reached forward and poured another round of Jack Daniels. "Yeah," I told him. "You do believe me. If I was some heavy in the Venezuelan government and I wanted to reach out for you, I'd have some Filipino thug hop on board and break your neck for fifty grand, maybe even twenty-five. You and I are just two old guys passing in the night."

"Perhaps."

"The two men you mentioned, they're the ones who want to bring you back to Venezuela?"

"Yes."

"To put you on trial."

"No, to kill me. Antonio Sucre is a federal judge in Caracas. Nestor Cuevas is a senator. They were both members of the party but they were exonerated because they blamed everything on me. They now have the power, but I have the money."

"How did you find out about my medical records?"

He shook his head. "I wasn't looking for them specifically, but I had to do a fairly detailed search and I had to have it done quickly. All of us have files in some government locker, and I still have people loyal to me who can get information."

"Well then," I said, standing up. "This has been interesting. I'll be going now. Let me ask you something, what are the chances you can keep my identity a secret so I can finish my job?"

He stared at me for a moment. It was a cold stare, one that made it very clear that he knew what it was like to hurt a man. I know that stare. I have it in me too but I didn't need to break it out just then.

"I'll consider it," he said. "I have more thinking to do about you still."

My actions described a line, the shortest distance between two points as I left that Parliamentary Suite and made my way to the security office. I looked up Duarte's file and confirmed what he had told me. Porfirio Duarte rose in the ranks of the Venezuelan army by eliminating the political enemies of the ruling party, after which time he eliminated the senior members of the ruling party.

"Why do you let him stay on board?" I asked Hugh Arlen.

He shrugged. "He's not breaking any laws, for one thing. For another, he pays seventy grand a month for his suite. And for yet another, we have no legal authority to get rid of him. And even if we did, we couldn't. No country will accept him except Venezuela and you better believe he's not going to step ashore when we stop there."

"What does he do on board?"

"He talks to ladies, buys them drinks, takes them to his suite. He's a very charming man. You don't think he had anything to do with Samson, do you?"

I shook my head. "How are the interviews shaping up?"

"We have them all scheduled; tomorrow is going to be a long day at sea. We've sent each person a little note with a time and a polite request. Most of the passengers are still ashore but we've received three complaints already; two by phone and one direct to reception requesting a meeting with the captain. The complaints are all similar; haven't we been through enough, this is insulting, etc."

"Well I guess we can't force them," I said. "Just keep a list of refusals and I'll have a look at them."

Arlen looked up at me. "Honestly, do you think this is going to work?"

"Yeah. Look, this is how it works; you talk to people. How else do you think crimes get solved? I'll get him, Arlen. I've still got three days."

People need to give me a break, I told myself as I took the stairs up to the Lido Deck. I'd already found one killer. They had a little buffet set out at the Bistro so I paused to circle the food island a couple of times before making my choice; three roast beef mini sandwiches on French bread and a couple of little sausages. Also, some cherry tomatoes.

"Once you eat one of those little quiches, you'll think you died," Helen said, reaching over my arm to point.

"Are they poisonous?"

"Probably," she said. "Cheese, egg, cholesterol."

"I'm getting a clot just looking at them." I kissed her on the cheek and added a little quiche to my plate. "How are you this afternoon?"

"Fine, Henry, just fine. You look terrible."

"I've been up since about six. I was thinking of having a snack and then maybe a little nap."

"Can I join you?"

"Of course," I said, pointing to a table by a window.

"No, I meant for the nap."

Wow. I was momentarily flustered.

"I'm teasing you," she said, taking my arm and leading me to the table. "You just about turned as red as the buffet tomatoes."

"Let me ask you a question," I said as we sat. "Did you know the woman who died last week, Dorothy Kent? I just heard about her."

Helen smiled sadly. "I did, yes. Not super well, but we did spend some time together."

"Is it true she had a boyfriend?"

Helen stirred her tea. "Aren't you a big gossip!"

"I'm a fly on the wall."

"She might have, I don't know."

The way she cut her little pastry was so delicate it made me want to kiss her fingers. "Come on, you know me. You and I go way back, you can talk with me."

She shook her head. "My mother taught me not to speak ill of the dead. And because my mother shares a cabin with me, she could be along any moment. I don't want her to be cross with me."

My mouth hung open for longer than it should.

"I'm joking. Look, Dorothy Kent was an old whore."

Mouth still open.

"Even ladies of a certain age make friends, make lovers from time to time, but not a new one every week."

I frowned. "She was in her seventies, right?"

"Yes, she was seventy-one, I think. But the way she threw it around you'd think she was nineteen."

"My goodness. She must have been charming."

"Oh, she was. And she was beautiful, absolutely beautiful. She could have passed for fifty. In fact, I think she did. She had a different man on each cruise. Some of them didn't even last from one port to the next."

"Do you remember the last one?"

She squinted. "You know, I can't really keep them straight. There was one fellow, Bill, who was a riverboat pilot in Baton Rouge. I think she sent him back up the Mississippi some weeks before. Then another fellow, the last one I remember, was Norton, I think, or Norman. That's right, Norman. I remember because he claimed to be a high school history teacher. I said something once, something about Woodrow Wilson being our greatest president, and he said he didn't remember which one Wilson was, which I thought was odd."

"Got us out of W.W.I, started the League of Nations," I said. "A great man. A Princeton man."

"And a wonderful lover. I had an affair with him. He had gentle hands."

"You lie."

"I do, but can't you leave an old lady to her fantasies?"

I smiled. "You don't think he had anything to do with her death, do you?" I don't know why I still cared about Norman Gellerman. Though I was leaning otherwise, it was still possible that he killed Samson too.

Helen frowned. "The doctor said she died of natural causes."

"That's what I heard too. I only ask because sometimes people feel safer on a cruise ship than they would at home. On board, a lady might open her door or her heart to someone a little quicker than she would otherwise."

"I suppose." Helen frowned again. "Oh, you're going to frighten me if you talk like that."

"It's not my intent."

"No. You know the men, single men who take cruises ..." she paused here. "Well, single men take cruises for a number of reasons.

In your case, for instance, to maybe take a break, see a bit of the world. But in other cases, a single man might take a cruise because he is lonely and because he's heard that cruise ships are filled with an abundance of lonely old ladies like myself."

"Oh, stop."

"It's true. In stormy weather, they use us as ballast. Look, nine times out of ten, men chat up women because they're lonely, not because they want to kill them."

"Nine times out of ten?" I leaned in. "Every tenth man has murder on his mind?"

She took a deep breath. "Right, that didn't come out well. O.K., take the riverboat pilot I mentioned."

"Bill."

"Bill. He was recently widowed, living far away from his children. He was lonely. Dorothy Kent was a dream come true. They danced, they ate nice meals, they drank wine and they were intimate with each other."

"So they liked each other. They had a good time with one another."

"They did. He was in love with her, wanted to take her back to Baton Rouge."

I was engrossed. I waved over one of the bartenders. "We need some drinks," I told Helen.

"Not yet. It's too early for me."

I waved the bartender away. "She didn't want to go to Baton Rouge, did she? She wasn't in love with him?"

"She may or may not have been, but she didn't want to go."

"Why not?"

"I told you, because she was an old whore."

"I think we need some drinks." I waved back to the bartender.

"Yes, it's about time."

"Can you bring us something white?" I asked the young lady. "Something French in a bottle?"

"He wasn't that good looking," she continued. "But more than that, he didn't have any money. Dorothy had her idea of romance. It was like she was still a young girl, waiting for her prince to come, like in that movie, *Pretty Woman*. Did you see that?"

"Yes, I loved it. The one with Raul Julia. I had such a crush on her."

"Julia Roberts."

"That's what I said. So after Bill there was this fellow Norman, who claimed to be a high school history teacher."

"That's right."

Our wine arrived. I took the requisite sip and pronounced it most acceptable. Helen and I toasted.

"So was Norman her prince? They're not known for their great wealth."

"Most princes are probably rich."

"No, I mean high school history teachers."

"I suppose not. And no, he wasn't her prince. They didn't fit well together. He was a handsome man, but he was twenty years younger than her. Like I said, Dorothy was beautiful, but she was still an old lady. I think he just wanted a fling. She would have spent time with him because he was young and handsome, but I don't think either had any long range plans."

"And then she died."

"Yes. They're having a memorial service for her this evening, for her and for the F.B.I. man. Samson."

"Are you going?"

"No."

"Why?"

"I'm going to a cocktail party with you, remember. It's for passengers who've taken multiple cruises. I like things that come in multiples."

"I'm coming too?"

"I wouldn't have it any other way."

I had forgotten. "I haven't forgotten," I said. "What time is that?"

"Six."

"Is that right? What time is it now?"

"Just about a quarter to five."

I sighed. "It's late. I was going to have a nap."

"You'll need one if you're going to spend the evening with me."

I smiled. "I need to leave you for now then. Can we finish the wine later?"

"I'll have it by my bedside."

CHAPTER FOURTEEN

I'm a prompt and respectable man but I'd be lying if I told you I made that date. The truth is I slept right through it. Well, almost. I got there fifteen minutes before they shut down the free bar.

Let me tell you what happened; when I got back to my Junior Suite, my intent was to do a little work and take a shower and maybe shut my eyes for just a wink. But there was something about that library surveillance CD that put me right to sleep. I turned it on and watched for just a few minutes. It was a shot of one end of the library. Every now and again someone stepped into the frame looking at the racks of DVDs or the paperbacks behind them. Or someone sat in the overstuffed chair near the window and opened up an atlas or one of the *Time Life* photography books and read for a bit. And that was it. I was asleep within minutes.

I think you could sell copies of that CD to people who have trouble sleeping. Maybe one day when I retire, I'll start a mail order business and do just that.

I had a dream. In the dream, Norman Gellerman was sitting in the overstuffed chair near the window reading *Popular Mechanics*. As I looked closer, I could see that it wasn't really *Popular Mechanics*. I squinted to read the title more clearly and saw that it was *Professional Murderer Weekly*, a very different sort of magazine. Gellerman was waving at someone, speaking to someone just outside the frame. A man leaned in and handed him a credit card. I saw the side of his head, close cut grey hair, and an ear. Yes, that narrows it down. Then I saw a tentacle pass over the library window and realized that a giant squid was attacking the ship.

It was already 6:30 when I woke up. I had no time to shower so I cleaned up, changed the bandage on my stab wound, put on a nice suit, and then I ran up to the Copacabana Lounge.

I heard a great deal of applause. Capt. Erlander was up on the stage handing a bouquet of flowers to a Japanese couple, congratulating them on their forty-third cruise with Contessa. Some people have too much money.

It was dark and I couldn't see too well. I had to ask around, ask the bartenders where I could find Helen. Finally one pointed to the stage and I saw her right there next to the Japanese couple with her own bouquet. She looked great, all sparkly in a sequined gown. What a smile. I waved, but she didn't see me.

A hostess walked past me carrying a tray of glasses so I took one and immediately felt a hand on my shoulder. "I thought it was free," I said.

"What?" It was Ron.

"Nothing. Hi Ron."

"Notice anything unusual?" he asked.

I shook my head.

"We're still docked."

"I thought we were supposed to sail at six."

"We were. Two passengers are still ashore. Shelley and Jack Tobin. Have you met them?"

"I don't think so."

"She's a TV actress. She got mobbed in town earlier and they're holed up in the bar at one of the all-inclusive hotels. Just about every young man on the island is screaming Jasmine, Jasmine."

"Wait, I did meet her," I said. Something was ringing a bell. "Yes, I had dinner with her. She's in a TV show, *Die Me Bloody Quickly* or something like that. She plays a vampire?"

"Something like that. In any case, it's a huge hit here, even more so than in the U.S. They call the show, *Ferocité,* and Shelley Tobin is the biggest celebrity to come ashore this year. They tried taking a cab but the cab can't move through the throng of people."

"Don't they have police here?"

He nodded. "We're working on it. It seems they too are fans, but they are putting together a motorcade to bring them back."

"Don't they have helicopters here?"

"They do. We're trying to be as low key as possible. We have assurances that they'll be here within the hour."

"They won't hold dinner for them, will they?"

"What? No."

"Good because I don't want to wait. Do you know what's on the menu?"

He took a beverage from one of the hostesses. "You know, I don't. I'm sure they'll have an extra copy of the menu at the table that they'll be willing to share with you."

Yeah, yeah. "Don't be testy with me. It's been a long day for all of us."

Ron nodded. "OK. I have to go dance with ladies."

Ladies were starting to dance. Here was my chance to look great in front of Helen, to be great in front of her. If there's one thing I can do well, it's dance. I'm an international champion. I headed for the dance floor and looked around for her. I thought I saw her dancing with the captain but it was a different lady.

As I moved slowly around the edge of the dance floor, I got a sense that I was being watched. I don't know exactly how I knew that but you can tell sometimes. I remember back at the camp, I became super-aware of the presence of the guards. You had to be. Those guys were mean; they could hurt you. Ever since, I can feel when someone means me harm. I could thank the Germans for that if I was so inclined. But in any case, someone in the room meant me harm. I didn't see Duarte anywhere and even he probably wasn't a menace to me.

I looked around. I didn't have my glasses so it was an exercise in futility. Most of the passengers were clustered at the cocktail tables, talking and having a good time. Back in the shadows by the bar, near the entrance, a man in a dark suit was standing alone, talking to nobody. He was looking right at me. I couldn't see his face so I walked straight toward him. I had to dodge around a couple of cocktail tables and when I looked up again, he was gone.

I ran out into the hallway and bumped into Soren Nilsen, the staff captain. He was dressed in his officer whites so I knew it wasn't him I was chasing. "I'm looking for a man," I told him. "Did you see a man just walk by?"

"We have a mixer later in the evening for singles," he said.

"I'm not in the mood. Did you see a guy in a suit just walk by?"

"It's a formal night. I saw many such men."

Nuts. I looked around but just about every man I saw was wearing black. I walked back in and exchanged my glass for one that had champagne in it. I suspect it was the last of the free liquor because the trays started disappearing and the lights were getting brighter. It was dinnertime. I hunted for Helen but I couldn't find her anywhere.

Feeling entirely sad and creepy, I fell into place with the crowd and made my way down to the dining room. I'd find Helen later and explain.

"What are we having tonight?" I asked Andres from Dubrovnik. I had a table to myself, which was not to my liking. I'm a social man. To be frank, I spend enough time by myself at Rolling Pines so I enjoy a little company now and again.

"I like the veal tonight," he told me. "The red snapper is also very nice."

"Are my table mates not joining us tonight?"

"Mr. and Mrs. Tobin have not yet arrived. If they do not come, I will be sad. I become forlorn quickly."

"I'm sure." I patted myself down and found my glasses in my jacket pocket. I put them on and scanned the menu. "OK, I'll have the veal with the artichoke salad and one of the soups. I can't decide. You decide."

He assured me he would and then left me alone at the table. I looked around the dining room and saw many happy people, which depressed me. Already I'd caught one murderer but I was getting nowhere with my investigation. I realized I was putting quite a bit of faith in the interviews we had set up. Interrogations really, but it sounded more polite to call them interviews. That's all I really had to go on unless the killer popped into the frame of my library surveillance footage, which was unlikely.

And what if I didn't catch him? We'd reach Miami and some Feds would come on board and ask a few questions. Do you know what would happen then? I knew what would happen then and so did Ron and Capt. Erlander, and Kenji Sakato, who owned the ship. Exactly nothing would happen then. Samson's killer would walk down that gangway and I would have gotten stabbed for nothing. The passengers would go home, and *Voyager* would be cleaned and sanitized for the next group of passengers. The crime would go unsolved and the cruise ship industry would suffer greatly as vacationers looked instead to the relative safety of Western Europe or the Grand Canyon for their vacation needs.

More importantly, I would have failed.

"Why are you looking so gloomy?" Shelley Tobin asked as she took a seat across from me.

The sight of her made me so happy. I swear she was the best looking girl I had ever seen. She had long dark hair and big green eyes.

But it was more than that; it was the way she smiled and the little laugh in her voice. If I was ten years younger and she wasn't married, I'd ask her to join me in one of those disgusting relationships you see sometimes with the horribly old guy and the young girl.

"Where's Blake?" I asked.

"You mean Jack. He's not coming tonight. I wasn't going to come either but I'm starving. We had an interesting day."

"I heard. It sounds like you're quite popular here. You almost became a permanent resident."

"I did." Andres handed her the menu but she gave it right back. "I'll have whatever he's having. I'm starving." She dug into the basket of rolls.

"Did you know they watched your show here?"

She shook her head. "I didn't. I knew there were international versions. They show it in Mexico and parts of Latin America, and I knew there was a French version but somehow I didn't make the connection. It's huge here. I don't know why they call it *Ferocité*."

"I think it means ferocity," I offered.

"I think so. It was actually on TV when we were hiding in the hotel bar. It's on like twice a day. And do you know what was on just after?"

"*Murder She Wrote?*"

"No, *Kojak*. The old *Kojak* with Telly Savallas. It's still on here in reruns."

"Well I'll be god-damned. What do they call it in French?"

She frowned and chewed at the same time. "Yeah, that's strange. They just call it *Kojak*."

"Hey, let me ask you something, how did you wind up taking a cruise anyway? I thought celebrities usually passed their time with other celebrities. Don't you have your own island somewhere?"

"Very funny." Her teeth were luminous. "I don't think we're anywhere close to having a private island. I guess it all depends on the show. It wasn't an easy sell to the network, and Jack had to bond a lot of the financing, so if the series tanks, we're back to square one."

"What was square one like for you?" I asked as Andres delivered our soup.

She shook her head. "Nothing squalid. I don't have any horror stories. I grew up in a comfortable middle class neighborhood in New Jersey. But show biz is a tough game. I was in L.A. for almost six years before I got any jobs at all, other than car shows."

"Car shows, like the girls that stand there in bikinis and wave their arms over the new Buick, like that?"

"Pretty much. Not bikinis but you get the idea. You're supposed to chat up guys as they walk by. You start talking about the features of the car, why it's special." She opened her arms wide. "This year's Mini Cooper Q features a dual pane panoramic moonroof, integrated Xenon headlamps with power washers, and an auto-dimming, light-sensitive rearview mirror."

I clapped. "What's a power-washer?"

"I'm glad you asked that, sir," she said, holding up her plate and fanning it with a breadstick. "A power-washer is an integrated safety device that our certified engineers have crafted to ensure maximum visibility even in low-visibility conditions. This ingenious device automatically removes dirt and grime from the exposed headlamp chassis for maximum output."

"So basically it's a windshield washer for the headlights."

"Exactly."

"Well I'll be god-damned."

"Right. So I'm happy to not be doing that anymore. If the show tanks, maybe I'll move to Martinique."

"They'll probably put you on the currency."

She laughed. She looked just like a movie star.

"Have you ever been in a movie?" I asked.

"No. Not yet."

"Hey, you know who was a hot ticket? That Betty Grable. Did you ever meet her?"

She picked up another breadstick and broke it in half. "How old do you think I am? Betty Grable probably died before I was born."

I thought about that for a moment. There was a time when Betty Grable meant a great deal to me. Back when I was in the service you'd see her poster everywhere. Soldiers carried it all folded up in their packs, and protected it from rain even if it meant their clothes got wet. It was strange thinking she died so long ago. "So have you given any thought to our F.B.I. murder mystery?"

"Funny you should ask. Jack has been talking about little else. We went up to see the volcano this morning, Mt. Pelee; did you go to see it?"

"I meant to."

"It was fascinating. There was a major eruption in 1902 and it killed something like 30,000 people. Only two guys survived. One by running away, but the other guy survived because he was locked in the dungeon and everybody forgot about him."

"Well I'll be god-damned."

"Anyway, we're visiting the volcano and Jack can't talk about anything but this mystery you started him on. That's the screenwriter in him, always looking for new angles. Now he's thinking he wants to develop it as a plot line for *Quickly Deadly.*"

"Is that right?" I had to tune her out for a moment to appreciate the beauty of the plate that Andres set before me. A generous and gorgeous slice of meat sat nestled between twin dollops of buttery mashed potatoes. There were vegetables there somewhere but I couldn't focus on them. I found them; they were baby carrots sprinkled with parsley. I could barely think.

"Well what do you think?" Shelley asked.

"I think that if it tastes as good as it looks I'll probably have an embolism."

"No, I mean we'd have to change the setting. It can't be on a ship."

"Come again with that, will you. I don't have my hearing aid in tonight."

"You do, yes. It's in your ear."

I checked. It was. "O.K., so why can't it be on a ship?"

"It can't be on a ship because in the show, we move around in a van. So we're driving around and we come up to a little town somewhere in Arizona where they're holding an annual reunion of retried sheriffs, and a retired F.B.I. profiler is giving a talk, just like Samson was giving here. Are you with me so far?"

"So far."

"And the night before he's supposed to reveal the murderer, he gets killed."

"That sounds familiar."

She frowned. "Well of course it does. So Jasmine, that's my character, has to investigate."

"You have a room full of retired sheriffs. Why can't they investigate?"

She was silent for a moment as she chewed. "You bring up an interesting plot point. Jack hasn't worked out all the bugs yet, but the curious thing is that we discover that the F.B.I. profiler wasn't working alone. He had an accomplice."

"An accomplice?"

"Yes, kind of a sleeper guy, someone to watch his back, but someone who wouldn't be obvious. The profiler was offering himself up as bait and he knew there was risk involved, so he had a bodyguard or at least someone he felt he could count on. Otherwise, it would be suicide."

I took a few bites before responding. "If Robert Samson had a bodyguard or someone watching his back, don't you think he would have come forward by now and shared this information with the captain or with me?"

"With you? Why with you?"

I took another bite. "Not with me, I mean with the ship's security people."

Shelley shook her head. "He's afraid. He doesn't want to be next. Or he's a criminal of some kind and doesn't like cops."

"Not much of a bodyguard."

"No. He's a major loser but I can flush him out."

"You can?"

"My character, Jasmine. She poses as a stripper and finds the body-guard at a strip bar, and then uses him as bait to find the killer. When the killer comes to take the bait, I'm still dressed like a stripper."

"Aren't strippers naked?"

"No. If they were naked there would be nothing to strip."

"That's actually a good point."

"At first, I pretend to come onto him and when he pushes me away I throw my drink in his face, only it isn't a drink, it's acetylene, which is highly flammable. I open up my lighter and hold it in front of him. He's maybe five feet away at this point and he's glaring at me, you can see the anger in his eyes. And I tell him, 'Back off, sport. Take one more step and I'm going to light you on fire. Your killing days are done, now we can end this one of two ways.'"

I waited but she didn't say anything. "What two ways?"

"The only two ways that matter, Quickly or Deadly."

Wow. I felt something stirring deep inside me, or somewhere. Wow. An accomplice. I hadn't thought about that. I thought about that as Shelley and I ate our dinner. It was a nice time. For a moment there I found myself thinking about how lucky I was, little old me having dinner with a TV star. About twenty years ago I was having lunch at a Kosher deli in New Rochelle, New York, and Walter Cronkite sat down right next to me at the counter. I remember it like it was yesterday. We talked about Vietnam and orthopedic shoes but I'll tell you, it wasn't as nice as my dinner with Shelley Tobin.

CHAPTER FIFTEEN

I stopped back at the Junior Suite to freshen up and clear my head. Someone had slid an envelope under my door. Inside were two printed pages with handwritten notes in their margins. It was from Opal Baxter.

She had also written a note on the envelope. "Here's the information you asked for. I don't know if it helps. There is no current listing for Robert Samson, so I suspect his death hasn't been certified by a medical examiner. In any case, he's not in the system yet. But Harvey Cotton is interesting. You'll see why."

It was time to get some work done. I needed to find a quiet and non-depressing place to work. I felt a slight roll and peered out the window past my lifeboat into open water. We were moving fast and that meant I was running out of time. So I got myself together. I put my glasses on. I ate some of my diabetic candy. I had the little hearing aid that Teddy got for me dialed up so high that I could hear the machetes tear into the cane fields far away in Cuba. I needed my wits about me. I packed up my things and headed for the Steamboat Saloon.

I found it crowded but Lana from St. Petersburg showed me to a table by a window that really wasn't a window at all, just a nicely curtained shutter that was mounted on the wall. If you didn't know better, you'd think it was a window.

I was amazed, I told Lana as I placed my order, how hard the crew works. Sixteen-hour days are not unheard of. These jobs can be grueling but they're plums. If a giant squid did attack the ship and ate every last member of the crew, the company could fill their positions so fast the passengers wouldn't even notice. So you work hard and you don't make a fuss because there are countless other Lanas lining up for this kind of job. That's the thing about modern Russia; they've got more Lanas than they know what to do with. Don't even get me started on the Philippines.

My Scotch came with a smile. I smiled back. I got out the pages Opal had sent me. The first was an obituary from the Cape Cod Ledger six years ago.

> Provincetown, MA – Local businessman Harvey Cotton was pronounced dead Friday. In a statement read by the police spokeswoman, authorities announced they were calling off their six-day search of local beaches and waterways. Because the body has not been found, there was insufficient evidence to obtain an indictment against a teenage suspect who has since been released from custody.
>
> One week earlier, guests arriving at Adam's Garden, a local Bed & Breakfast owned by Cotton, found copious amounts of blood

covering the porch and driveway. Police followed a trail of blood to a wooded area behind the establishment where a 1983 pickup truck was parked. The owner of the truck, whose name was not released because he is a minor, has a history of breaking and entering. According to the police, the Bed & Breakfast appeared to have been ransacked and the cash register was found open and empty.

The state medical examiner conclusively determined that the blood was Cotton's and that the loss of blood was so copious that Cotton was probably dead before his body was removed from the property.

"If the body was dumped in the ocean, the tide would have pulled it out to sea. It's unlikely we'll ever find him," the medical examiner noted.

Although local and state police had attempted to link the case to a series of attacks against homosexual men along the east coast, authorities now believe a more likely scenario involving a robbery gone horribly wrong.

Harvey Cotton was born and raised in Montana. At the time of his murder, he had been living in Provincetown for three years with his partner, Adam Grace, who died last February of pneumonia. Mr. Cotton had no known relatives. He was 52 years old. A service will be held on Sunday at Provincetown Unitarian Church.

Opal had scribbled a note along the margin: "This is his obituary. Normally, even a short piece like this one would have more to say about a person. There's not much about him here before he turned up on Cape Cod."

The second page bore the results of Opal's database search. Across the top she had written, "Montana has a small population. This would have been harder to do in New York or California."

The printout consisted of a series of inquiries and a series of negative responses. There was no record of anyone named Harvey Cotton born in Montana since 1894. Harvey Augustine Cotton was a trapper and purveyor of fine pelts. He died in 1952. He was not our man.

Apparently, the database also searched similar names. The Harvey Cotton I was interested in was fifty-two years old when he died six years ago, but Opal had used a wide search parameter, from 1940 to 1960. She got two hits:

Harvey Kotanski was born in 1955 in the town of Bothan, Montana, and died in infancy.

Genero Cottonelli was born in Helena in 1948 and was currently an assistant district attorney.

Next, Opal did a nationwide search. She got another thirty-four names. Hershel Kotovski was a diamond broker in Manhattan. Herve Kotto was a trapeze acrobat in Las Vegas. I didn't need to read them all. There was only one genuine Harvey Cotton, a meat inspector in Denver. He had a current credit rating, which suggested that he was still among the living.

Opal's handwritten note at the bottom of the page confirmed what I had begun to suspect, that Harvey Cotton was not the man's real name, and that maybe Robert Samson had discovered something.

I spent the next ten minutes or so waiting to catch Lana's eye so that I could wave over another drink.

I must have nodded off briefly because I closed my eyes, and when I opened them, Ron Gibson was leaning over me patting my shoulder. Furthermore, the people sitting at the tables around me had been exchanged for others. The ice in my glass had melted, and a cursory glance at my watch confirmed that I had slept for approximately an hour-and-a-half.

"Fine, fine," I called out, perhaps a bit too loudly. I got a little frightened just then. Falling asleep in public was probably not the best idea when there's a guy running around who has already stabbed you once.

"Are you alright?" Ron asked.

"I just answered you. I'm fine yes. Just resting my eyes."

"People thought you might be dead."

"No, no."

Ron sat across from me. "You've had a long day. You'll need to rest up for your dancing tomorrow."

"I was trying to do just that until you interrupted me."

"I meant in your stateroom."

"I know. I still have work to do tonight. I have to think things through. I'm under some pressure here, Ron. If we don't find our killer by the time we leave St. Thomas, I'm going to have to flush him out."

"How do you plan to do that?"

"I haven't decided just yet. I'll probably use myself as bait, make it clear that I know who he is. He'll come for me."

Ron leaned back into his chair. "That didn't work out so well for Samson, if you recall."

"He was unprepared."

"And you will be different?"

I nodded my head. "Yes. I've got a feeling about this guy. He's out and about. He's not hiding. He's having dinner and playing the slots. And I'm going to find him."

I was feeling pretty crappy about myself as I left the Steamboat Saloon. I don't often nap in public. It's the kind of thing a very old man does and that worried me. Maybe I was getting old.

I am fortunate in that my mind is everything it used to be, if not even more finely honed. I thought about that as I headed for the stairs and started down. If my intellectual capacity had been diminished by time, I was blessedly unaware of it. I was quicker and more precise than I was at forty. But my body was so much less than what it was.

I don't want to tell you what an old man's body is like. The indignities are too numerous, but chief among them is my seeming inability to wrest control of my sleeping patterns from their subconscious overlords. I can't even blink without fear of waking up in a changed world. It wasn't just inconvenient, it was unsafe, and more than that, it was embarrassing.

During the last few years alone, I had napped through two funerals, an appointment to renew my driver's license, and a lecture on Celtic mythology, although the last event might have been due more to content than to my advanced age. My doctor suggested that my overall lack of sleep, and my consumption of vast quantities of alcohol played a hand, but I was not yet convinced.

Other than the napping, however, and some minor infirmities relating to vision, hearing, orthopedics, dentition, and pancreatic function, I was fit as a fiddle. Don't get me started though; we mature individuals pay a great deal of attention to issues of health or infirmity, and we pursue any opportunity for discussion.

I wandered for a bit. Just beyond the Steamboat Saloon was a room nearly as big, with rows of computers so that passengers could use the internet. And every last computer had a passenger sitting in front of it. Imagine that, you spend God knows how much money to take a cruise, and then you spend half the vacation doing what you'd be doing if you stayed home. I wondered if the crew had a computer room of their own, and I decided to find out. I took the elevator back down to the Sea Mist Deck, walked through the door and passed through the curtain as I had before.

It was even louder than I remembered. My lungs filled with smoke as I climbed down the narrow stairs, and I could feel the vibration of the engines in the soles of my feet. I found myself alone in the long hallway. I didn't hear as much music as I had the last time. Either the noise of the engines was drowning it out or there weren't a lot of people in their cabins. I decided on the latter explanation. Cruise ships are busy late in the evening. It was just after 10:00; the kitchen staff was cleaning up from the second seating while the dining room staff vacuumed and polished. The bars and lounges were fully staffed, and the casino was all bells and whistles. Most of the entertainers were entertaining, half the sailors were sailing, and all of the cabin stewardesses had already turned over all the rooms they were going to turn over. Maybe they were napping.

I wandered down the hallway, passing door after door. On one side were the exterior cabins, which were generally more spacious, but it made little sense to call them exterior cabins this far down since they were underwater and thus had no windows or port holes. On the other side of the hallway were the less-desired interior cabins where the lowest ranking engine room scrub boys slept three or four to a room, dreaming sweet dreams of Manila before their night shift began.

I passed a laundry room where three dark-haired beauties stopped their ironing and their conversation long enough to regard me suspiciously while a huge colored sailor refilled their styrofoam cups from a gallon bottle of Vodka. He didn't see me, nor did he offer me anything.

Next to the laundry room was an interior cabin that had been converted into an internet café. I peeked inside and found six diminutive Asian men huddled up to six terminals shouting at each other. Just behind them, a platinum blonde who must have been about six feet tall drank wine from a bottle as she typed with one hand.

I kept walking. The whole place reminded me of a college dormitory; the little message boards on the doors, the scuff marks on the linoleum floors, and the smell of socks and old beer, or old socks and beer. I got a few strange looks but nobody stopped me or even talked to me. I suspected that some mention had been made of a mature gentleman who might show up during the course of his investigation.

I heard music from up ahead so I kept walking towards the Starfish Club, the crew bar. That's where I found approximately all of the cabin stewardesses, along with half of the custodial crew. The Starfish Club was about the same size as the crew mess but the ceiling was much lower. Or at least it might have been; a thick layer of smoke hung just overhead. Anyone taller than about six feet would have to either bend down to take a breath or use some portable oxygen delivery device.

A big sign on the wall suggested that this room should never be occupied by more than 120 people but apparently that big sign had absolutely no authority. I've been in a lot of bars and clubs in my life, but I've never seen so many people crammed into so small a place. Everybody had at least one person sitting on their lap, whether or not they themselves were sitting on someone else's lap.

The room was alive with music and laughter and conversation until the moment I walked in, then just music. I'll tell you something; walking in there, I felt like a ballerina walking into a cowboy bar. All eyes were on me. I pushed through the crowd and tried to find the bar but it was slow going. At one point I managed to get myself caught up inside a group of sailors who each held a pool cue. I didn't see a pool table but there must have been one somewhere. Playing pool on a ship is a risky endeavor. It's not for the faint of heart. One lurch, one swell, one sudden change of course can alter the geometry of the game. One minute you think you're in control and the next you realize you're not. But life is like that too and I still needed to find the actual bar.

Although it seemed like a couple of hours, I probably made it to the far side of the room in about ten minutes. I did a lot of smiling on the way but I got few smiles back. A nearby bartender was hard at work pouring drinks and handing over six-packs of beer. I managed to edge myself in close but he didn't even look my way until I waved a $100 bill with enough authority to summon some attention.

The bartender was a big fellow, and he didn't have a nametag so I had to ask to learn that he was called A.J. I think A.J. understood that I wasn't from around these parts.

"What are folks drinking here?" I shouted across the din of nine languages being spoken simultaneously within six inches of each of my eardrums.

Without taking his eyes off me he grabbed two six-packs of beer and placed them on the bar in front of me.

"Carlsberg," I read. "And San Miguel. What's San Miguel like?"

He leaned in closer and I repeated my question. "Is it nutty?" I yelled. "I don't like a nutty beer."

"It's not nutty," he said.

"OK, I'll tell you what," I screamed at him. "I'm going to buy a round of San Miguel for the whole room."

He gave me a quick nod, then turned and rang a large copper bell. All at once the conversations stopped. The noise level dropped dramatically for one second and then everyone cheered at me as six-pack after six-pack was passed overhead to the parched crowd. I estimated that I had bought about sixteen or seventeen seconds of good will so I tried to make the most of it.

"Can I have everyone's attention for a moment?" I spoke loudly as the last of the beers was delivered. I introduced myself. "I'm investigating the murder of Robert Samson. The man who killed him cut a number of video camera cables to be sure the murder wouldn't be caught on camera. Someone might have seen something, might have seen a man acting suspicious. I need some help here. If you help me find this guy, I'll give you a thousand dollars U.S. Tell your friends."

I got nothing, just stares. Then just as suddenly as the noise had stopped, it started right up again. I didn't even get a San Miguel of my own.

A.J. leaned across the bar. "The boys in here grease gears at night," he said. "And most of the girls change sheets all day long. Nobody here sees the light of day."

Nuts. "Well can you put the word out?"

He said he would.

I felt pretty silly at that point. It took me about twelve minutes to claw my way back to the hallway. I got as far as the stairway when I realized I was being followed. I climbed up to the Sea Mist Deck and waited just inside the curtain.

Two chubby Filipino guys finally summoned the courage to climb up the stairs and meet me. "Mr. Henry," said the first. "You are serious about the reward?"

"I am," I said.

He turned and said something in Tagalog to the second, and a few moments of dialog ensued.

"This is Barry," the first guy said pointing to the second. "Barry works cleaning up big messes. When somebody makes a big mess, everybody knows to call Barry."

I nodded, then I waited as they talked some more.

"Barry says there are American mafia men on the ship, American men like in the movie about godfathers. Do you know this movie?"

"I do," I said.

"One night they call Barry to go to the Cigar Bar because one man has made a big mess of spilling things. Do you know this Cigar Bar, Mr. Henry?"

I nodded. "I know the place you're talking about."

"Barry says that he listened as he cleaned up and he heard one of the godfathers yell at one of the other godfathers that someone was close by and they had to find out who he was before the ship got to Miami. He said they were running out of time."

"Is that right?"

"That is right, Mr. Henry. Barry thinks the godfathers might have killed the American policeman who was killed."

I smiled. "I think Barry watches too many movies," I said. "I'll look into this, and if it leads anywhere, I'll be sure he gets his reward."

I wasn't on board to chase fictitious mafia gangsters so I didn't have much faith that the tip would pan out. I was going to have to look elsewhere. I passed through the curtain, through the door and back into the world of fresh air. I took the elevator up to the Tropicana Deck. It was time to party.

It occurred to me, as I sucked oxygen into my lungs, that I had very little in the way of formal training. In the service, we had some rudimentary instruction in developing lines of evidence, but not much. It wasn't until I started studying archaeology that I developed a knack for reading clues, and an eye for details dim with age.

One of the things that appealed to me about archaeology when I started college after the service was that it felt so safe, so harmless, so far removed from any harm I could do to anyone. You dig, you do your work, you write your conclusions and you tell your story. And if you get it wrong, you get it wrong. The people you're telling the story about are long dead, a safe temporal distance from any harm your actions or inactions might impart. But a criminal investigation is different. My current line of work is not harmless. If I get it wrong, a murderer goes free.

The elevator made every single stop, so it was more than a few minutes before we reached the Tropicana Deck, where the late night party was well underway. The band dominated the little island in the middle of the pool and the crowd was happy. I spotted four security officers watching over the festivities.

I turned my hearing aid down a bit because of the music, so I didn't hear Vasily Orlov until he was right beside me. A half second later he was hugging me. Immediate feelings of paranoia dissipated as he kissed me on the cheek.

"I thank you, my friend," he said. "I was so sad down there. Now, they have me in same cabin as before I have fight with captain. I have minibar again and Bulgarian girl to pick up towels. You come and watch tomorrow, I give great talk, make audience weary with disbelief."

I promised him I would be there. I declined the offer of a drink, which is something I rarely do, because I needed to admit I was very tired. I took one last long look at the scene in front of me, trying to get a feel for who was looking to party, and who was looking for something else. Mostly I was looking for someone smirking, someone already half packed to get off the ship in Miami. But I didn't see anyone like that at all.

CHAPTER SIXTEEN

I slept all through the night, and to my horror, I missed breakfast. The only recourse left was to order room service, which
was fine. I had nice waffles and a couple of sausage links and
a croissant, the kind with nothing inside.

I considered my leads as I ate breakfast and confirmed to myself that they were pretty scant. Aside from killing Samson, the
only thing the killer had done, to my knowledge, was tamper with
the security cameras. That wasn't much to go on. I needed to learn
more about Robert Samson's last case. Who was Harvey Cotton?
Who killed him, and how did Samson find out? I didn't know how
I was going to answer these questions.

That aside, I needed to focus on the task at hand, which was
the program of interviews I had set up. We'd be talking with

eighty-two solo male passengers and thirty-four crewmembers. I was reasonably certain that Samson's killer would be among those people but even if he was, I wasn't certain I'd find him. He had proven to be a cool fellow so far; he might be able to sail right through the interview. He might be waiting in line already. But maybe not. He didn't yet know my questions. He might blink.

So I ate my breakfast in the Junior Suite and I watched the surveillance tape from the library. It was dull, heartbreakingly dull, but I needed to watch it. There's something I learned in the camps that has since proven useful to me; if you pay attention to something closely enough, obsessively enough, you become an expert at that thing. Every little detail feels important. It's like when you play chess for days in a row and you wind up with chess dreams.

Here's what I'm talking about: let's say you have a job, and that job is polishing boots. You polish boots for ten hours a day, and all the time you hate the polishing of boots. You don't know how your life came to this. Half the time you're weeping because you hate boots, you hate black polish, and you miss your wife who you should be home curled up next to, except she's already dead but you don't know that yet. And the other half of the time you're crying because you really, really wanted to work in the kitchen. It smells so good and it's probably warm. Life becomes all about boots. You learn about every last stitch, what they sound like on pavement, how much you wished you had boots like that because your feet are always freezing. Almost every pair of boots is the same, but now and again a different style appears on the table in front of you and it's like a whole other world just opened up.

There aren't ten people on this earth who know more about World War II vintage German army standard-issue combat boots than I do. This knowledge has gotten me nowhere in life. But given a couple of days, I'd know more than anybody else about one particular corner of the *Voyager* library, with the big puffy chair by the window next to the atlas, where someone might have drifted into the frame, just for an instant, as he tried to find the camera to disable it.

But I couldn't spend all day watching the TV. I'd spent enough of my life's days doing just that. I cleaned myself up and dressed for business. When I pressed my hand on my side I could feel pain but otherwise my injury didn't hurt at all, I was happy to note. I put some more alcohol on it and then a little Band-Aid.

On any other day, the Stardust Theater would be closed in the morning for rehearsal. We were at sea, after all, and pianos were not in abundance. Neither were open stages. Musicians need to practice and stage artisans intent on presenting a Cole Porter tribute must choreograph intricate stage maneuvers while memorizing the words to *Anything Goes*. But on this particular day, those entertainers were just plain out of luck.

It was an interesting room, the Stardust Theater, a Las Vegas style theater with deep sofas and little tables barely large enough to hold a couple of drinks. The drapes had been pulled by the time I arrived, so the sunlight filtered in, which probably didn't happen often. I counted fifteen guys sitting around, mostly by themselves. The occasion didn't call for much chit-chat. A few were reading but most sat quietly watching the TV.

Someone had made two very good decisions; they had opened the bar and were serving free drinks, and they had detailed the prettiest girls to bring the drinks, and serve little sandwiches. Even so, the sense I got when I opened my eyes wide and inhaled deeply was one of impatience or offense. This was after all an interrogation, no matter how nicely you dressed it up. C.N.N. was playing on the big screen, kind of loud. A reporter was talking about orphans in Uganda and their plight, which was terrible.

On stage, a thick velvet curtain hid what was going on behind it. I knew that because I had left Arlen a message detailing the kind of environment I was interested in. Four little inquisition rooms had been set up on stage, divided by curtains. Each had a little cocktail table and a comfortable chair on either side of it.

I got what else I had asked for; four members of the crew to conduct the interviews. I got Hector from security, and Soren Nilsen, the second highest-ranking officer on the ship. And I got Eddie & Lane, the dance instructors, who I hadn't yet met.

I had allotted fifteen minutes for each of my suspects, and they were just that, suspects. There was no use in pretending otherwise. I grabbed a little sandwich from a tray and wondered if fifteen minutes was going to be enough time. Remember, some of these passengers were not the youngest. They had only five questions to answer, but everyone on a cruise ship has a story to tell. And the fact that there were already fifteen guys sitting around waiting their turn meant that we were already backed up.

I headed backstage and found Arlen nestled behind yet another curtain. He was surrounded by costumes and props and staring at a bank of monitors.

"You're late," he said.

"Overslept. This looks high-tech. Are you taping the interviews?"

"I am."

"Well I'll be god-damned. Anything interesting yet?"

He shook his head. "Not much. Most everyone is handling the questions fine, but we've had two demonstrations of indignation and three meltdowns."

"Meltdowns?"

"Meltdowns. One of the passengers took the cruise because his marriage was failing and his wife suggested he needed time alone. Hector was in with him for over an hour. The guy was weeping by the end, talking about how much he missed her, how he'd promise to stay away from the internet. It was ugly. The other two meltdowns weren't as bad but both involved tears unrelated to the issue at hand."

"And the indignations?"

Arlen leafed through his paperwork and handed me two pages. "I think the first individual was just genuinely pissed off. He's a school superintendent in Los Angeles here for some relaxation. He said he gets enough bullshit at home. I don't think he's a problem."

I read the sheet but I didn't really know what I was looking for.

"But this other guy bothers me," Arlen continued. "Hector did this interview as well. The guy sat down and Hector asked the first question, 'Is there anything we can do to make the remaining days of your cruise more comfortable or enjoyable?' And the guy told him to fuck off."

I picked up the file and looked at a photo of a middle-aged man, short hair. He had a hard look to him. Harold Roper was a firefighter from Sacramento, California. Thirty-nine years old, though he looked ten years older, recently divorced. He was on his first cruise. "Probably just an asshole," I said.

Arlen shook his head. "No. We've had trouble with him already. The first night of the cruise he got overly friendly with one of the cocktail servers. He rubbed her bottom. She reported it so I had a talk with Mr. Roper. The next night he gets in her way, corners her against the wall and calls her a slut."

"Time to pitch him overboard."

"It crossed my mind. We paid him a visit in his cabin. He was roaring mad and drunk, too. I had met with the captain earlier and we agreed to a fine. I explained this to Roper. He'd have to pay a $2,000 fine for his aggression or we would leave him in Aruba. He called me an asshole so I explained to him why the fine was now $3,000. We gave him till the next morning to make the payment or have his bags packed."

"So he paid."

"They always pay. If it was me, I'd have stayed in Aruba. But they always pay."

"Did he stay away from the girl? Who was the girl?"

"One of the servers in the Steamboat Saloon. A Russian girl named Lana. She's been with us for awhile."

My Lana? My Lana from St. Petersburg? That made me very angry. "I'm going to have to talk with him."

"He's unpleasant."

"So am I."

Arlen's phone vibrated. I stared at Harold Roper's photo as he took the call.

"Shit," he said, standing up. "We're on TV."

The next part was a little uncomfortable. They didn't have a TV backstage so we had to climb out into the theater to watch on the big screen. There we were, larger than life, *Contessa Voyager*, on C.N.N.

Several more men had gathered by then. They joined the others in their catcalls and snickering. We'd clearly missed the first part of the segment but the part we saw was bad enough.

....normally considered a safe environment, though recent events have called into question that assumption. Crimes aboard cruise ships have been increasing in recent years. A recent report issued by Princeton University cites the relaxed atmosphere found on cruise ships as a natural environment for crime. The last thing you expect when you're playing shuffleboard is to be assaulted, yet this type of crime, according to statistics, is rising.

In two notorious cases in 2005, passengers fell overboard under mysterious circumstances. Given the tens of thousands of passengers who cruise the seas each year, this number is very small, and aggressive new security measures are being taken, as the Association of Cruising Vessel Operators is quick to point out. Still, a murder at sea is a serious event indeed, especially considering that the murderer remains among you, undetected for the remainder of the cruise.

So we'll keep the passengers of *Contessa Voyager* in our thoughts as the ship steams toward Miami bearing the body of former FBI profiler Robert Samson. For C.N.N., I'm Cindy Jordan.

Arlen and I shook our heads in unison. Let me tell you something: if you want to really piss off someone in the cruise industry, all you have to do is mention the word 'shuffleboard'. A cruise ship can have all manner of activities on board. It can have a pool, a golf course, skeet shooting, water slides, even a rock-climbing wall of all things, and still you get the shuffleboard comments. There's just no escaping it.

I find it depressing when people clap at the TV, which they did as we walked backstage. "At least we haven't had anyone go overboard," Arlen said.

"No yet. Where can I find Harold Roper?"

He typed at his laptop. "Duchess Deck, cabin 2211."

"Is that a Junior Suite?"

"It is. Look, there's something else you need to know. Whenever a passenger's keycard is put in a lock, it makes a record."

"I know."

"We checked your whole list. Nobody on it entered or left their stateroom between 3:00 and 5:00 A.M. the morning of the murder, and that includes Harold Roper."

At that point, I started to lose faith. "So what, the entire ship was locked down for two hours? Not a soul was out except for Samson and one other person?"

"I'm not saying that at all. In fact, forty-three locks were swiped during that time period. Early risers exercise group starts at 5:30. We had some insomniacs too. The rest were probably walks of shame."

"Walks of shame."

"You know, people coming home from staterooms where they spent part of the night."

"So you're telling me that nobody on my list was out and about at the time of the murder."

"I can't say for sure. What I'm saying is that nobody on your list opened their stateroom door during that period. So our murderer would likely have remained somewhere on deck or in one of the other public areas of the ship."

"Well that's just great. I can't think about this right now. It's making me want to jump. Can you punch up Harold Roper's shipboard account? Show me where he spends his time and money?"

Arlen did just that. "He was in and out of the Steamboat Saloon the first day. But since we fined him, he's been spending most of his evenings up on the Promenade Deck drinking. He's also dropped some cash at the casino. He took four cash advances against his shipboard account, each for the daily maximum of $300."

"What does he do during the day?"

He read the screen scrolling through several pages of accounting. "It looks like he spends a lot of time at the pool. There he is now, he just paid for four piña coladas, about six minutes ago. That generally means he's buying for someone else, too. He's trying to pick up."

I smiled. "I had one of those in St. Thomas many years ago. It was really good. It tasted like pineapple."

"Yes. That's what piña means in Spanish."

"Well I'll be god-damned." I took another look at Roper's photo. It was time to go deep undercover.

I changed as fast as I could. I squeezed into my trunks and I found my cap and my sunscreen. I put on my complementary robe and headed for the Promenade Deck. It was glorious; the sea, the sky, the aroma of freshly-applied sunscreen. There's nothing like a day at sea on a cruise; nothing to do but relax, not a care in the world. Well, usually.

All around us, the calm Caribbean Sea shimmered. What a beautiful day to be on this earth, I told myself as I walked between rows of deck chairs looking for Harold Roper.

Every last deck chair was occupied, and there must have been six hundred of them. There's not a great deal to do on a day at sea, making it the perfect opportunity to lounge by the pool and read something smutty while drinking a piña colada. I wandered all over the place with no luck, and I was beginning to think that Harold Roper had already left. Then for some reason, I looked over at that island in the middle of the pool, where a small group of people sat happily in the hot tub. There he was.

I walked over the little bridge to the island, smiling at the swimmers below me. I walked right up to the hot tub and I smiled. Harold Roper sat in the hot tub surrounded by three genuine beauties. They were young girls, probably in their early twenties, and it seemed as if they liked him. I didn't quite understand the appeal. I found him to be an ugly man but they were sitting with him, hanging with him, up close. I smiled and dipped my toe into the water. "Hot, hot, hot," I said.

The girls looked up, not sure what to say.

"That's why they call it a hot tub, grandpa," Roper called out.

I didn't like him already. To be honest, I never did, not since he first came to my attention about seventeen minutes earlier. But staring at him right then, I wasn't convinced he was the kind of man who would stab someone in a room full of people. That requires at least a flickering of insanity, and insanity requires at least a modicum of intelligence that I wasn't convinced Roper possessed. I opened my belt and let my complementary robe fall to the deck. "Room for one more?" I asked.

The girls looked momentarily uncomfortable and Roper frowned, clearly concerned about the competition here. I am a beautiful specimen of male virility. I told the girls as much as I immersed myself slowly, inch by sexy inch, into the water. I grabbed the tube of sunscreen from the pocket of my robe and extended it to Roper. "Will you do the honors?" I asked him. "Just the shoulders, please. I freckle."

He looked dumbfounded, and more than a bit irritated. He wasn't a nice guy. I knew that but the girls didn't, and I wasn't sure he was ready to clue them in to that fact. I sat in front of him and turned to the girls as he reluctantly squirted lotion onto my shoulders.

"I'm Henry," I told the girls, holding out my hands. "Who the hell are you all?"

I learned that Beth, Haley, and Rachel were seniors at the University of Miami, all majoring in Recreation & Leisure. That's a major, it seemed. And the cruise was part of their senior project. "And this is Harold," they told me, pointing to Roper who was currently rubbing me with lotion.

"Nice to meet you Harold. Don't forget my arms."

"Harold is a fire chief," Rachel told me, grinning. "He told us if we came to California, we could visit the station and slide down his pole."

"Is that right," I said. "Maybe I could come along. You are three beautiful women. Have you ever thought of posing for pictures?"

"What kind of pictures?" Haley asked.

I could see myself with Haley. She had short razor cut blond hair, pert little body and a cute button face. Rachel was too bouncy for me. Beth was the blond dream girl; big bosoms and a tan, but she didn't really do it for me. Girls like that never really have. I don't know why. I hoped she wasn't falling for me. "I work with some photographers," I said. I leaned over and fished through my robe for my wallet. I took out my ID card and handed it to Haley. "Maybe you'd be interested."

Her eyes opened wide. "*Penthouse?*"

Beth grabbed the card from her. "You're the senior editor of *Penthouse?*"

"That I am. Ever think about being a model?"

That got me all kinds of embarrassed laughs, and a modicum of respect from Harold Roper. "I'm a big fan." He grinned, working my shoulders. "Been a subscriber for years."

"Is that right?" Harold was slow to pick up on the fact that any interest these girls had in him had just evaporated. No woman who walks this earth, even if she gets a kick out of pornography, has ever appreciated a man who grins at the mention of naked girls in print.

"Guess what I did this morning," I told the girls as I took a spot between Haley and Beth. "I got interrogated by the security goons. They think I might have killed the man who got killed."

"You're kidding," Haley said. "They think you did it?"

I shook my head. "Nah. They're just questioning people about it. They wanted to know where I was when it happened."

Haley smiled. "How do we know it wasn't you?"

She wasn't afraid. None of them were. I didn't get that. We were sitting not thirty feet from the rock wall where they found his body and it was as if nothing happened.

"It wasn't me," I said. "I was asleep at the time, a beautiful woman spent on either side of me."

"You're a pig," Rachel said.

I think she meant it. That was kind of a piggy thing to say. It was time to redeem myself. "I'm just messing with you," I said. "I was asleep at the time. I'd probably been asleep for hours. But where were you? How do I know you didn't kill him?"

Roper was trying to punch into the conversation but I wasn't giving him the chance. Rachel shook her head and the other girls grinned.

"Rachel didn't come home that night," Beth said. "She made a friend."

Roper grinned.

Rachel kept shaking her head. "We're not talking about this, OK?"

"What about you?" I asked Roper. "They probably didn't even question you, did they?"

His mouth opened but no words come out. I could see why he was divorced. At one point, his wife probably asked him a question of reasonable complexity, like where is the juicer, and he hung there, processing, mouth open until she ran screaming from the marriage.

"Why do you say that?" he asked finally.

I shrugged my oiled shoulders. "You don't look like you have it in you, that's all."

He squinted, reached for his drink and took off his sunglasses. I'd made him angry. I could see it in his eyes. It's just you and me now, Harold Roper, and I can take you.

"I don't look like I have what in me?"

"Murder."

"What the hell is that supposed to mean?"

"I was in the service," I told him. The girls were quiet now, aware that some balance had shifted, completely unrelated to the rocking of the ship. "I knew this lieutenant who claimed he could tell if a soldier had killed a man, just by looking in his eyes."

"You want to look in my eyes, old man?"

Beth slapped him gently on the arm. "Hey," she said. "Be nice."

I looked in Harold Roper's eyes. That lieutenant was a guy named Earl Holiday, a good guy. He got killed by a sniper outside of Luxembourg City about a month after I was captured. I don't know if he really could tell by looking in a man's eyes but I couldn't. I never could. I look into my own eyes in the mirror sometimes. I've killed four men, and in my eyes I see nothing but blood vessels and the soul of a thoughtful caring man. "All I meant is that I don't think you're a killer," I told him.

Roper considered that for a moment and put his glasses back on. He was backing himself off the edge, a skill he likely picked up from one of the anger management seminars the fire department made him attend after he mouthed off one too many times. "Whatever," he said.

Brilliant. Well-done. A witty riposte. "Then again, maybe you did kill him. Where were you when Samson was killed? Alone in your cabin? Nobody to corroborate your story? No alibi? Alone on a cruise; how sad."

"I was with her," he said a little too forcefully, pointing to Haley.

"Well I'll be god-damned."

Haley's mouth opened but she didn't appear to have much to say. Beth and Rachel stared at her. "No way," Rachel said. "You're kidding, right?"

Haley lowered herself so that her chin rested on the water.

"You never mentioned this," Rachel said. "You're quick to talk about me getting back to the cabin late, and then you go with this bonehead?"

Roper grinned. I knew him in that instant. Insults from women were fun, nothing more, not worth the effort of responding. Plus, he was enjoying his victory. I'd let him have that, despite the fact that I was deeply disappointed in Haley. We could have had something, she and I, if I were about sixty years younger.

I didn't want her anymore. The loveliest of them always fall for the assholes. This is one of two reasons I know there is no God. If there was, he could not abide the vision of his child, Haley, naked and willing underneath Harold Roper, who is also his child, but who could not possibly be loved as much. The other reason I know there is no God is because no God would have let me kill Mikhail Palacek back in 1945. He was a good boy, a Russian boy, only seventeen years old, and every day for more than six decades I've wished I didn't have to kill him. But I did have to kill him. So I can't believe in God.

"I was drunk," Haley said softly. "He was nice."

"I am nice," Roper said, lifting her foot playfully out of the water.

I was done with him and I was done with her. Harold Roper didn't kill Robert Samson.

CHAPTER SEVENTEEN

I walked three times around the Promenade Deck, taking in the sun and the gentle breeze. I'll tell you something; I felt like I wasn't getting anywhere. A sidekick would have come in useful at that point, or a partner. I think I'd prefer a sidekick, someone I could delegate tasks to. She'd have to be quick thinking, nimble, nicely muscled. I needed a hard-punching investigator who could follow up on leads while I worked on, I don't know, other leads. I had an idea.

I needed information. I could have asked Hugh Arlen but I knew he was busy at the moment, and if I went to him, he'd probably want to know why I was out wandering around when I should have been overseeing the interviews. So instead I hurried through the rainforest and stopped at the reception desk. "I need to know something," I said to the young woman behind the desk. "Is there a real toucan in that little jungle or is it a fake one?"

"It's real," she said. "In fact there are three of them."

"Three toucans. And they don't fly away?"

"They're inside."

"That's true. Listen, I need some information about a passenger."

"Of course. I do need to remind you, sir, that bathing suits are not appropriate attire except up by the pool."

"That's a sensible rule."

"And you still have your bathing cap on."

Nuts. I took it off. "Can you tell me if Mr. Duarte is in his suite now? It's one of those Parliamentary Suites, the ones with two stories."

"Let's see what we can find out," she said as she started typing. I had to wait while she took a call so I walked over to the case where the menus were posted. It was Caribbean Cuisine night. How clever. I made a decision right then and there to try the jerked chicken.

"Sir," she called, beckoning me back to the desk.

I had left my glasses in the pocket of my robe, which I must have left by the hot tub, so I had to lean in close to read her nametag. She leaned back away from me, but by that time, I had already read it. "Monica from Los Angeles," I said. "You're American. I didn't think Americans worked on cruise ships."

"You're American too," she said.

She had me there. "Why did you want to work on a ship? Don't they have jobs in Los Angeles?"

"I thought it would be fun. You know, see the world."

"So is it fun?"

"Sure, loads of fun. O.K., the passenger you were inquiring about is just now playing Bingo in the Copacabana Lounge."

"Bingo. You're sure?"

"Yes, he just placed a drink order."

"Maybe he's just sitting in the lounge reading. I can't see him playing Bingo."

"He plays every day."

"He does, does he? Can you do me a favor? Can you have someone pick up my robe and bring it back to my Junior Suite?"

"Where is your robe?"

"It's up on the Tropicana Deck, right next to the hot tub. I'd get it myself, but it's far and I need to sit."

She looked unsure for a moment. "I can see if one of the servers has seen it. What does it look like?"

"Well it's a robe, you know, it's fluffy and white. I found it in the closet."

"It's one of our robes?"

"Yes."

"So it looks like every other robe up by the pool?"

"Pretty much. It has my glasses in the pocket, and some mints. You can tell whoever finds it that they can have a mint."

I stopped by the Junior Suite to freshen up and put some clothes on, by which time, my robe had been retrieved and my glasses returned to my face. Then I headed out for the Steamboat Saloon. Lana from St. Petersburg wasn't on duty, which was a dissapointment. It didn't feel the same without her. I put a bottle of Canadian Club on my tab and walked from one end of the Lido Deck to the other, from stern to bow, to the Copacabana Lounge, where Bingo was well underway.

I saw Duarte right away. He was sitting by himself, about three rows from the stage. He didn't notice me, even as I approached, because he was playing six cards attentively. He made no reaction when I sat next to him. "I brought you a gift," I said, placing the bottle in front of him.

"N9," the caller called out. Duarte scanned all six cards with no success.

"Are you any good?"

He looked up at me. "Bingo is a game of tenacity, not of skill."

"Are you tenacious?"

"G14"

"I am," he said, not taking his eyes off the cards. "You lied to me."

That took me by surprise. I almost never lie. "What did I lie about?"

"I'll discuss it with you when this game is over, not before."

"Fine. Can I play one of your cards?"

"No."

So I waited. I leaned back into the comfortable swivel chair and watched Bingo transpire. Bingo has always been an old person's game. I don't know why it appeals, I really don't. If you ask me, it is the sedentary bastard cousin of shuffleboard, and the whole set, cards, balls and all, should be thrown overboard. I played a round once on a

Princess cruise and each time one of those balls got taken out of the cage, I felt myself that much closer to death.

I closed my eyes for just a moment.

Inga was patting my shoulder when I awoke. All traces of Bingo had been removed and the catering staff was setting up for a pineapple carving demonstration.

I stumbled trying to stand. "How long ago did Bingo end?"

"They just cleaned up about twenty minutes ago. Are you sure you're all right?"

"Yes. Yes. Say, when are we going to spend some time together, you and I?"

"We could have a drink this evening after my show?"

"We could surely do that. And you're playing piano for me tomorrow too, at 3:00. Tango music."

"No, I'm playing tango music for you today at 3:00, right here, after pineapple carving."

"Is that right?"

"You set it up yourself."

"I did, yes. Tell me something, is it too late for lunch?"

She checked her watch. "I don't think so. It's open seating, you can head on down right now."

"Come with me?"

"I can't. I have to play for noon tea but I'll see you at 3:00."

I couldn't keep nodding off like that, it was too reckless. Why not just go ahead and stab myself at this rate and save the guy some trouble? I was thinking there might be some pills you could buy, like an anti-sleeping pill. I wondered if anyone had invented that yet.

When I got to the dining room, one of the waiters tried to escort me to my table but I shook him off. I headed over to where Elliot and Donna and Doug and Opal were working their way through enchiladas.

"We thought you had given up on us," Elliot bellowed. "We were going to wait but Donna here didn't have breakfast. Plus, we didn't know how long we'd have to wait."

Donna shot him a frown.

"I'm glad you didn't wait," I said. "I have to meet with an old friend. I just wanted to stop by and say hello. And thank you," I said to Opal. "The information you gave me was great, just great."

She nodded. "You let me know if you need anything else."

I promised her I would. I grabbed a menu from the waiters' station and walked over to the Duarte's table. "What are we having today?" I asked, sitting myself across from him. "I saw some enchiladas on my way over but I have to pass on that, gives me gas. What are you having?"

Duarte made no response. He reached into his jacket pocket and pulled out a folded paper, which he handed to me. "You said you were not investigating me. You lied."

I read the paper. It was a request that he show up to be interviewed. Nuts. "It's a mistake. They're interviewing single passengers. I'll take care of it."

"How do you know it was a mistake?"

"Because they're my interviews. A mistake, I promise."

A waiter I didn't recognize approached. I looked for a nametag but didn't see one. "Can I help you, sir?" he asked. "Mr. Duarte does not usually dine with guests."

"No nametag," I pointed out.

"No, sir. I am Mr. Duarte's personal waiter."

"Well I'll be god-damned. Will you bring me something too?"

He looked to Duarte who issued a brief nod. "What would you have, sir?"

I scanned the menu. "I'll have the Dover sole."

"I didn't see Dover sole on the menu, sir."

I nodded to Duarte. "This guy is very good. I'll have the pasta then, whatever the pasta might be. What is the general drinking?"

"Armagnac."

"Then I'll have the same."

I waited for him to leave before starting in. "Did you win at Bingo?"

"Today I did not." He shook his head. "Mr. Grave, I do not enjoy your company."

Bullshit. Everybody enjoys my company. I'm a lovely man. "I'm sorry to hear you blurt that out," I told him. "Maybe I should cancel that Applejack."

"Armagnac."

"That's what I said. You know, most people like me."

"I am interested in you leaving me alone. If you're not investigating me, then all we have is a social relationship in which I have no interest."

I'd be lying if I said my feelings weren't hurt. "If that's the way you want it, then I'll leave you alone," I told him. "But first I need a favor. After that, if I so much as see you walking down the hall, I'll turn around. You step into the hot tub, I step out, that's the way it will be from now on. I see you reaching for an egg roll at the buffet, I back off that egg roll."

"A favor?"

"You walk up the gangway, I walk down."

"Stop it."

"OK. Yes, a favor. My investigation is not progressing as well as I had hoped."

"I care not in the least."

"There's a murderer on the loose, remember."

Duarte focused on his meal and made no response.

"Here's how I see it," I told him. "In a little more than forty-eight hours, this ship will arrive in Miami and be processed by federal agents. If I have not identified Robert Samson's murderer by then, the ship will be forced to stay in port for several days. Are you following me?"

He didn't even look up.

"I will ask authorization from the Association of Cruising Vessel Operators to impound the ship pending resolution of my investigation. At which point, *Voyager* will cease all commercial operations and discharge any remaining passengers. How many steps do you think you could take on U.S. soil before you are taken into custody and prepped for extradition? I'm sure Caracas is lovely this time of year. The pineapples and shit are probably all blooming."

So we sat there staring at each other, killer to killer, until my *rigatoni carbonara* arrived.

He set down his knife and fork. "What would you have me do?"

"I was hospitalized in 1959. You used the word institutionalized, which is not far from the truth. I had, as you said, something of a nervous breakdown. But the case wasn't handled by a V.A. hospital. My university paid for it, privately, secretly. They generally didn't like to reveal to their students that their professors might have serious mental disturbances. My point is that this episode was sealed, was never revealed to the public. I never spoke of it either. And yet it took you only a matter of hours to discover it."

"I have many friends."

"I'm sure you do, but not ones who worked in the Pennsylvania health care industry forty-something years ago." As I said that, I began to seriously dislike Mr. Duarte.

He grinned. "I did not gain power over a nation and hold it tightly for half a decade without powerful allies in many governments, including your own."

"I suspected as much."

"There were communists to be eradicated, you see. I performed certain services for your State Department which they are eager to not have revealed. So you are quite incorrect in suggesting that I would be extradited. Your government has no interest in seeing me on trial, not in Venezuela or anywhere else. No, I would be flown to some nameless place and executed, or flown out to sea and thrown out of the plane, as the Argentines used to do to their dissidents."

My *rigatoni* was delicious.

"So I have people I call friends, but they aren't really friends. They are reluctant allies who provide me with the information I need to remain free and quiet."

Sometimes a little pasta can change your whole attitude. Just one forkful and it felt like springtime, like my taste buds were all abloom again and the world was full of birth and love and real bacon bits, not the kind from a jar.

"That's the kind of situation I was hoping for," I told Duarte. "I need you to use those connections to find out some information about a man."

"About Robert Samson?"

"No." I handed him the paperwork on Harvey Cotton. "About the case he was working on when he died."

CHAPTER EIGHTEEN

I was feeling kind of stuffy when I left Duarte. I was irritated that I didn't get to finish my lunch, but I had to leave when I did. The moment called for it.

I took the elevator up to the Sky Deck and wandered around the top of the ship. The sea was clearly getting a little choppier though you could barely feel it that high up. A couple of self-doubts crossed my mind.

My first meaningful job in the service, and as luck would have it, my last, involved walking foot patrol in Belgium. I didn't really know what I was doing. I didn't have a clue. We were working in pairs and I got this little Irish guy from New York assigned to me, a guy by the name of Chester Grady who had no fear. They had us patrolling the streets of a pretty little town called Sarlat, not far from the border. We were keeping an eye out for Germans, for sure, but mostly we were doing police duty, watching out for looters or people violating curfew.

We had been walking the same sequence of streets for about a week, kind of getting a feel for it, but Chester was bold and he was thinking eagerly about pretty Belgian girls who sometimes stayed out later than they were supposed to. One night we went a little further out. All we did was turn the wrong corner and the guy was there, a German man with a big pistol.

Chester laughed, which was inappropriate. The German would probably have shot us except he was alone and clearly behind enemy lines, and it would have raised an alarm. Looking back, I don't think he was a soldier. He didn't have a rifle. He was some kind of scout probably, or part of a recon team.

He disarmed us, and he walked us for hours that night across fields and little forests. And at no point did I have any idea what to do. It never occurred to me to fight, to resist, or to rush the guy. Chester did something. I'm not sure what. I think he made a move, and he got shot, got killed. I was standing in a field when it happened, probably the biggest field I'd ever seen. I remember thinking at the time that it was probably bigger than Connecticut. It had just started raining and I didn't even turn around. I was reasonably certain I would be shot right then and there, which I felt would probably be just fine. But I wasn't shot.

We kept walking until we came to a road. I don't know where we were but surely across the line. We sat by the side of the road for a couple of hours and I fell asleep. I woke up to find soldiers cuffing me. They put me into the back of a truck. The German guy sat across from me. He gave me food.

I've tried to piece together the next sequence but I can't. Too much happened. At some point we rode in a train and then another train, and then we reached a prison camp. Then they moved me to another one, and then maybe a couple of weeks later they moved me again. I don't know why.

I wound up in a camp with other Americans and some Brits and a couple of Dutch policemen. And I felt O.K., like I had some friends, like I wasn't going to die.

And then winter came.

And I'm not going to tell you about that except to say that something about me changed. I got sharper. I could hear the crack of a twig a mile away. The sound that a carrot makes as it falls into boiling water is like no other. I could smell a field mouse at a hundred yards and the polish of a guard's boot at two hundred. I could close my eyes and find a sensory world that promised not to betray even when my eyesight started to fail.

So let me tell you something: I was fairly certain that Harvey Cotton and Robert Samson shared a killer. I didn't have any evidence yet, but you'll just have to trust me. I'm not a normal person. I've got skill sets that I'm not even aware of. Late in life, I'm a predator. And I had picked up something in the wind.

I heard the laughter even before I got to the movie theater. No movie was playing; the sign outside clearly read, "311 Days in Space – My life aboard Mir by Vasily Orlov."

I walked in through the back and sat. Orlov was sitting on the edge of the stage. He was about half an hour into his allotted time and taking questions. And he was doing really well.

"No," he told a young man in the front. "I was not participating in the launch of Mir. Was Colonel in Soviet air force when first part of Mir is launched in 1986."

A woman up front asked the next question. I couldn't hear it. The rules of cruise lecturing are quite specific – the lecturer must repeat the question. Orlov did not.

"No," he said. "Am not still a Colonel in Soviet air force because is no more Soviet air force. I retire and move to Miami Beach to live in condo with hot tub. Order pizza from Domino's. Very nice. Yes sir?" He pointed to a man in the third row.

"Were you ever scared?"

"Sometimes hot tub get too hot, or drop Domino's pizza into water and get very scared."

Laughter. He was scoring well.

"Yes, I know what you meaned. Yes, very scary in March 1998 when third crash happens. This one not reported to international community for scared of rebuke. Supply ship now overdue because of not repaired the docking module from last crash, so when Progress cargo ship arrive, cannot dock because now has different shape base block.

"Cannot use second docking module because not enough clearance from solar array. So have to say O.K. with different shape base block or have no food. For this, need to depressurize module and do space walk to get supplies from Progress because cannot dock."

"Did you do the space walk?"

Orlov laughed. "Not crazy enough. On board is special guest American astronaut Jerry Reiter who agree to go. Lose at chess last time so have to do least favorite chores including sanitize chemical toilet. I stay at controls and make sure station maintain position and eat sandwich."

"But the cargo ship crashed, right?" The young man at the front again.

Orlov paused to take a drink. "Yes, cargo ship ultimately not stable due to different shape base block and is turning on different axis than Mir, and breaks tether and crashes into Spektr module, making very big hole. Jerry Reiter already get most of supplies on board, including water and Vodka and ham from Denmark. But then have to depressurize Spektr to make repairs. I continue to be at control making sure Mir maintain position, finish sandwich."

Hands were waving all over the place. No wonder Orlov had been doing this for years. He was very good. I was learning almost nothing but I didn't care.

"The question," Orlov remembered to repeat, "is what was in the Spektr module. Spektr is science module. Have experiments on seeds but mostly atmospheric sensors and mice experiments that German University pay to have on ship, to study effects of weightless on sexy actions. Very sad. Jerry Reiter have to clean cages and note very little sexy actions maybe due to be in space and difficult to catch other mouse to have sexy actions with. When crash, mice die. Very sad, some float out of hole into space. Can see for next half hour floating in cage. We make a toast to them, say goodbye sad and dead not sexy space mice, and have drink."

"Did you have an escape pod?"

"Yes, have escape Soyuz capsule for escape if need."

"How long did it take to get from earth? Did you fly in a rocket?"

"On a rocket, yes. Trip from Baikonur Cosmodrome about hour and half."

I couldn't help feeling some degree of pride. It was my idea, after all, putting Orlov back on stage. There were two hundred people in the room and they were never going to forget their afternoon with a cosmonaut. I couldn't think about that, though. I was due on stage myself in a short while and I needed to get ready.

I was putting my tuxedo on, back in the Junior Suite, and I had that surveillance C.D. playing because I had never managed to really pay any attention to it. And I saw Norman Gellerman on the tape. I didn't recognize him until I saw him sitting there in the big over-stuffed chair by the window. He opened a *Popular Mechanics* magazine and started reading. It was just like in my dream except there was no giant squid attacking. I must have been just falling asleep when I watched it the last time.

This would have been just a day or so after he killed Dorothy Kent and there he was reading a magazine. He looked up and started waving to someone. The CD had no audio so I couldn't hear what he was saying, but he was calling to someone, beckoning with his hand. A moment later, a man leaned in and handed him a credit card. I saw the back of the guy's head, that's all. Then he kind of backed away, backed right out of the frame. He must have still been standing right there because Gellerman continued talking with him for a few more minutes before putting down the magazine and leaving.

I wished I had more. If the mystery man's shoes had been in the frame, and if they had been World War II vintage German army standard-issue combat boots, I might have had something to say about them but I was just plain out of luck in that department.

I couldn't figure that out. Who did Gellerman know on board, and why would someone hand him a credit card? I could have asked him, but because I'd had him arrested on Martinique facing a murder charge, he was unlikely to be inclined to help me.

I'm no cosmonaut so I shouldn't even try to compare myself, but I was a little disappointed with the crowd that showed up at the Co-pacabana Lounge for my event. It's not every day that you can take tango lessons from a master. In fact it's not even every other day. *Voyager*'s dance instructors hadn't offered tango lessons in almost a week.

I had hoped for at least a few dozen people. I got nine, and it was time to start looking at the bright side of things; I had a spotlight on me. I was wearing a tux and I looked good. I had Inga on the piano and a little band backing me up. I saw Helen in the audience. She was in the back but as I said, only nine people showed up so the back was only a few rows away. Opal Baxter gave me a thumbs-up. She and Doug were drinking margaritas.

Ron Gibson introduced me, reading from my prepared script. "All the way from Bethlehem, Pennsylvania, please welcome international dance champion Henry Grave, master of the tango."

I had my hearing aid turned way up in case I got a question. The applause was deafening. "Thank you, thank you," I said, taking the stage. "Today I'm here to talk about my favorite dance. And if you give me a chance, you might leave here thinking it's your favorite dance as well. Let me tell you the first reason I like it; it's very easy yet sexy as hell."

That got me twitters from a couple in the front that I hadn't met.

"It began in the steamy sultry brothels of Buenos Aires in the 1880s when tens of thousands of Spanish and Italian immigrants began making that city their home. But in order to call a city your home, you need to meet women. I'm going to need a volunteer. Perhaps the young lady in the back could join me." I extended a hand to Helen. She looked around but there was no getting out of it.

"These immigrants worked hard, worked as cowboys, or gauchos as they say in Argentina. After a long day of work, stinky from horse sweat, they would come to the bordellos to meet pretty ladies." I took Helen in my right arm and leaned her back. "But being stinky from horse sweat, you hold the lady at arms length so she doesn't have to smell you. You then lead her around in a circular motion, around the small tables that would crowd a bordello's dance floor."

Helen moved like a pro.

"Have you done this before?" I asked her quietly.

"Before you were born, gaucho. Get on with it."

"I forgot my spurs."

"I have an extra pair by my bedside."

Ron Gibson's voice came over the speakers. "I'd like to remind our champion that he is wearing a microphone. We're looking forward to a great lesson!"

Nuts. "The word tango comes from the Latin verb 'tangere,' which means to touch. The dance itself is deceptively simple. It's nothing more than quick long strides, then a rapid reversal on the balls of your feet."

Helen and I demonstrated. "The lady's right hand is on the gaucho's left hip, close to his pocket. He'll need to pay for several tangos if he wants her companionship. Can we get some music please?"

Inga led the band in a nice number, sort of a generic tango. I had asked for something from the early days, from the first tango record that Angel Villoldo recorded in Paris in 1902 because there was no recording studio in all of Argentina, but they didn't have that score on board. We danced to Inga's tango accompaniment and it worked out just fine.

I can't tell you how much I love tango. I'd say I love it like no other but I love no other. For me, a waltz is something better left to European wood nymphs. The Foxtrot bores me. I never could get a handle on Swing dancing and I don't have even a tenth of the agility necessary to pull off a merengue. The beauty of tango is that there's nothing to it, yet it's beautiful. If I break a sweat, it has everything to do with the lady.

I had to share Helen, and I didn't like it. But fifteen minutes into my lesson a number of gentlemen showed up, and for the first time in cruising history an event transpired with more men than women in attendance. By 4:30, my students were good enough to pick up a prize at the Rolling Pines contest. The way Doug Baxter was leading Opal, you'd think he'd been dancing that way for years and I'm pretty sure it was among their first times on a dance floor.

"I slept through our date last night," I told Helen as we finished up. I made sure my microphone was off.

"Did you really?"

"I did. I'm sorry. I haven't slept a lot lately."

"Don't apologize. You did a good job here, Henry, though I'm not sure how a passenger winds up leading a dance class. I've never seen that before. In fact, I don't think it ever happens."

I led her to one of the cocktail tables and we sat. I told her about what I did. She nodded slowly.

"So you lied a little bit," she said.

"It's important that I can work without people knowing what I'm working on."

"Am I part of your work?"

I held both her hands in mine. "Of course not."

"I'll help you then. We'll find the killer together."

"No. But you can provide moral support."

"It wasn't a question. We're a team now."

"Is that right? Will you have some drinks with me later?"

"Are you leaving me now?"

"Yes. I have to work. Let's meet up by the pool later. At seven-thirty."

"Perhaps," she said, "if I don't nod off."

CHAPTER NINETEEN

I headed back to the Stardust Theater to see how the passenger interviews were going. I counted twenty-eight guys sitting around watching C.N.N., which wasn't good. It meant that my team was getting backed up. I went back stage and found Arlen at the monitors. He handed me a set of headphones. "Check this out."

"Who is he?"

Arlen turned his laptop around so I could read the passenger profile. Richard Conway, age sixty-two, was a businessman from San Francisco. He was on his first cruise and he had a Deluxe Suite to himself. I looked into the monitor and I swear Richard Conway looked up into the camera at that moment. He grinned.

He looked mean. Hector was questioning him. "How did you choose this particular cruise?" he asked.

"He's off the script," I said to Arlen. "I don't know if I want Hector doing this. He's too young. That isn't one of my questions."

"He's doing great. He's pressing him."

"Why?"

"Just watch."

"I thought the sun would do me good," Richard Conway said.

"We have cruises to Hawaii too, you might be interested in those."

"Perhaps. I'll give it some thought."

Hector nodded. "What was your reaction when you learned Robert Samson had been murdered?"

Conway folded his hands on his lap. "You indicated at the start of this interview that there would be five questions. I believe you've already asked me seven or eight."

"I'm sorry, sir. I'm just trying to be thorough."

"I see. I'm always happy to help in any way I can."

Conway was doing a good job holding it together, but he was definitely working to hold it together. "He's been incarcerated," I told Arlen. People who've been locked up get kind of a nervous energy thing that works as a force field, keeps them wiry and safe. But once you activate whatever clump of neurons that starts that up, you can never turn it off. It will never go dormant, and for the rest of your life anyone in law enforcement will be able to pick you out

"Did you attend any of Robert Samson's lectures?" Hector asked.

"I did, yes. I found them to be both informative and entertaining. And to answer your question, I was saddened when I learned of his death. I was looking forward to the next lecture."

"The one where he was going to reveal the killer?"

"That's right. It was a mystery and I was looking forward to learning how it ended."

"Were you frightened when you learned there was a killer on board?"

Just the hint of a grin passed Conway's mouth. "I was not frightened, no. I suspected at the time that whoever killed him came on board to do just that."

"Why did you think that?"

Conway shook his head and said nothing for a moment. "I don't know. It's just what I thought."

"Well, thank you for your time, Mr. Conway."

"Richie."

"Richie, yes. Thank you again. We've arranged for a $100 credit to be posted to your shipboard account with our apologies for the inconvenience."

"That's very generous of you." He stood to leave.

"Would it be O.K. to contact you if we have any further questions?"

He nodded on his way out. "I'm always happy to help in any way I can," he said.

Arlen and I exchanged glances as we took off our headphones. "Hard case," Arlen said. "You think we might have to talk to him again?"

"Most definitely. I'm going to have to pay him a visit. But first I want some more information on him. We need to have someone in the home office, at Contessa, contact the San Francisco police. Mr. Conway has a long story and we need to know it."

"I have an old girlfriend, a paralegal, who works back home for Contessa. I'll find out who we need to talk to."

Richard Conway pulled the curtain and walked into our little room. "You could just come out and ask me what you want to know," he said.

I stared at him. I thought my mouth might have been open, so I checked. It wasn't, but it felt like it was.

He took a seat across the table from me and adjusted his cuffs. "You do know that the walls of your interview rooms are just curtains, right? So when you talk about someone who is two feet away behind a curtain, that person is likely to hear."

"Well I'll be god-damned."

He looked at Arlen only for a second. Then he focused his attention on me. "Who are you?"

I didn't know what to say. I was unprepared. So I told him the truth. And I understood at that moment that this was very much the sort of man who could put a knife in another man and still sleep like a baby.

"Undercover," he said. "That's interesting. I wouldn't have suspected you. You're old to be a cop. Don't they give you guys a nice retirement?"

"I'm not a cop."

"Retired cop?"

I shook my head. "Never a cop. Just something I picked up."

He leaned back in his chair. "Are you normally any good?"

"I am. How long were you in prison?"

"Fourteen years of a twenty-eight year sentence," he said, not even skipping a beat. "I was well-behaved."

"What did you do your time for?"

"Assault."

"Twenty-eight years is a long sentence for assault."

"It was a profound assault. I had an altercation with a business competitor and I got carried away. We've since come to agree on a number of premises."

"Is that right?"

Arlen jumped in. "What line of work are you in?"

"Masonry architecture. We design monuments," he said, still looking at me.

"Tombstones?"

"Some. Let me clear your mind about something. The night Samson was killed, I was in that cigar room until four in the morning. I wasn't alone. You can confirm that."

"The cigar bar closes at midnight," Arlen said.

Conway turned slowly to face him. "Normally it does. I host a poker game. The manager of the casino organized it for me. You can confirm that with him. Four other guys were there and we played until late. We're playing again tonight if you're interested. It starts at midnight with a $5,000 buy in."

"Did you win?" I asked.

"I did, yes. It wasn't looking good for a while but I managed to pull through at the end."

"How much did you win?" Arlen asked.

"I won't tell you," he said as he stood up. "I think you'll find that my alibi is complete and we won't have to get together again."

"Thanks for coming by unexpectedly, Mr. Conway."

"Richie," he said, shaking my hand. "Call me Richie. You have a good day now."

Neither Arlen nor I said a word for the next ten minutes or so. We sat quietly watching the monitors, switching the audio back and forth between different interview rooms.

"That was uncomfortable?" Arlen said finally.

"Yes."

"Did you get scared?"

"I think I crapped myself. I'll check in a minute." I stared at the monitors. In one of our interview rooms, a gorgeous girl wearing a halter top twirled a pen on the table. "Who is this most precious thing?"

Arlen peered over my shoulder. "That's Lane Camden. She teaches dance. She and her partner Eddie are working with us today, but they're breaking up, so she's anxious for the cruise to be over. They've been doing the crew interviews, which are not interesting. All of the crewmembers on your list are checking out fine."

I thought about that for a moment. "Why are they breaking up?"

He pointed to the neighboring monitor. "That's Eddie."

He looked morose. I'd look morose too if a girl like that was breaking my heart. Eddie looked to be in pretty good shape, which we dancers have to be, but he had a sad face. "She's six times better looking than him," I told Arlen. "Maybe seven."

"Yeah. And she's just figuring that out."

"Who's doing the interview in room four?"

"Staff Captain Nilsen." Arlen checked his list. "He's interviewing Mr. Avner Basken of Houston. This is his fourth cruise with us. His wife passed away last year."

I listened in for a moment but heard nothing more than the words of a lonely man. Avner didn't deserve to be sitting in a little curtain room while a killer ran free. I'm sorry, Avner.

I scanned the monitors and frowned. Hector's next victim was a woman. "Hey there, Arlen, what's with the lady behind curtain number two there?"

He checked the list. "Dr. Kelly Merwin, age forty-three, a middle school principal from Santa Fe, New Mexico. This is his or her first cruise with us."

"His or her?"

He frowned. "There's no gender designation anywhere on the paperwork."

I had to hear. I put the headphones back on.

"...the talks at all," I heard Dr. Kelly Merwin say in a husky voice that sounded vaguely male, but just vaguely. "To be honest, I didn't come here for an education but for the sun and the relaxation. The food is not bad either. So I'm afraid I can't help you. I really would have no idea. As I said, I was a little shocked to hear."

Hector nodded and moved on to the next question. "We don't have the personnel on board to pick out all of the faces from our surveillance tapes, so to make it easier to find you, can you tell us where to look for you at the time of the murder?"

"My goodness. Let's see. That would have been, well I don't know."

I turned up the volume. Dr. Kelly Merwin was becoming flustered.

"I assure you," Hector continued, "that everything we speak of here will be held in the strictest confidence. Our goal is only to find the perpetrator of a crime. This is a vacation after all, and we respect that people make friends on vacation."

Dr. Kelly Merwin looked down at the table. "I was drinking Cosmopolitans and it was late."

I watched the hands holding tightly to each other.

"And then there was this wonderful man paying attention to me. So few men do, and he was not only good looking but educated, interesting. An astronaut! Or cosmonaut, I should say. And we had some drinks."

Hector nodded. "You were with him, with Mr. Orlov for much of the night."

"Yes. With Vasily. I've never known a man like him. I was married for two years but my husband left me. Vasily made me feel good about myself."

Well I'll be god-damned.

"He's a great man," Hector said. "We're lucky to have him onboard." He told her about the $100 credit and she left. The next passenger was in the room a minute later.

Soren Nilsen's latest interview had taken only five minutes, and he came backstage for a break. He looked tired.

"Can I buy you a drink?" I asked.

He shook his head. "I was in the navy for seventeen years. I am a ship's master, and yet I'm doing the work of a police constable."

"And doing it with admirable grace."

"Will there be many more?"

Arlen looked over the list. "About thirty."

"Anybody interesting?" I asked.

"Not really, I'm sorry to say. We have three no-shows. Milton Hammermill of Miami Beach, age ninety-three. Probably forgot."

Nilsen laughed.

"Hey, hey." I frowned. "No jokes about the elderly forgetting stuff. It's rude."

"You want to go talk to him?" Arlen asked. "He could be a criminal mastermind. It says here he's retired. But he owned a delicatessen in Brooklyn for fifty-three years. That's a little convenient don't you think?"

"Why?"

"He had access to knives."

"He had decades to plan out the perfect crime," Nilsen added, "many decades."

"You're both assholes," I said.

The curtain parted and a passenger walked in. "We can hear you out here, you know. Is someone coming to interrogate me, or can I go? I'm starting to get a rash."

Arlen frowned. "We'll be right with you, sir. If you could take a seat in interview room four."

"OK. Which one is four? Is that the one near the stairs?"

"Yes. It is. It's the one with the card on it that has the big four. Capt. Nilsen can perhaps show you the way."

"We should probably keep our voices down," I suggested. "Who were the other no-shows?"

"Porfirio Duarte. He's a Venezuelan colonel or something."

"He's a general. He's O.K. I told him he didn't have to come in."

"Did you? Well, O.K. then. The last of the no-shows is Michael Finn, fifty-three, of San Jose, California, a business owner. This is his first cruise with us. He's technically not a no-show. He left a message saying he was ill and wasn't going to be able to attend."

"He did, did he?"

"You want to talk to him or do you want me to."

"I'll do it. Where is he?"

Arlen checked his laptop. "He has a Deluxe Suite on the Penthouse Deck."

"Very nice. Is he there now?"

He stared at me. "I wouldn't really know. I've been here all day."

"That's a good point. I'll go have a look."

Chapter Twenty

I braved the tropical environment of the rainforest once more, still unable to spot the toucan, and came to the reception desk where Monica from Los Angeles was still perched. "Remember me?" I asked.

"Yes, sir. I didn't recognize you with your clothes on."

"You and half the women in eastern Pennsylvania!"

She stared at me.

"I have another favor to ask you." I asked her about Michael Finn.

"What do you want to know?"

"Can you tell me where he is?"

"He's in his suite. He's on the phone. Ship to shore."

"How about that. That's expensive, isn't it?"

"It is. It doesn't seem to bother him, though." She scrolled down through a list of calls. "It looks like he makes at least two calls a day, usually for about half an hour."

"Is there anything else interesting?"

She looked again. "He has a minimal bar tab, and he bought a $2,600 pair of earrings earlier in the week. That's his only purchase except for this afternoon. He bought a pack of Rolaids at Tropical Treasures."

"How are Rolaids tropical treasures?"

"It's just the name of the gift shop," she said.

I took the elevator up to the Penthouse Deck. I only had to walk a few steps before I came to his door. I knocked.

I knocked again when nobody answered. "I can stand here all day," I shouted at the door. But in truth, I could not. My legs start to hurt after awhile. I'm supposed to wear those special elastic socks but somehow I only brought one with me and I couldn't decide which foot to put it on so in the end I didn't wear it. As it turned out, I only had to wait about a minute.

"I was on the phone." Michael Finn looked like he'd spent much of his life doing physical labor. He was middle-aged but fit, with good muscle tone. He had bad skin, too fair for all the sunlight he had clearly been exposed to. "What can I do for you?"

"You don't look well," I said. I held up my private investigator's license, a real one, with my real name on it.

"I haven't been feeling that good." He leaned in to read my license. "Supreme Court? You're on the supreme court?"

I looked at it. Wrong one. "Sorry," I said, putting it back and finding the real license. I handed it to him.

"Private investigator," he read. "Did you get this one on the Boardwalk too?"

"No, it's real."

"Yeah, I know. I heard. Do you need to come in right now? Or can you call me later. I have to lie back down."

"I'll come in, thanks. What was it that you heard?"

"What's that?"

"You indicated you had heard about me."

He took a seat on the couch and put his feet up on the ottoman. A bottle of ginger ale was open on the table and the TV was on, the volume down low.

I took a look around. He had a nice suite, very roomy. The sleeping area was separated from the little living area. And it had a nice little kitchenette too. And the balcony was first rate. No hot tub like Duarte had, but still it was a very respectable accommodation.

"Are you seasick?" I asked.

He nodded.

"Really? I can hardly feel any movement at all."

"I know, it's just me knowing that it's moving is what does it. I never been on a boat like this before, and this is gonna be my last time, I can promise you that."

"How did you hear about me?"

He shrugged. "You hear stuff, that's all."

Do you now? Not too many people knew who I was. Not too many at all, and most of those who did would probably keep quiet about it. "Tell me something, you're from San Jose, right?"

He drank his ginger ale. "I am. Is that important? Listen, you're here about the guy who got murdered. I don't know anything about it, O.K. I wish I did but I don't."

"San Jose is near San Francisco, isn't it?"

"It is."

"I just met a guy from San Francisco. A guy named Richard Conway. Do you know him?"

He changed the TV channel without turning up the volume and stared at it for a moment. "Yeah, I know him."

"Did you come on the cruise together?"

"Nah, we just ran into each other. I hadn't seen him in years. We went to high school together. It was quite a coincidence."

"Quite. He's about ten years older than you. Did he get left back about ten times?"

"Then from the neighborhood, OK. I didn't say we were in the same class."

"Is he your boss or something like that?

He chuckled. "I don't think so. Richie Conway? Not in this life is he my boss or anything like that."

"Do you have any other acquaintances on board?"

"You know, I met a few guys is all. We play poker. And no, I wasn't playing poker when the Fed got himself killed. I was right here in the room throwing up. And yes, I was alone. So no, I don't have an alibi and no, I didn't have nothing to do with it."

So many people have so much to hide. "Did you make any phone calls that night?" I asked.

He shook his head. "I don't know. Probably. I call my wife every night at about midnight. It's earlier in California, a different time zone."

"Did you leave the cabin that night after you made the call?"

"No. Like I said, I was sick. I watched the TV, whatever movie they had on. I watch the TV at night."

"Did anybody visit?"

"No."

"Then I think you have an alibi. The phone call would have been logged, and if you were in your room alone, then your door lock wouldn't have been triggered. We can check on it but if you're being straight with me then you're off the hook."

He stared at me. "Are you serious?"

I saw genuine relief in his eyes. "I think I just cured your stomach ache," I told him.

"I think you might have."

"You were a little worried?"

"Nah. You know, you hear about something like this, and I guess I have to admit it made me nervous."

I needed to press him; I had nothing else to go on. "Have you ever been to prison, Mr. Finn?"

He stared at me coldly. "Nah. I never have been. Have you?"

"I kind of have been, yes. It's a long story. Listen, I'm going to be writing up an account of my investigation here. I can clear you as a suspect or I can ask the Feds to have another look at you in Miami. Would it be OK if I got one of those ginger ales?"

Something was simmering there. He didn't know what to make of me, which was fine with me.

"Help yourself," he said finally.

I walked over to the kitchenette and took a soda. "You've got Heinekens in here. Can I have one of those too?"

"Please."

"They give you free beer?"

"Yeah."

"I only get soda. I have a Junior Suite, a couple of decks below us. It's not as nice. You want a Heineken?"

His faced turned a shade paler. The thought of drinking a beer was making him sick. "No thanks."

"So listen." I sat back down. "I've got about forty-eight hours before we reach Miami, and I've got nothing. Nothing except you."

"I got an alibi, remember?"

"You do. But you're a little cagey. If I look into you, I'm going to find some heavy things, right?"

He stared at me. "Nah. Nothing heavy."

"Are you on parole?"

"I told you, I never been to prison."

"I think you have. You look like the kind of man who has to pay someone a visit every week or so, report in. You aren't allowed to leave the state of California, are you?"

I'll tell you something; it was not that big a leap of faith. I've seen my share of Michael Finns over the years. Philadelphia is full of tough, tightly-wound cases like him. They're mobbed up but they're not making the kind of money or career moves they had hoped for, so they simmer. The way he was staring at me right then, I knew I was lined up on him. All I had to do was push him and he'd come undone.

"Tell me something I can use," I said.

"I don't know what you're talking about."

"You want to ask the boss before you answer. You want to call Richie Conway and find out if it's OK to talk to me."

He shook his head slowly, trying to keep it together. "Old man, you don't know what the fuck you're playing at."

There we go. I looked up at the TV. There was a game on so I watched it for a couple of minutes to give him some glimmer of privacy. When I turned back, I could see his muscles twitching.

I picked up the phone and called Hugh Arlen's mobile. "I need you to search the passenger manifest," I told him. "Other than Mr. Finn and Mr. Conway, do we have any other single male passengers from northern California?"

It took him about thirty seconds. "Just one. Harold Roper of Sacramento, a firefighter."

Nuts. "Anybody at all from San Francisco? Only give me guys over fifty years old."

"That's not really narrowing it down," he said. "OK, we have three passengers from San Francisco: Richard Conway, who we've met. Bernice and Esther Rosenthal, sisters, age seventy-two and seventy-nine, on their eighth cruise."

Nuts.

"Here's something interesting. Mason and April Cornish, of Avalon, California, booked their trip from the same San Francisco travel agency that Finn and Conway used."

"I like it. Tell me about them."

"Mason Cornish, age eighty-six, is a retired businessman, and April, age thirty-nine, is an interior decorator. This is their first cruise."

"Is that right?"

"This guy must be quite a talker," Arlen said. "Either that or he has a great big bank account."

"Probably both. Do me a favor. Check with the desk find out where he is right now. I'll need to speak with him. I'll wait."

Arlen put me on hold. Michael Finn was staring at the TV, avoiding me. "Hey, you ever stab anybody?" I asked him.

He shook his head slowly.

"You know a guy named Mason Cornish? Does he work for Richie too?"

If Michael Finn could have killed me with his eyes, he would have. Instead he just shook his head.

Back in the early sixties, one of those Israeli groups that tracks Nazis tracked one to Bellingham, Washington. His name was Kurt Wasserman and he was a guard sub-commander at an internment camp near Munich, of which I was an alumnus. He was a major asshole. He'd come around during breakfast and take bits of food right out of our bowls as if it were a joke. And it wasn't funny.

I flew to Seattle to testify at his extradition hearing. When they put me on the stand, I ate a hoagie. Hey, Kurt, remember me, fucker? He looked like he wanted to murder me. You had the chance, Kurt. You had the chance. He died of something or other before they sent him back to Berlin or wherever, but I enjoyed the moment.

Michael Finn was giving me that same look. He was getting himself organized, however, so I didn't think I was going to get anything else from him.

Arlen came back on the line. "He's at the spa. He's getting a massage."

I hung up the phone. "Hey, Finn, I'll be leaving now."

"Yeah, you better," he said.

"Thanks for the beer. You want me to say hi to Mason Cornish for you? Does he have a nickname I should use, Scooter or Skip?"

"Yeah, you call him Skip, you see how that goes."

You piss people off enough and they'll give you anything you want. "Corny," I said. "I'll bet people call him Corny."

I left Mr. Finn to nurse his illness and perhaps knock back an anxiety pill or two. For the first time all day, I felt like I was getting somewhere. I took the elevator up to the Sky Deck and opened the door to the Ambrosia Spa.

The girl they had working there had seriously pretty eyes. Eyes like that seemed to belong on another species, like an owl but a good-looking owl. She was from Belgrade. I think I might have met her already. I showed her my crew ID.

"I know who you are," she pouted. "You booked a steam bath and you never showed up."

It wasn't ringing a bell, and as much as I'd have liked to stand there for a bit and look at her and talk to her, I had to move along. "I'm going inside," I said, walking into Mason Cornish's massage room.

He was a tiny guy. A little Asian woman was rubbing his back and she looked like a giant compared to him. He had the phone cradled against his ear but he hung it up when he saw me.

"You want this should be in private?" I asked, nodding at the masseuse.

"Nah. I got a knot in my neck that's been kicking my ass for three days. Have a seat."

I did.

"That was Finn on the phone. I tell you this so you know I'm playing straight with you."

"I appreciate that." I couldn't keep my eyes off him. He was withered. He was two years older than me but those two years, and possibly all the rest of them, had not been kind. If I wanted to steal him, I could have just picked him up with one hand and stuffed him in a duffel bag. "So, Finn and Conway work for you?" I asked.

"In a manner of speaking, I suppose they do."

"They're your soldiers?"

He chuckled. "Listen son, soldiers are young men. You met Mike and Richie. They're not young men; senior citizens the both of them. When we go to the movies, all of us get the half-priced tickets. Only we don't go to the movies all that often."

"Why did you come on the cruise? Why did you bring your guys?"

The masseuse kept at it. She didn't even raise her eyes but you could see the tension there. This wasn't what she signed up for.

"I was playing cards when Mr. Samson met his end. You can check it out but you'll find I'm telling you the truth. The pit boss from the casino was there."

"Is that right?"

"Look, we didn't cause no trouble and we're not looking for no trouble. You guessed right when you told Mike he was violating parole. He did nine years for homicide. He's sensitive about it. But he's got nothing to do with this. He wasn't at the card game, so I can't tell you how I know, but he wouldn't do nothing without me knowing, and I didn't know."

"I don't suspect him."

He looked up at me. "How old are you?"

"Eighty-four."

"You look good."

"Thank you very much."

"You work out, eat right?"

"I try."

"Smoke?"

"No."

"I do. Always have. I cut down since I been newly-married. The wife smokes the Menthols which I cannot stand the smell of. Are you a drinking man? Do you like to drink?"

"Every day."

"That makes me feel better. A man with no vices is a man I can't trust." He told the masseuse he was done for now and grabbed a towel. "So if you don't think Mikey did this, why are you hassling us?"

I shook my head. "I've been asking myself the same question. The best I can come up with is that I have a day-and-a-half left to solve a crime and I really don't have any leads, so when a little pod of mobsters falls into my lap, you know, it just feels too strange to be a coincidence."

He rubbed himself off with a towel and put a robe on. "OK. I see where you're coming from."

"I have the same robe," I told him.

"It came with the cabin."

"That's true. Mine did too. Hey, were you in the service?"

His eyes lit up. "Yeah. You?"

"I was. I did one week of civil patrol in Belgium before being captured. What'd you do?"

"I was a cook's assistant on a destroyer, two destroyers actually. The first one got destroyed. The wife left me while I was away."

"That sucks. Mine died."

"I'm sorry to hear. You remarried?"

"I did. Then I got divorced. You?"

"Yeah, remarried. This is our anniversary. I been with April for two years. I says to her, let's go to Vegas or Maui, but she watches the Travel channel and wanted to see the Caribbean. So here we are on this cruise."

"And you brought your guys as company?"

"Something like that. I like to feel safe."

Nuts. "Did you go to Robert Samson's lectures?"

"I didn't. The wife gets bored easily and she misses me when I'm away, even for an hour."

"Had you heard of him before you came on board?"

"Can't say that I had."

"Alright." I stood up to go. "Thanks for talking to me."

"No problem. You have any other questions, you come to me, O.K.? And give Mikey a pass on this one. He didn't do nothing."

I nodded. Mason Cornish was not the kind of man who could stab a man and not think twice about it, but I was quite sure that a couple of decades ago he was very much that sort of man.

CHAPTER TWENTY-ONE

Now, if I had been getting paid to identify criminals cruising on that particular ship, I would fast be gaining wealth. But I wasn't getting paid for that, and I wasn't really getting anywhere. Mason Cornish was almost certainly lying to me about a couple of things. But Michael Finn and Richard Conway were too old to be bodyguards, just as he said. I used a courtesy phone at Reception to leave a message for Arlen, asking him to check on the card game my mobsters were allegedly playing at. I was reasonably certain it would check out fine, which meant that none of these three killed Samson. Even so, I wasn't ready to believe they weren't involved somehow.

I headed back down towards the Junior Suite but the hallways were already filling up with people. It was time for dinner and I was swimming upstream, heading away from the dining room. I changed quickly and joined the horde.

I saw Shelley Tobin from across the room. She had that kind of look that drew gazes from everyone around her. Half of the people in the room were stealing glances between bites of shrimp cocktail. I wondered if she was even aware of it. I felt a hand on my arm; it belonged to Duarte's waiter.

"Señor Duarte requests your company at his table," he told me.

"Señor Duarte doesn't even like me. He told me as much himself."

"If you would follow me?"

I had my heart set on staring at Shelley Tobin for the next hour but duty called. I made a frown as I waved to her. She made a frown too and waved right back. We had a connection, she and I. We were two peas in a pod, like Elizabeth Taylor and the British fellow, the one who drank.

"Sit down," Duarte told me when I reached the table. His tone suggested that he was not entirely pleased with me.

I sat and picked up a menu.

"Do you know what blowback means?" he asked.

"I'm not sure. Give me some context."

"It refers to the unintended consequences of an action."

"Is that right?"

He tapped his finger on an envelope next to his plate. "The inquiry you asked me to make was tagged by the Department of Justice.

My associate was contacted by federal marshals within an hour of requesting the information. That, my friend, is blowback."

"The Department of Justice?"

"Yes. I don't appreciate attention coming my way, and you've brought attention my way. So I'm going to give you this envelope as a symbol of closure. I ask that you not contact me at any point in the future for any reason whatsoever. Is that understood?"

"Perfectly. Thanks for your help." I put down the menu. "Does this mean we're not having dinner?"

"It does."

Nuts. I'd have to grab something later. I took the envelope and walked quickly to the Steamboat Saloon. It was just about empty by then, with half the passengers at dinner and the other half at their pre-mealtime nap. I found a table in the back and waited for Lana to bring me a Heineken before I opened the envelope. Inside was a single page, a printout of an e-mail from someone using the screen name 'Motherlode.'

> While I am hard-pressed to see the connection between this individual and your case, I went ahead and coded an inquiry. The results are quite interesting and I wouldn't be surprised if I am contacted to determine the nature of the inquiry. This is a big deal; you should have told me what you were asking me to do. I doubt I will have the same access to agency files after this, and very likely I will be monitored for the foreseeable future if I am not terminated from my position. I hope you understand that this will limit my ability to work for you, and I hope you understand that this is your fault.
>
> Harvey Cotton was the name assigned by the Department of Justice to Harry Clooney in March of 1996 when he entered the

Witness Protection Program. Clooney provided valuable testimony in the RICO trial of Abraham Solano, the head of the Rennero family crime syndicate operating out of San Francisco. Solano is now serving life without parole in the Security Housing Unit at Pelican Bay State Prison.

Clooney was a high-ranking Rennero capo. He was apprehended in June 1998 at his Carmel, California home in possession of seventeen kilos of heroin and $1.3 million in cash. He was given immunity in exchange for his testimony.

Clooney, now Harvey Cotton, was placed under the jurisdiction of federal marshals in Spruce Knob, West Virginia, where he was assigned employment in the mailroom of a coal power installation. He remained in Spruce Knob for only three months before breaking protocol and relocating, against the directives of his handlers, to Provincetown, Massachusetts. He is believed to have made contact with former associates, against the directives of the program. It is also presumed that he was able to retrieve significant amounts of cash that were never disclosed to authorities.

Harvey Cotton remained in the witness protection program until his murder in June 2003, which remains unsolved. His case was closed by the Justice Department in November 2003, though the murder investigation is still open in the state of Massachusetts.

Well I'll be god-damned. I folded the paper back into the envelope and stuffed it in my pocket. I finished my beer and waved to Lana for another. I drink more when I get confused. I think it helps.

I had never heard of Abraham Solano and I knew nothing at all about California crime families but I had no doubt that my three mobsters came on board for Robert Samson. Lana brought me a plate of pecans and a couple of little tuna sandwiches, which was nice because I hadn't had dinner. I started working up a scenario. It went like this:

Harry Clooney gets busted at his home in Carmel. He's pretty high up in the network but the prosecutors want the number one guy. So they give him immunity in exchange for his testimony. He gets moved to some dump in West Virginia which he hates, so he makes a few calls and he gets his hands on a few million dollars. He moves to Provincetown and tries to keep his head under the radar but the mobsters are never going to let him go. It takes them three years to find him, and when they do, they kill him.

They get away with it too, until a retired FBI profiler who couldn't let go figures it all out. He's about to name the killer so they have to kill him first.

And that's why my mobsters were on the cruise. I liked my scenario. I felt good about it. I didn't know who actually killed Samson. It could have been Cornish, or Conway, or Finn, or more likely they had someone else do the actual dirty work but they organized it.

And that's how I broke the case. Technically, I didn't find the killer but I had it narrowed down to three. I could write it up and send it to the F.B.I. so they'd be ready when they boarded in Miami.

I sat there for another fifteen minutes or so thinking it through, trying to poke holes in it, but I could not. I considered smoking a cigar but I didn't have one. I closed my eyes, just for a second or two.

I finished my drink, which had gotten warm quickly, and I thanked Lana. I headed to Reception and knocked on the door of the security office. I was hoping to find Hugh Arlen so I could share my thoughts with him but neither he nor Hector was there. I used one of the courtesy phones to leave a message, and I headed for the Copacabana Lounge.

It was dark. I was expecting to see Inga there but instead there was a young fellow playing the piano. I ordered a red wine and sat at the bar.

"Is this you?" one of the bartenders asked, holding up an envelope with my name on it.

It was a note from Inga apologizing that she couldn't meet me. The theater troupe was upset at me for monopolizing their rehearsal space all day. They needed Inga to accompany them as they rehearsed their Vaudeville Follies show for the farewell night of the cruise.

Nuts. I borrowed the courtesy phone and left a message for Arlen to meet me A.S.A.P. I needed someone to celebrate with. Then I recalled that I had made arrangements to meet Helen at 7:30. I looked at my watch and saw that I was already about half an hour late, so I walked around looking for her in the dark before remembering that we were supposed to meet upstairs at the pool bar.

The halls were crowded with dressy people heading for cocktails before the second dinner seating, and the elevators were stuffed with senior citizens. So I took the stairs, and by the time I reached the Tropicana Deck I was nearly in need of a defibrillator. Gasping for air, I walked over to the Pirate's Cove Bar.

It was breezy out, and the sea had gotten progressively choppier throughout the day. The Pirate's Cove was almost empty so I had no trouble finding Helen. She was the one with the sour look on her face. I made a quick stop to pick up a bottle of wine.

"I lost track of time," I told her. "And we just sailed into another time zone so technically I'm half an hour early."

"Is that true?"

"No, it might not be. The unimportant thing is that I'm here."

"I'm freezing out here, Henry. Let's go somewhere else, somewhere warmer."

"What did you have in mind?"

"Stop. I'm too cold to flirt. Are we going to capsize?"

I looked up at the sky. A little bit of rain was coming down. "Probably," I said. "How would you like to spend your last hour on earth?"

"I think I'd take a bath. I'd pop a couple extra arthritis pills, light some candles and bring a bottle of champagne into the tub."

"That's exactly what I was going to suggest."

"Let's go inside."

I picked up my bottle of wine and led her into the elevator lobby. I pressed the button and we waited and waited. She was shivering so I put my arm around her, then my coat.

"Your pockets are full, Henry. How much stuff do you need to carry with you on a date?"

"You have no idea." I discretely transferred some of the contents of my jacket pocket to my slacks. "There's my hearing aid, my hair pomade, a comb, breath mints, Viagra, extra hearing aid batteries, my wallet, a roll of quarters, Swiss Army knife, great big extra large jumbo condoms, and sunscreen."

"It might be too late."

"Too late for what?"

"Sunscreen." She held my hand.

"We could take the stairs," I suggested as the elevator continued to not come.

She shook her head. "Not with my knee." She led me across the hall into the dark and deserted children's activity room.

"They have air hockey," I said. Then she kissed me. I kissed her back. It was nice. We sat down and cuddled up on a miniature couch with a cartoon mermaid on it, and we kissed and kissed.

"Can I ask you something?" she asked.

"Anything."

"Did you have tuna fish for dinner?"

I frowned. "Yes. I'm sorry." I dug around for my breath mints and took one. "What did you have?"

"Lamb. Enough talking."

And we stayed there and kissed some more. The ship was rocking back and forth by then. I didn't know if it was because of us, or the waves in the Caribbean Sea, but I didn't care. It had been a while since I last kissed a girl and it felt great. A realization dawned on me.

"Is my breath still bad?" I asked.

She nodded.

"I think that wasn't a mint I took."

We drank the wine in Helen's suite, which was nicer than mine, better traffic flow, more room overall and a balcony. And more fruit; they gave you much more fruit. We spent some time together. I'm not going to tell you about it.

Later we ordered room service. We cuddled on her couch drinking champagne and eating fruit cocktail and we watched the rain fall on a moonlit sea. It was romantic. I only started talking business when she asked, and I told her about the interviews. And about the mobsters. I wasn't going to tell her about Duarte but then I did anyway. I was pleased with myself and looking to show off.

"I'm not buying it," she said as she refilled my glass.

"Pardon?"

"It just doesn't come together for me."

"How so?"

"I don't know. It's just too neat. This man Cotton was killed what, six years ago?"

"Yes."

"So nobody cares anymore. It's a cold case, like on the TV programs. Nobody cares except one old determined ex-F.B.I. agent."

"Yeah, so?" I didn't like the sound of this.

"Why didn't he just go to the police?"

"I don't know. Maybe he did and they didn't believe him."

She popped a grape into her mouth. "Maybe. But let's say he did know and he came on the cruise prepared to tell the world, to prove to everyone that he's still in the game. So what? Nobody cares."

I sat up. "What do you mean, who cares? Whoever did it cares."

Helen shook her head. "No. Let's say it was one of your three mobsters who killed Harvey Cotton. You think they can't drum up an alibi for something that happened six years ago?"

I frowned.

"It's just too much of a risk, the three of them getting back together to tie up loose ends. It doesn't come together for me."

I frowned again as I stared out at the rain through the sliding glass door. "These guys are connected to Samson's murder," I told her. "There's absolutely no way this is a coincidence."

"Maybe so. Maybe there is a connection. I'm just not sure you've made it yet."

"Do we have any more liquor?" I looked around. "I think I'm ready to turn this case over to the F.B.I. Let them bring Cornish and Finn and what's his name in for questioning. I'm done with them."

"Why do you say that?"

"What am I supposed to do, just barge in and ask them to tell me what the deal is?"

"Why not?"

"They probably won't even talk to me. One on one, neither Finn nor Conway will say a word and Cornish will just stonewall me."

Helen rubbed my shoulders. "Aren't you supposed to have some skills?"

"I do but most of them pertain to lovemaking."

"Well there's nothing more you can do tonight so you might as well just enjoy yourself."

I remembered something. "Actually, there is something more I can do. Do you have $5,000?"

She stared at me. "For what?"

"It's my normal rate."

"You could maybe charge half."

"I'd have stayed most of the night for double. Seriously though, I need it for a poker game."

Chapter Twenty-Two

I insisted on going alone and Helen insisted on going with me. And so we had the first fight of our relationship. I told her that I was a trained professional and that it might be dangerous, and she told me that it was her money so she was making the rules.

It was well after midnight by the time we set out. The ship was oddly quiet at that hour. Plenty of people were still up and about but they were playing in the casino or watching the midnight movie or drinking in the bars or the disco. The halls were mostly empty. We took the elevator and found our way to the cigar bar.

I've smoked about six cigars in my entire life so I hadn't yet had call to frequent that part of the ship. We found it soon enough but the door was locked. A little sign indicated it closed at midnight.

I kissed Helen on the cheek as I knocked. "Which is better," I asked her, "a full house or a flush?"

"Don't ask me. I haven't played in years. Just make sure your cards don't go over twenty-one."

A man wearing a casino nametag opened the door. "Private party, sir," he said. "I'm afraid we're closed."

"We're coming in," I told him, showing him my crew ID. "But in any case, I'm invited. Ask Richie Conway."

"I will."

He tried closing the door but I didn't wait. I pushed past him, pulling Helen behind me. Man, it was something seeing the look on those faces.

"What the hell?"

"Good to see you again, Richie." I walked over and shook his hand. "When you invited me to join the game earlier, I thought I was going to pass but then I realized I had an extra five grand. Tonight I'm going to turn it into ten, maybe even eleven. This is Helen." Four other players sat at the table.

"Tell me you didn't invite this guy," Michael Finn said. Mason Cornish shushed him so he looked down at the table in front of him where precious few chips remained.

Elliot Powell was there too. I wasn't expecting to see him there. In terms of sheer size, he was the biggest man in the room but he wasn't dominating this crowd like he did the lunch table. "We missed you at lunch, Henry," he said.

"My day didn't go according to plan. Hey, I didn't recognize you without Doug. He's not a poker guy?"

"He's at the movie with the wives. They're playing the old science fiction movies. Tonight is the one with the evil robots on the planet."

"Is that right? You, I don't know," I said to the man sitting between Elliot and Richie. I was pretty sure I hadn't seen him before. He was in a wheelchair and he breathed oxygen from a tank. He looked to be a couple of hundred years old. He waved a leathery hand at me. "Arthur Gruper," he said, his voice husky. "Pleased to make your acquaintance."

"I'm afraid there are no more chairs," Michael Finn told me. "It looks like you won't be able to join us after all."

"You need to take a breather," Cornish told him. "Save your chips for tomorrow. You're playing like shit anyhow."

He shook his head but did as he was told.

"And the lady can have my seat," Cornish said to Helen.

"Thank you," she said, "but I'm not playing. I'm just here for moral support."

I handed my roll of hundred dollar bills to the casino dealer and he converted it into chips.

"What do you do, Henry?" Arthur Gruper asked as he lit a thin cigarette. I was unaware that cigarettes could be smoked in such close proximity to an oxygen tank but apparently they can.

Elliot Powell answered before I could get a word out. "Henry here has the kind of job men dream about. He's an editor at *Penthouse*, so I'm told. Can you imagine what that would be like?"

Helen stared at me, as did Cornish and the rest.

"*Penthouse?*" Cornish said.

Michael Finn was having none of it. "That's bullshit. The guy is a cop. Don't believe a word he says."

Elliot Powell stared at me. "You're a cop?"

"I'm not a cop. I'm a private investigator. I'm here working on the Robert Samson murder."

"Are you going to write about it in *Penthouse?*"

"I'm thinking about it. It really depends on how the evening progresses." I sat in Finn's seat and organized my chips. "Maybe you all could help me out with the story."

"What do you have so far?" Arthur Gruper asked.

"I don't have much of anything, except for some lobsters on the moose."

Silence.

Gruper stared at me. "What do lobsters have to do with it?"

Helen rubbed my hand. "You mean mobsters on the loose."

"That's what I said. I've got mobsters on the loose, in strangely close proximity to a murder that would be of considerable interest to them."

"The mobsters are these three, right?" Gruper asked, pointing with his cigarette to Conway, Cornish, and Finn.

I nodded.

He pointed at Elliot Powell. "I don't think this one is a mobster. He's got a different look to him."

"He sure does."

Cornish cleared his throat. "Did we not discuss this, you and I? I told you, I gave you my word. We had nothing to do with the unfortunate event. We were right here when it happened. Isn't that right, Arthur?"

"I have to say it is," Gruper said. "I don't remember Mr. Finn that evening. I can recall taking his money most nights but I'm fairly certain he wasn't present that night. Maybe he killed him."

"Shut your trap, old man," Finn called out.

"Blow me," Gruper said. "I was in World War I. I beat bigger assholes than you with sticks."

"Hey, now," Cornish said. "Let's be civil here. First thing is this; I'm a retired businessman and I don't appreciate being called a mobster. Second thing is this; I told you that Finn didn't do it. Case closed."

I was thinking that I liked Arthur Gruper a lot. I wouldn't mind having a beverage or two with him one day when it was all over.

"Case not closed," I said. "But in the interests of laying my cards out on the table, let me be clear; I don't think any of you killed Samson."

Elliot Powell kind of hung there, not sure how to respond to what was going on around him.

"Well then," Gruper said. "Can we get back to the cards? I don't know how much time I've got left on the earth, but I don't want to spend it listening to you ladies bitch. The game is Texas Hold 'Em. Ante is $50. Mr. Powell deals."

I threw five ten-dollar chips at the center of the table when everyone else did. "Refresh my memory, please. I haven't played Poker since before Texas was a state."

Conway groaned but Gruper didn't miss a beat. "Each player gets two cards, then we bet, then we all share the next three cards, then we bet, then we share one more, then we bet, then we share one more, then we bet. Make your best five card hand."

Elliot Powell dealt us each two cards.

I got two fours, which I figured had to be good. "Now, if I have twenty-one, does that give me any advantage?"

"It does not," Gruper said, looking at his cards. "I'm in for $20."

Everyone threw chips in. I was hoping for someone to fold but nobody did. Next came the three shared cards; a jack, an ace, and a three. Everyone passed so I figured it was time to make my move. It wasn't my money in any case. "I'll bet $100."

Helen squeezed my hand.

Elliot Powell gave me a long studious look but ultimately added his ten chips to the pot. Gruper did the same as did Conway. Cornish pushed his cards away and sat back. "If you don't think any of us killed Samson then why are you busting our balls?"

"I need information."

"On what?"

"I want to know who killed him. It wasn't you but you know who it was."

"No, I don't."

"Yes, you do."

"Ladies," Gruper interjected. "What time I have left is being wasted."

Elliot Powell dealt the next shared card, another ace.

I smiled because at least now I had a pair of aces. Strictly speaking, I realized, so did everyone else.

Elliot Powell pulled out.

Gruper stared at the cards. "Why not," he said, throwing another $20 chip at the pot. "It's either this or leave it to the great-grandkids, and they're a bunch of bastards. I'd rather leave it all to the Krauts."

Conway tossed his chips at the pot, as did I. The next card was a four. I looked at my cards again. I suspected that was good for me.

Cornish leaned back in. "Henry here is a veteran too," he said, moving the conversation. "He got captured by the Nazis."

"Pass," Gruper said. "P.O.W.? They send you to Berlin?"

"No. Moosburg, near Munich."

"A concentration camp?" Elliot Powell asked.

I shook my head. "No, a stalag, a camp for captured enemy fighters."

"I'll bet that was fun."

"Lots."

"Were the guards assholes?"

"Yes they were, most of them. One guy I ultimately got to be half-way chummy with toward the end. He wound up spending half of his life in therapy. He wrote to me about ten years ago to apologize, and we started kind of a pen pal thing. I visited him in Berlin and we had a nice time. It felt good. We went to see some dancing girls."

"How was the food in the stalag?" Gruper asked.

"Don't get me started."

Richie Conway stared at his cards a few moments longer and pushed them away.

I raised $100.

"All yours," Gruper said.

"Well I'll be god-damned. There's like a thousand dollars in here. Do I need to show you my cards?"

He shook his head so I reached in and collected my winnings. "Samson was working on the murder of a man who had joined the witness protection program," I said, turning to Cornish. "His name was Harry Clooney. Does that ring a bell?"

He rolled his lower lip and sat back.

Richie Conway didn't even flinch but he was a cool cat anyway. Michael Finn looked away, then moved to the bar.

I counted my chips; $910, which was at least $900 more than I had ever won at anything in my life.

"This is going to need to be a private conversation," Cornish said finally.

"The hell it is." Gruper shook his head. "This is just getting interesting."

Elliot Powell stood. "I'm going to head out. I'm not doing too well tonight as it is." He asked the casino dealer to hold his chips until the next game. Nobody said anything until he left.

Cornish shook his head. "This is kind of a personal issue."

Richie Conway cracked his knuckles. "Harry Clooney was like a brother."

"Hey." Cornish held up a hand.

"It's OK, Mason. I'll handle it."

"I think it's unwise ..."

"I said I'd handle it." He didn't even look at Cornish. He didn't have to. Cornish didn't say another word. "Clooney broke my heart. We'd been working together for almost thirty years when he turned on us."

"He was facing a long prison sentence," I said.

Michael Finn took Powell's seat. "Then he should have gone to prison, not rat out his friends."

"You got put away also because of this, didn't you?"

He looked over quickly at Richie before he nodded.

"I searched for him for years," Conway continued. "We had a bank account in Bermuda that we shared for some purposes. And I never closed it. I knew that one day he'd give in to temptation."

"How much money are we talking?" I asked.

"About a million, five. So anyways, one night I'm sitting at home with my sons watching a program on the television, and the phone rings. And people know not to call me at night unless it's important." He took the card deck and began shuffling. "Mikey, get me a Scotch, will you?"

"Yeah."

"Hey, me too, Mikey," I said, "and one for the lady here. No ice for me; it hurts my teeth. I think I'm getting a cavity."

He didn't say anything but you could sense the muscles rippling again.

"It was my guy in Bermuda on the phone," Conway continued. "The money had been transferred to a bank in Panama, about three quarters of a mil. Isn't that something? He only took half the money. Clooney was always a stand-up guy, always fair. That was him reaching out to me from beyond the grave I was ready to put him in."

"So you traced the money."

Finn brought our drinks but we didn't toast. The moment didn't call for it.

Arthur Gruper had apparently nodded off so Conway took the cigarette from his hand and stubbed it in the ashtray. "We traced the money, yes. It's not as easy as it sounds, and it took awhile. It took us some time to find out that he was on Cape Cod."

"He was a homosexual man," Cornish added. "That made it a little easier to find him."

"So you flew out there to pay him a visit."

Michael Finn bounced a chip on the table. "You're goddamn right we flew out to pay him a visit."

"We wanted to have a talk with him," Conway continued. "But you need to realize, we weren't the only guys he screwed. There were guys a hell of a lot madder than us, a hell of a lot heavier too."

"So you flew out to Cape Cod."

"I flew out with Mikey. We had a stopover in Chicago and while we were there, we got a call letting us know that Clooney had been taken care of."

"So you didn't get to see Cape Cod?"

Conway shook his head. "No. We didn't."

Arthur Gruper nodded back to life. "That sounds like a bunch of bullshit to me," he said, raising his cigarette to his lips, surprised to find out it wasn't there.

Conway turned to him. "How so?"

"You weren't going out to talk to him."

"Yes. Yes, we were. You see, Arthur, I'm talking with law enforcement here. So if I were going off to kill someone, which in this case I was not, I'd probably just say I was going out to talk. See, the only reason we're having this conversation in the first place is because I'm telling the truth, and because this detective here knows that he can trace the flights and work the timelines and see that I'm telling the truth."

"I'm learning a lot," I admitted. "But we're still not coming up with any answers."

Gruper nodded. He turned to Richie. "So if someone killed him, that should be the end of the story. But if it is, why the hell are you on this cruise?"

I liked him more every minute. "Maybe we could go into business together," I told him. "We could hang out a shingle, get cases."

"Maybe. So how about it, guys? Why the gangster reunion?"

"You want to know why?" Cornish said. "Because all these years, we just never knew exactly what happened to him. He cost me a fortune and I just really wanted some closure on it."

I smiled at him. "That's so sweet." I turned to Conway. "Now tell me the real story and we can be done with this. I need something to work on or this all gets reported to the F.B.I. Helen is recording our conversation, did I mention that?"

"Is she now?" Cornish asked.

Helen looked started. "No, I'm not."

"I gave you the tape recorder, didn't I?"

"No you most certainly did not."

"Did we not talk about this?"

"No, we did not."

"Well then." I turned back to Conway. "Although our conversation is not being recorded, a transcript can easily be generated. So tell me more."

"He means why are you really here?" Gruper added.

"I got that," Conway said. "Look, we were interested in what Samson had to say. And we also thought there might be a good chance that someone else would show up, someone connected with Clooney's death. We were curious to see if we'd run into anybody we knew."

"Did you?"

"No. But we were right about one thing. Someone did show up, only we don't know who. We've looked at everyone on this boat and we haven't recognized a soul. We don't know anything more, none of us."

"He's telling the truth," Gruper told me.

"Is that right?"

"It is. I did prisoner interrogations in Greece in 1918. You learn how to tell if a man is lying. It's all in the eyeballs."

Mason Cornish looked up. "Interrogations. Is that like torture?"

Gruper lit another cigarette. "Yes, it is."

I took a deep breath. I'd learned a lot here but not what I was interested in. The only reason these guys were talking to me is because they knew I could bring serious federal pressure to bear on them, but talk they did. I didn't think they were lying to me.

"The card game sucked tonight," Gruper said.

"You should be complaining?" Finn noted. "You're the one with all the chips."

The casino dealer approached Finn and whispered something.

"Can you believe this guy?" he asked. "He wants me to cancel my account right now."

"Just for today," the dealer said. "You're $400 over your buy in. If you have your keycard, I can just post that to your shipboard account."

"I'll make it back tomorrow," Finn said as he pulled out a wallet and took out a Platinum American Express card.

"Your keycard, sir. We don't use credit cards on board except at the registration desk."

He shook his head and exchanged the card for his keycard. I thought about that for a minute. Some bells were ringing in my head but I couldn't quite identify what tower they were coming from. No credit cards on board; I needed to think about why that bothered me.

"We're going to call it a night," Conway said. "Mason, maybe you and I could go have a drink."

Cornish nodded.

"I must say I have enjoyed taking your money," I told them. "I try to play down my poker skills but now and again I like to break out with the night moves. I was bluffing, you know."

"I doubt it," Gruper said. "You were lucky but I think you had a pair of fours buried."

"I did. How did you know?"

"You held up four fingers twice when you showed her your cards."

"Did I?"

"Yes."

"Well I'll be god-damned."

Helen took my arm. "I'll be taking my boyfriend now."

"Wait for the chips, baby," I told her as the dealer converted my chips to cash. I handed Helen the money but she handed it right back.

"We'll divide it up later," she said. "You should at least keep your winnings."

Gruper chuckled. "You were playing with the lady's money?"

"I was. That's funny?"

"No. That's true love. I've enjoyed meeting you, Henry, and your wife. I hope you find your killer. It wasn't me."

"It probably wasn't," I told him. "Good luck taking more of their money tomorrow."

"It's got nothing to do with luck. Poker is seventy percent memory and thirty percent cheating."

"That was illuminating," Helen told me as we stepped into the elevator.

"Shall we stop somewhere for a drink?"

"Absolutely."

I hit the button for the Lido Deck. "You don't normally carry money around with you, do you?"

"Why should I? We're on a ship."

"Then no credit cards either."

"No."

"What's in your purse?"

"The usual; lipstick, perfume, tissues, birth control, I think a couple of quaaludes, why?"

We got off at the Lido Deck and walked over to the Bistro. It was closed. We sat anyway, and just then, I remembered the surveillance footage. The man leaning into the frame wasn't handing Norman Gellerman a credit card, he was handing him a keycard.

"I don't think they're going to serve us here, Henry. We might have to find another place, a place that's open, with people at it."

"Who would you hand over your keycard to?" I asked her. "I mean, not you personally, but who would the average passenger give his card to?"

She stared out the window. "I don't know, maybe a bartender or someone in the shops."

"What if it wasn't a crewmember?"

"Someone who had some reason to be in my suite, I guess. Maybe if I had a roommate. Maybe if I had a roommate and she forgot her keycard."

I smiled. "Your roommate. Gellerman borrowed a keycard from his roommate. And that roommate was careful not to get caught on the surveillance camera. That means he knew where the camera was."

Helen looked up at me. "Why are we stopped?"

"What?"

She pointed to the window. "We're not moving."

She was right. We got up fast. I led her down the large spiral staircase to the reception area. I saw Hector as soon as we cleared the rainforest. He wasn't alone. Two other security officers were standing right beside him.

"We've been looking all over for you," he said. He walked over quickly and took my arm. "Come with me, right now."

"What's going on?"

He pushed me toward the elevator. I didn't let go of Helen. "Where are we going?"

"Captain wants to see you."

The elevator opened but I stood my ground. "Explain,"

"Step inside please. The captain will explain."

"No, you will."

Helen took my hand. "What's going on, Henry?"

"Please," Hector said, waving to the elevator.

"What happened? Why is the ship stopped?"

"We had a man go overboard."

"Who?"

"Hugh Arlen."

CHAPTER TWENTY-THREE

I take pills for my heart, and right about then I wished they weren't back in the Junior Suite because my heart was racing. I don't get shaken up easily. Maybe I do, I don't know.

Capt. Erlander looked like he'd lost some weight during the cruise, about half of what he started with. He looked shrunken. "It happened sometime before one o'clock," he said. We were sitting at his glass desk, Helen on one side of me and Hector on the other, which was comforting to me. "We thought you might have gone overboard too."

"You found his body?"

Hector nodded. "Yes. He went off the starboard side, from either the Sky Deck or the Tropicana."

"And nobody saw anything?"

Hector and the captain answered in unison. "It's raining."

"It was raining," Hector continued, "so there was nobody on deck but yes, people saw it. There was a party in one of the penthouses and they had their sliding door open, even with the rain. Several people saw him go over. They called it in and we turned around."

Erlander brought a bottle of vodka from his desk drawer and poured himself a shot. "The doctor said he was dead before he went over. Strangled."

I didn't know what to say. I was scared. It could have been me.

Erlander downed his shot and poured another. "We have to ask, you understand."

"Ask what?"

"Ask you where you were?"

"Yeah?" I said. "I'm a suspect?"

Hector shook his head. "Up until ten minutes ago we thought you were a victim. Arlen had been looking for you all evening but nobody was able to find you."

"I was with her," I said pointing to Helen. "We were in her cabin. Later, we played poker in the cigar bar."

Helen nodded. "I was with him the whole time."

"So what do we do now?" I asked.

"We go to Miami," Erlander said. "We've already changed course. We're going to skip the Virgin Islands. I've been in contact with Contessa in Los Angeles. They've advised me to undertake a voluntary impound in Miami. We're going to lock down the ship."

"For how long?"

"That's for the F.B.I. to decide. At full steam we can be in Miami in about twenty-two hours."

"We're going to shut the fire doors to all outdoor public areas," Hector said. "They'll remain closed until we reach port. Additionally, we'll have armed guards patrolling the ship. We're putting bulletins under every door and sending messages to every voicemail informing the passengers."

"Why was Arlen looking for me?" I asked.

"He said you had arranged to meet him and then you didn't show up. You've been gone all evening. He was worried something happened to you."

I didn't know what to say. "Was he following up with anybody?"

"He was but we've looked into them and I can't figure anything out."

Helen stood and started walking around the office. She found a decorative wine glass on a shelf and placed it on Erlander's desk. She pointed to the vodka bottle. "It looks like he found the killer," she said as he poured.

"That was our assumption," Hector said. "He found the killer and the killer got him. Now we're back to square one."

"Not exactly," I said. I told them about the mobsters.

"How does that help us?" Erlander asked.

"I'm not sure."

"Tell them about the keycard," Helen reminded me.

"Yes, I remember now. I think I know who the killer is."

Erlander leaned back in his chair. "Do you mind sharing?"

"It's Norman Gellerman's roommate."

He stared at me, just as he had when I first met him.

"So you're telling me that Norman Gellerman, the murderer we know about, was sharing a cabin with the murderer we don't know about?"

"Right," I stood and searched for another decorative wine glass but I couldn't find one. "Here's how it went, as I see it. Help me with this, Hector. The ship isn't full, is it?"

"No. There are still cabins available."

"That's what was troubling me at first, but not anymore. The ship isn't full but the only cabins available are the expensive suites, right?"

Erlander nodded. "That's how it usually works out."

"I thought so. Norman Gellerman tried to book a passage but found that there weren't any low price suites available, either because they had all been sold out or because they had been held back by your roommate matching service."

"Yes. Contessa Community."

"So this is a problem. Gellerman is a predator but he's not rich, and now he has to share a cabin. You found him a roommate. That's inconvenient, I'll give you that. Now Gellerman has to be a little more careful but he's confident. He probably figures he won't be spending much time in the cabin anyway, and as it turns out, he's right."

Hector held up his hands. "So what?"

"So the same thing happened to the man who came on board to kill Samson. No affordable cabins, and he absolutely couldn't wait for another cruise. He had to be here so he was forced to share a cabin. You got him a roommate."

I got nothing but stares.

"Remember the surveillance camera in the library that went bad?"

"Yes."

"That was the killer's practice run," I said. "He already knew where he was going to kill Samson but he wanted to make sure he wasn't caught on tape. So he disabled the library camera to see how long it would take to get fixed. It took long enough, so when he disabled the camera by the rock wall, he knew it wouldn't be fixed until after he finished with Samson."

Erlander shook his head. "I still don't see how this ties in to Gellerman."

I was getting grouchy, hungry too. "Look, the man cut the line to the surveillance camera in the library. The camera is hidden, so he had to scout it out. I've been watching that surveillance footage to see if I could spot someone snooping around. And there was nobody snooping around. What I did see, was Norman Gellerman sitting in the library reading. And at one point he waved someone over, called to someone, and that person came over, but carefully. He walked up to Gellerman and handed him a card, a keycard, and then he backed away. Why would he back away?"

"Because he had figured out where the camera was," Helen said. "And he planned on disabling it soon so the last thing he wanted was to be caught on tape just in case someone started looking it over."

Erlander thought it through. He stared at the vodka bottle. I did too but I was too worked up to do anything about it. "How do you know it was his roommate?" he asked. "It could have been anyone."

"No. No. The only person you'd give your keycard to, other than someone bringing you a drink, is a roommate. Gellerman forgot his card, and he saw his roommate walk by. He called him in so he could borrow it. And that roommate is Samson's killer."

Erlander didn't move, so Hector walked around the desk and logged on to his computer. He pulled up the passenger manifest. While he did that, I picked up the phone to check my messages. I had four, two of which were hang-ups. The next was from Arlen. It came in at 12:30. I listened carefully since it was the last time he would ever speak to me:

> Henry, I still can't find you and I'm getting worried. All the interviews are finished and I'm concerned we haven't gotten anywhere. I still need to hear from you about Conway's associates. I also have two more passengers I want to check in on, passengers who declined interviews at the last minute. You know who else I want to have another chat with? Bob Redmond. Remember him, he was Norman Gellerman's roommate? I know this sounds far-fetched, two murderers sharing a stateroom and all, but when I talked to Redmond back in Martinique and told him what had happened, he laughed. Most people would be afraid or shocked, right? Also, we called him late for this interview and he declined. He said he had already talked to me. So I'm going to have another talk with him.

I felt very angry, very upset at myself. If I had thought things through a little more quickly, Arlen might still be alive. I had one more message. It was from Duarte and it was only about half an hour old.

> You're never going to believe what just came through my fax machine, Mr. Grave. Come as soon as you can. You'll be very interested in seeing this.

"Bob Redmond," Hector said, spinning the monitor around so that we could see the image. Redmond looked like an average middle-aged guy. He didn't look at all like Conway and Finn. He looked like an accountant.

"Mr. Redmond, age sixty-two, is a software engineer from Durham, New Hampshire. This is his first cruise with us."

"Pick him up," Erlander said. "Bring a couple of guys with you. And wear side-arms. He's dangerous. Bring him to the brig and let me know when you have him."

Hector left us alone with the captain. Helen was clearly exhausted and laid down on the office couch. "Let me take her back to her suite," I said.

"Why don't you wait here for now? Let's be sure it's safe first. If he went after Arlen, he could go after you too."

"I'm a big boy."

"And I'm the captain."

I have to say I was feeling a little lightheaded. It was late but I realized that I hadn't had much to eat lately. "Is it still possible to get room service? It is, right? You can get it any time. Do they deliver up here?"

He stared at me. "You can think about food right now?"

"It's not easy but I'm a little bit diabetic. I have to eat more frequently than many are comfortable with."

"Suit yourself. Dial 8 on the phone."

I went to ask Helen if she wanted anything but she looked to be about dozing off. I ordered a burger, well-done, a baked potato, the leek soup, and a cheese plate. I covered Helen with a blanket. "Are you going to interrogate him?" I asked. "Or will you leave that to the F.B.I.?"

He shook his head and puffed out his neck like some lizards can do. He seemed to be getting bigger. "When I'm at home I work out at a boxing gymnasium. It's good exercise and I miss it when I'm at sea." He checked his watch. "We'll be in international waters for another twelve hours at least. If he killed Arlen, I'm going to beat him half to death. Every one of my officers will gladly sign a statement saying he resisted arrest. Then I'm going to beat him half of the remaining distance to death."

I nodded. "That sounds about right."

So we sat there, restlessly, not quite knowing what to do.

"I'm going to take a quick walk," I said. "I'll be back before my food comes."

"You should take an escort or at least wait until he's in custody."

"I can take care of myself. Watch over her, OK?"

Maybe it was the lack of food, or the hour, but I felt a little dis-oriented as I made my way to Duarte's cabin. I didn't know what he could add to the picture by that point, but I was anxious to have all of the information I could get my hands on.

"It's open," he called out when I knocked. "Come in and please lock it behind you."

That was odd, but I did just that. The lights were low but the cur-tains were open. The rain had almost stopped and a little moon shone through. I could tell as soon as I shut the door that something about that Parliamentary Suite was a little off. There's a smell to that, kind of a sour smell that creeps up your throat, and it makes your heart clench, like when you realize you have more to fear from the Russian prisoners than from the German guards.

I walked into the living room and saw Duarte sitting on a barstool, his hands behind his back which didn't look comfortable. He looked frightened. He was looking behind me, not at me. When I turned around, I saw the man standing right there.

"Hey," he said.

"Are you talking to me?" I asked, like an idiot. I wasn't sure what to say.

"Do you know who I am?"

I squinted but I still couldn't see anything. "No, I don't have my glasses on. And it's dark. Can you turn the light on?"

"Maybe later. Do you know who I am?"

"Room service?"

He came towards me slowly as if to shake my hand, then he smacked me in the side of the head with his gun. "No fucking games."

"Hey, hey, hey," I yelled out. I fell over and landed on my side. I tried to get up but I was a little disoriented. My head felt like it had exploded. "Hey, do you have any idea how old I am? You don't hit an old man."

"Do you know who I am?" he asked again.

"How did you get a gun on board?"

"It's his," he said, pointing to Duarte. "Ask him. Ask him later. Answer my question."

I stumbled up and sat on the edge of the couch. I rubbed my head. "Yeah, I know who you are. I'm just now figuring it out. You're Harvey Cotton. But that's not your real name."

He stared at me.

"It's George Clooney," I told him.

"Harry Clooney."

"That's what I said. I ran into some of your old friends. They're anxious to get back in touch with you. I think Mason Cornish figured out you didn't really die on Cape Cod."

"Mason Cornish didn't figure anything out. He's retired and retarded. He just came along for the ride. Richie Conway figured it out."

"No," I reminded him, "Robert Samson figured it out."

"Him too. You know, if he had just left well enough alone this would not have been an issue. But no, he had to hunt me."

"He tipped off Richie?" I speculated.

"No, it was the other way around. Richie had been working on him for years, and Samson just wouldn't let go. He wasn't even a cop anymore."

"Why did you have to kill him like that, string him up on the rock wall? Why didn't you just toss him over the railing? You're obviously capable of doing that."

"You know, he just pissed me off. I knew Richie and the rest of them would be here so I wanted to make it nice for them, just to show them I wasn't afraid. It shouldn't even have mattered. I look completely different. I stood next to Richie Conway at the buffet and he never even suspected. I had everything under control. Then yesterday, this Colombian asshole gets my file reopened."

"Venezuelan," Duarte volunteered.

"You might still have pulled this off," I said, "if you hadn't wound up with a murderer for a roommate."

He shut his eyes for just a moment. "I've had a run of good luck."

"Did you know he was killing women?"

"Not at first. I should have killed him, too."

"Well you didn't and now it's over. I can offer you protective custody until Miami. That way your mob friends won't kill you."

"That's very kind of you," he said. "I'll pass."

"That would be a mistake. Can I get a drink?"

"No."

"Fine. You know, you've really screwed up badly. All along you've underestimated the resolve of the people you were up against."

"I'm not in the mood for a lecture."

"Did you not think they'd look for you in homosexual places? You know they have homosexuals in Minnesota and Buffalo too, and maybe even in Mississippi. Did you really have to pick the most homosexual place on the planet to hide out in? Cape Cod? Even the seagulls are queer."

He stared at me. "It was a long way from San Francisco, was what I was thinking."

"But a Bed and Breakfast?"

I felt great anger directed at me. My eyes had adjusted but it was still dark. I sensed a crackle of murderous energy discharge in the room and it didn't come from me. "You'll never get off the ship," I said. "I told security where I was going. They'll find us."

"No. We're leaving. Mr. Duarte has made preparations. He's a war criminal you know. He's killed millions."

"Thousands," Duarte corrected.

"What kind of preparations?" I squinted at Duarte.

He looked down. "Preparations in case one day I needed to leave the ship in a hurry. I would make a call and a Med-evac helicopter would be on its way."

"Did you make that call?" I asked.

He nodded.

"But it won't be a real Med-evac. The men on board will be armed."

"Well that's different," I admitted. "Did you just holler all that out to him? Why not tell him your bank account numbers?"

Clooney stood up. "Señor Duarte and I will be discussing just that as we fly to Grand Cayman."

I shook my head.

"You're coming too," he said, "though you'll be exiting the helicopter some time before it lands. You've made things difficult enough for me."

"That's not going to happen, son," I told him. "I have to take you down. I'll keep you in here until Miami, make sure nobody touches you but I can't let you go."

"Suit yourself." He raised Duarte's gun and moved toward me. I think he meant to hit me with it so I shot him. I shot him about four or five times and I hit him at least twice. That's for stabbing me, you fucker. The gun was still in my jacket pocket and it made a big hole. I really liked that jacket.

Let me tell you something: I am always armed. The first time a man pulled a gun on me I was a nineteen year old corporal pulling civil patrol duty in a little Belgian town. I was armed then too but I didn't do anything. Although I might have died if I had, I've always wished I had tried something, anything instead of just standing there like an asshole and then getting stuck in a rancid Nazi jail camp for five months.

I made a promise to myself one day in that camp as I stood outside, staring at the clouds, eating a dandelion, that for the rest of my life any time someone pulled a gun on me I was going to shoot them. And I have ever since, every time.

"I think you got me too," Duarte said.

Clooney had fallen back into him and knocked him into the bar. I checked Clooney first. I had hit him in the arm and in the chest, and one bullet went right into his forehead. I checked his pulse and found none. I also hit Duarte too, a little bit. I'm not a very good shot on a good day, and it was dark.

"It's just a scratch," I told him. I untied him and helped him to his feet.

He walked into the bathroom and flipped on the light. "Just a scratch? You shot me in the head." He grabbed a towel and held it against his scalp, which was actually bleeding quite badly.

"I grazed you. Quit your bitching." I dialed the emergency number and was in the process of giving some information when Hector and a security team burst through the door. We enjoyed a tense moment before they dispersed, bringing Duarte to the ship's hospital.

CHAPTER TWENTY-FOUR

I'd be lying if I told you that Capt. Erlander was pleased. I suspect he'd been looking forward to doing a little beating, and that was no longer going to be possible. But what bothered him more than anything else was the fact that two people were carrying guns on his ship. Duarte, it seems, had paid one of the engineering assistants to smuggle one on for him, and I just brought mine. I came in on a helicopter, remember, and any time I set off a metal detector I prattled on about my titanium hip and they just waved me through. Nobody expects much from an old man.

I thought Erlander should have been happier but he was grumpy and tired and a little drunk, and I understand how that all comes together. For my part, I felt good. I found the killer, after all. Two killers.

It was morning by the time we wrapped it all up. Duarte managed to call off his rescue attempt. And I watched as Hugh Arlen's body was placed on the last available morgue bed. Clooney or Cotton, I wasn't sure what to call him, was wrapped in plastic, and tossed on the floor of the deep freeze not far from the yellowfin tuna but not too close either. When we searched him, we found a little gold-plated penknife in his pocket. It was quite a thing. It had a tiny steel blade about an inch long. Nobody said anything when I took it.

I brought Helen back to her suite and promised I'd check on her in a bit. I needed some alone time, and some food, so I stumbled out to the Bistro for the early risers' breakfast. I was planning on doing some thinking about Hugh Arlen. There was grieving to be done.

Shelley Tobin was sitting by a window, her head framed by the rising sun behind her. She looked like an angel.

"You heard the news?" she said, "We're going straight to Miami."

"I heard."

"Did you hear the shots last night? It seems the security guards killed the guy who killed the other guy."

"I heard." I ordered a bunch of stuff; coffee, a Mimosa, a bagel, salmon, some eggs, potatoes, something called a Belgian endive patty, a couple of strips of bacon and a waffle. "Hey, why are you up so early?"

"I didn't sleep well," she said. "I haven't actually gone to sleep yet. I was up in the lounge until it closed, then I watched one of the late night movies, science fiction. I don't know what it was called but a robot went crazy and started taking over computer systems. In the end, they trapped it in a submarine with an octopus and sent it to the bottom of the ocean. But then it took control of the submarine and headed for Washington, D.C."

"What happened to the octopus?"

"I'm not sure. I don't think that was addressed."

"Is that right? So where's Warren?"

"Jack."

"Where's Jack?"

She looked down at her coffee. "He went to bed early."

"Well then he missed a great deal of fun, I'm sure."

"Yes. He did."

"Are you heading back to L.A. now?"

"I think I'm going to spend some time in New Jersey with my mom. The show is on hiatus so I can spare a couple of weeks. Jack will head back home and take care of the build-up for the next season."

"Well that sounds like a plan. Jersey is a lovely place. I live not too far from there. You could come visit me at Rolling Pines. We have a nice pool and even a hot tub. They don't keep it as hot as the one here, and it gets pretty crowded but I'm sure we could fit you in."

She grinned. "I can never tell if you're kidding me or not."

"Not me. I'd love to spend time with you but it would be danger-ous, I warn you. I'm very charming. Dashing, some would say. Give me three days and you'd fall in love. The closest you'd get to TV work is changing the channel on my floor model Trinitron."

"Do you have cable?"

"Not yet, but I can have it installed before you arrive." I had to think about that for a moment. "No, I do have cable. I'd forgotten. I'm serious though, we could build a life together."

"I'll give it some thought," she said, but I knew she was kidding.

My beverages arrived. "Want to try my Mimosa?"

"I do." She took a long drink.

"I'm definitely going to watch your show from now on. Every night."

"It's only on Thursday nights."

"Then I'll watch it twice on Thursdays."

"That sounds fair. I bet there will be something on TV about this cruise, like a Dateline special."

"You think?"

"Sure. Come on! A murder on a cruise ship, then another one, then security takes down the killer? That's interesting material. I wonder how they figured out who it was."

"Probably good detective work is all."

"I've been thinking about that. Remember how I said I thought Samson would have had an accomplice?"

"I do."

"Now I think he didn't."

"Why is that?"

She folded her hands in front of her. "Well, you work on something for long enough and it becomes your own. Even if other people help out, you can't help thinking you did it yourself. I think collaboration has to be the most difficult thing. In the end, I'm not sure he'd want to share the credit."

"You might be right." My breakfast came and I ate all of it. I swear I was half asleep at that point. I made a promise to myself to eat a Belgian endive patty every day of my life.

"I have to get going," she said. "I think I need to sleep. Sorry for talking your ear off."

I stood and gave her a hug. "I'll miss you. I'll think about you every Thursday night during *Horny Plenty*."

"*Quickly Deadly.*"

"I know. I was referring to me."

I slept. I slept long into the day. I heard the phone ring a couple of times but I couldn't bring myself to answer it. It was afternoon before I woke up and I had a stomach ache. I made a promise to myself never to eat a Belgian endive patty again. I called Helen but she was still half asleep so we made a plan to meet for dinner. Since the cruise was ending early, it would be our last night together at sea and I needed to think about that and about her.

I played my messages. Capt. Erlander wanted to meet with me about an hour ago. I'd get to that but relaxation was top priority. I'd done a job and done it with extraordinary grace, and I was due a little reward.

I put on my trunks and my cap and headed out.

"Sir," a crewmember called out to me as I waited for the elevator. "Sir, I'm afraid you have to wear a shirt and shoes until you get to the pool."

Nuts. I headed back to the Junior Suite and found a robe and my slippers and then I headed back out.

It was crowded by the pool, as it should be. It was our last day at sea, after all. I found it curiously quiet out there. It felt kind of somber; no music was playing. Many of the passengers were probably still stunned. They had been through quite a lot.

Refunds would already be in the works. Cruises are not cheap, and when they go bad, the rebates and refunds can be ruinous. Cruising is a highly competitive industry, and things were going to be tough for *Voyager* in the coming months.

So I walked around the pool and watched people. Most were quiet but at least they weren't staying huddled in their cabins. They were out sunning themselves, having some drinks. Ultimately, you can't not enjoy your cruise, unless you get sick or go overboard or get shot. If none of that happens, you're just about guaranteed to have a blast.

"Make way," I called out as I walked over the little bridge to the island in the middle of the pool. I started to climb into the hot tub but it was so hot I had to just stand there and lower myself little by little. I threw my robe to the side. I closed my eyes and turned my face to the sun. It was a glorious day, a fine day to be alive.

"Dude," someone called out. "Dude, you're blocking our sun."

I looked down into the tub where a couple of teenage boys bathed in the shade that my girth provided. I climbed down and settled myself next to a lovely young woman. "Hey there," I said. "I'm Henry and I've been looking forward to this hot tub all damn day. Say, which one of you boys is married to this gorgeous thing?"

The young woman groaned as the boys snickered. "Me," one of them said. "We're not married yet but we're engaged."

"I'm dating her, too," another added.

"Listen to me carefully," the young woman said to the boys. "I've had enough of your bullshit. Get out of the tub this minute or I'll call my husband over and tell him you've been staring at my tits for forty minutes. He's a jealous man. He'll choke you until you die."

They laughed nervously but they left.

"At least we can be alone now," I told her. I slid around so that my face was in the sun.

"Don't you start with me."

"I wouldn't dream of it. I've had some recent trauma in my life, so I'm just going to sit here and have some drinks right now, probably five or six. Would you join me in three or four?"

"Yeah, huh. Why not? I like the piña coladas."

Now there was a girl I could fall in love with, I told myself as I raised my hand and made my selection from the three Filipino waiters who approached. "We'd like a number of piña coladas," I told him. "We'll start with four; we have a lot of catching up to do."

"We've never met," she said.

"Then it's about god-damn time we did." I held out my hand.

"I'm April."

"A lovely month for a lovely name?"

"What?"

"I mean it's a great body for such a month." It wasn't really what I meant to say but it was close.

"OK. Thanks I guess."

"Where are you from, April?"

"Catalina Island. It's off of southern California."

"That sounds nice, island life all year round."

"It's all right if you like golf. Do you like golf?"

"I don't."

"Neither do I. I like sailing. I want to get a little sailboat but my husband says he doesn't want me out sailing all day. He likes playing golf. He even plays on the ship, you know on the little course they have on the top deck."

"Yes, I walked by it."

"He was supposed to play this morning but they closed it to get ready for a helicopter that's supposed to be landing soon."

I opened my eyes. "Is that right?"

"Yes, my husband said probably there would be police coming onboard."

"Well I'll be god-damned."

"It's on account of the man who got killed last night."

I turned around to see if I could spot a helicopter. I thought I couldn't but the sun was so bright I could hardly see.

"No, it didn't land yet. They said sometime today."

I looked back at her but there was something standing over her, something little and wrinkly like a troll or one of those goblins that people put in their gardens. I waited until my eyes adjusted.

"Well look who's sitting here ogling the missus," it said.

I couldn't place the voice but my eyes adjusted as Mason Cornish lowered himself into the water. "I imagine you had something of a rough night."

"Not me. Taking your money at poker was a pleasure."

"I mean afterwards."

"Making love till dawn's early light."

"Cut the crap. Do you have any idea how many members of this crew will tell you anything you want to know for $50?"

"That pisses me off. I offered $1,000 to anyone who could help me out, and I never got so much as a nibble." I thought about that for a moment. Something was ringing a bell but I couldn't put my finger on it.

"Probably cause nobody knew nothing. Clooney was a profession-al; did what he had to do when nobody was watching, as you've seen. Anyway, all's I wanted to say was thank you."

"Thank you for what?" April asked.

"For nothing. Sweetheart, why don't you get me one of those little pizzas they have on the hot tray over there. I'll buy you a drink when you get back."

"Henry already bought me one," she said as the waiter arrived with our tray of beverages.

"Geez, what are you trying to do, get her drunk?"

"It crossed my mind."

He watched closely as April climbed out of the hot tub. "In any case, thanks for doing a job we might have had do to ourselves."

"You did come here to kill him, right?"

"Goddamn right we did. We just didn't recognize him."

"How did you know he'd be here?"

Cornish shrugged. "I don't know. It was something Richie was working on. He stayed in touch with Samson these past years, always hoping Clooney would show his face. But he never did. Then they had this idea to draw him out, to get him to come on board. I guess it worked. I'd tell you more but I don't want to. Did you figure out it was him before you shot him?"

"Yeah, I did. Maybe about a minute before I shot him."

"The police are going to be all over this. You'll be meeting with them?"

"Yes. More than likely I will."

"Do you think you can see your way to leaving us out of it?" he asked as April returned bearing a limp pizza.

I drank my piña colada, finding it just as tasty as the one I had years ago on St. Thomas. "I don't see any reason why I need to mention you," I told him.

"Mention him to who?" April asked.

"To my guy who works at a marina down in LA. Your husband was just telling me he was going to buy you a sailboat."

Cornish frowned.

"Is that right, honey?" she asked, excited.

"It's something we should maybe wait and ..."

"Don't be coy with her, Cornish. You told me it was going to be an early birthday present. Listen, my guy tells me they have a twenty-eight footer that would be perfect for day sailing. I'll tell him you're a good friend and he'll give you a deal."

She climbed on top of him, all but engulfing him. "Oh, Corny, you're the best," she said..

"Fine." He gave me a nod.

"Yeah, I don't think I need to mention you at all."

CHAPTER TWENTY-FIVE

I fell asleep in the hot tub. I napped for longer than I suspect is healthy in 104 degree water, and I dreamed. I dreamed I was back in Moosburg, back at the camp, back in the winter of 1945.

It was evening when the food wagon arrived, and the dogs were barking. We were freezing and we hadn't eaten anything substantial in days. A couple of the more sadistic guards were on duty and they had apparently decided to play a game: they let the Russians divvy up the food packages. Of all the prisoners of war, the Russians had it the worst. The guards hated them. They beat them, kicked them, shot them, and fed them next to nothing. So when they put a Russian corporal in charge of the food, they were just stirring up trouble, and when they checked back, they found he had eaten his way through some carrots and a tin of fish so they hanged him.

The job fell to a young Russian kid, Mikhail Palacek, who was seventeen years old and my friend. We worked together at the laundry polishing boots. I don't know what I would have done in Mikhail's place, honestly I don't. But he did what his fellow prisoners told him to do, which was to give them the bulk of the food and short the Americans. I have no doubt that they would have killed him if he hadn't. They were starving. I cried when I saw him do it. We all did. We were dying of hunger. The next day he cried when he apologized to me. I told him I would kill him if it happened again. And it did and I did.

I woke up in the hot tub to find a waiter tapping at me. I had pruned up pretty good. A cursory glance revealed several empty piña colada glasses in my immediate vicinity. Three young women were staring at me from the other side of the tub, and a waiter was peering down at me, saying something or another. He tapped at me again.

"Are you OK?" one of the young women asked.

"Yes. Are you?"

"We thought you were dead."

"Did you now? That would be a problem. The ship only has a three-bed morgue and already they've got four bodies piled up."

"What are you talking about?"

"Nothing. How long have I been sleeping?"

"It's unclear. You were asleep when we got here and that was five hours ago."

"Don't lie to me, little girl."

"Sir," the waiter began, "the captain is looking for you. He's asked that you please meet him on the bridge."

I nodded. "I'm going to need to freshen up. Tell him I'll be there in forty minutes."

"But sir."

"Just tell him, OK. I have to shower and do my iron-man workout. If I don't do at least thirty minutes on the rowing machine I feel like crap come dinner and drinks."

I said goodbye to my tub mates and headed back to the Junior Suite. I showered and got myself set up and then headed out for the Steamboat Saloon. We'd be in Miami shortly after dinner and I was feeling sad about that.

There comes a moment toward the end of any cruise when a passenger finds some measure of lament. This might happen over drinks or while dessert is being served, or even waiting for the elevator but in that moment, a minor sorrow blossoms. Something will be lost upon return to life normally lived. Perhaps some insights have been gained. Minimally some stress has boiled off, but the cruise would soon be over and shortly there would be nobody at hand to pick up the wet towels.

The Steamboat Saloon had a warmth to it that I was going to miss. Sunlight filtered in through the shuttered windows, or perhaps not. I couldn't remember for sure but I thought the windows might be fake. Inga was playing the piano when I walked in. She was playing something soft to a room that was mostly empty save for a couple of gents at the bar. She smiled at me. I didn't see Lana so I asked for her.

"It's her day off," Dario from Santo Domingo told me. "We were supposed to be in St. Thomas today and then it became a sea day so everything is changed."

I ordered a Scotch and sat in a comfortable chair. I watched Inga play, and I didn't nod off, not even for a moment. I felt completely at peace. When I was ready to leave, I took an envelope out from my pocket and asked Dario to give it to Lana from St. Petersburg. My poker winnings were inside and I wrote her name on the outside.

"What should I tell her?"

"Tell her she made the cruise a pleasure for one of her guests," I said as I headed out for the bridge.

There I found Staff Capt. Nilsen talking on the radio with the harbor pilot from Port of Miami. He let me sit in the big chair and stare out through the front windows. I squinted to see if I could see Miami but I didn't have my glasses on and I think it was still too far away. I did see the helicopter approach.

"Is that coming here?" I asked stupidly as the helicopter hovered near the bridge, its side dominated by an intertwined S and K, the Sakato-Kobe logo.

"It is," Nilsen said. He picked up a ringing phone and nodded.

"I'm going to go watch it land."

"He's right here," he said into the phone. Then to me, "Captain Erlander asks that you come to the officers' dining room immediately for a debriefing."

"Tell him I'm on my way." I headed out to look at the helicopter. I don't like debriefings. I find them depressing and anti-climactic, and as such I avoid them when possible. I climbed up a flight of stairs to the Vista Deck and walked toward the stern. I stopped by the top of the rock-climbing wall and watched the helicopter land.

It was a little one, and sporty too. Black, but shiny black with the bright orange S and K forming two snakes, kind of. You can't really make a K into a snake but the effect still worked.

Nilsen came up behind me. "This is not the way to the officers' dining room," he said.

"Sometimes I get lost."

"Fine." He continued past me toward the helicopter.

When the blades stopped spinning, an elderly Asian man stepped out. Kind of old for a company representative, I caught myself thinking.

Nilsen shook the man's hand and then he pointed in my direction, probably at the rock-climbing wall, probably indicating where the murder had taken place. Once the engine died down, they spoke for a few more moments before the Asian man headed toward me.

He paused to light a cigarette and found it difficult to do so, being up on the highest deck, exposed to all the wind, but eventually he managed. He came right up and leaned on the railing next to me. "This is the place he was found," he said in heavily accented English.

"Yes."

"Can you imagine such a thing?"

I shook my head.

"You've done fine work here," he said. "Fine work. You have my gratitude."

"You know who I am?"

He puffed on his cigarette. "I was in Stockholm two years ago when this ship was launched. I remember thinking that a rock-climbing wall on a ship was too much, was not what a ship is about. I am considering having it removed."

"You're Kenji Sakato."

He nodded. "I own twenty-three ships. Of all of them, my favorite is a converted Korean tanker from the 1970s. She is no longer in use for petroleum, only for cargo but cannot accommodate containers so she is of little utility. Even so I cannot remove her from service. Now and again a small job is offered, often in Fiji or the Marquesas. But she steers like no ship built today. No computers, just a single man at the helm is all she requires. A pleasure."

"Do you know how to sail all your ships?"

He shook his head. "No, but I've spent my whole life around ships. I was the personal secretary to a commander of a destroyer group in the Imperial Japanese Navy. I spent much of the war in the Philippines. Admiral Yamamoto promised my commander the military governorship of Washington state, after the war ended. I was to accompany him to Seattle."

"I had no idea."

"The emperor himself put his seal to the papers at a ceremony at Aoyama Palace. It was the proudest day of my life. I can say that even today. More than sixty years have passed and I have never seen the day that was its match. But then your air force shot down the admiral's plane. And then of course, the war didn't end as expected."

"You're probably better off. Seattle is damp."

He stared at me while he smoked his cigarette. "It is a blessing then. My knees pain me in such weather."

"For me it's the hip. And my toes cramp up. One time last winter it was the fingers as well. I woke up and my right hand was like a claw. I couldn't uncurl my fingers. I had to spend the whole day like that."

He stared at me for a moment. "For me it's just the knees. I use a cream made from the fat of a whale."

"I use Ben Gay. I don't know what's in it. I doubt whale."

Kenji Sakato took one last drag from his cigarette and tossed the butt over the railing, right into the Caribbean, or onto someone's balcony.

"They'll fine you for that," I told him.

"I doubt it."

"So what happens now to this lovely ship?"

"She'll spend two days in Miami and then continue her program as scheduled; a twelve-day voyage through the Panama Canal to northern Peru. More than half the passengers have cancelled. Money will be lost. I expect *Voyager* will continue to lose us money for the rest of the year. But it's not her fault." He stroked the rail as if it were a kitten. "We can't really blame her."

"Did half the passengers really cancel?"

He lit another cigarette. "Yes, at least half. More cancellations will come."

"So if I wanted to stay on board, maybe have a little vacation, there might be a stateroom available?"

"You want to stay on board?"

"I might think about it. The food is first rate and the hot tub is good for my back. Plus, I don't have any jobs lined up for the rest of the month. I should check on the condo at Rolling Pines but it's probably fine. I don't have any plants."

"Then of course. You'll stay aboard as my guest. Consider it a salary enhancement."

"Well I'll be god-damned. That's just wonderful." There was just one thing though. "I hate to bring it up, but where they have me now, it's a Junior Suite and it has a lifeboat hanging over the window."

"The lifeboats are required in case of emergency. In case of an event that might cause the ship to sink."

"I'm aware of that. My point is; would it be possible to change my accommodation?"

He kept puffing on his cigarette. I wondered if he had read anything recently about smoking. "Of course," he said.

"I kind of had my eye on one of those Parliamentary suites. I've been seeing this lady and she might be quite impressed if I could romance her in something like that. They give you free liquor, you know."

"I know."

"I know it's expensive. On a twelve-day cruise, that would probably cost close to twenty-five grand. But if nobody is using it, well, it would sure be a shame to let it go to waste."

"Thirty-two thousand, four hundred and ninety-five. It would be my pleasure. What is the name of the lady? I'll upgrade her suite as well."

"Her name is Helen, and that won't be necessary, if you get my drift." I elbowed him playfully in the ribs but he kind of jumped away.

"Would you be available for another job in two months time?" he asked me.

"What kind of job?"

"I have a new ship being launched. It's very exclusive; intimate even. She's a sailing yacht for ninety passengers. I'd like you to be on board for her maiden voyage."

"Is that right? Why?"

"It is sure to be interesting. Two of the richest men in the world will be on board, along with a princess, a psychic calling himself Carlyle the Great, and an American senator from Wisconsin."

"I ran for Congress once. Did I ever tell you about that?"

"We've only just met right now."

"True. Very true." Just then, as the sun was setting, I spotted some white dots off the bow. It took me a moment, but soon they registered somewhere in my neural cortex as seagulls. "OK. Pencil me in for that job. You know, I think I need to go get some food. I have a dinner date. You could come. Do you drink rum?"

He shook his head. "I will speak briefly with the captain and then I will return to Nassau on my helicopter."

I held out my hand. "Hey, it's been a pleasure then."

He kind of lined himself up so that he was right in front of me, and then he bowed, actually bowed. "I have enjoyed meeting you," he said.

"Me, too."

"You are a man well-suited to the tasks you undertake."

Well, how about that. Nobody had ever said anything even anywhere like that to me before. That felt like a gift. That made me feel just great, like the time I was ten years old and I won a prize at the fair for having the best guinea pig, or the time I was shipping off to France, and Emily told me that no matter what, she and I were going to be together forever, or the time... No, that's all. Those were the best times.

I gave Kenji Sakato a quick wave and headed for the elevator. I needed to get a drink. A Scotch, I remember thinking. Then I was going to find Helen and tell her to get ready for the best cruise of her life. We were going to have some fun. I hoped we wouldn't keep Duarte up with our love making, but you know, I really didn't care. I was going to find Helen. But first, the Bistro; every afternoon, they have little spiced meatballs.

ABOUT THE AUTHOR

Photo by Julia Jensen.

William Doonan is an archaeologist and a professor of anthropology at Sacramento City College. He was born in New York and grew up in northern New Jersey and southern Puerto Rico. He received his B.A. from Brown University and his M.A. and Ph.D. from Tulane University. His research focuses on architectural archaeology; he has spent many years conducting excavations in Costa Rica, Honduras, and Peru. He is also a veteran cruise ship lecturer, traveling the world and speaking on topics as diverse as the Trojan War, piracy in the Adriatic, and the peopling of the Americas. He lives in Sacramento, California with his wife Carmen, and his sons Will and Huey.